'Tightly structured prose, tension and a vaguely threatening feel which seems to lurk in the background set Keevil's novel in motion and make it very difficult to turn away, even during its most uncomfortable moments. What really stands out...is Keevil's distinctive writing style and his ability to lead readers to question the choices they would make if they found themselves confronted with a situation such as the one Eira unwittingly finds herself in. This is a snappy and pacey read which makes for an excellent page-turner and a poignant reminder of the frailty of human life.'

– Emma Schofield, *Wales Arts Review*

'There's a transcendent quality to novels which wrest tenderness and beauty from brutality and ugliness, and this one has it in abundance. *Your Still Beating Heart* has the emotional heft of a character-driven literary novel despite being a palpitation-inducing page-turner, a rare combination. I found it moving, gripping and evocative of place – if you enjoyed Judith Heneghan's *Snegurochka* (set in Kiev) or Garth Greenwell's *What Belongs To You* (set in Sofia), there are shades of overlap, but this book's heart beats to its own tune.' – Isabel Costello, *The Literary Sofa*

'*Your Still Beating Heart* is a slow burn novel, which meticulously gathers pace to become an exhilarating thriller about the sudden twists and turns of fate and how our personal choices can create a domino effect, dramatically altering the course of our life, even ending it prematurely, or making us come alive to its renewed potential.' – *Nut Press*

'A phenomenal thriller... An extremely menacing and electrifying narrative... I couldn't put it down. It was lingering in my mind for days.' – The Biblio Sara

YOUR STILL BEATING HEART

TYLER KEEVIL

Myriad Editions
An imprint of New Internationalist Publications
The Old Music Hall, 106–108 Cowley Rd,
Oxford OX41JE
www.myriadeditions.com

First published in 2020 by Myriad Editions
This Myriad paperback published in 2021

First printing
1 3 5 7 9 10 8 6 4 2

A CIP catalogue record for this book
is available from the British Library

ISBN (pbk): 978-1-8383860-0-9
ISBN (ebk): 978-1-912408-63-4

Designed and typeset in Palatino
by www.twenty-sixletters.com

Printed and bound in Great Britain
by Clays Ltd, Elcograf S.p.A

For you

part one

an ending

So, this is how your husband dies: not forty years from now, coughing, wilting, consumed from within by cancer, holding your hand, looking into your eyes, the irises reflecting a lifetime of companionship. Not twenty years from now, after the kids that you haven't yet had grow up and leave home and no longer need him, and you don't either – at least, not as much. Not ten years from now, around the time you expect him to have a mid-life crisis and buy a Ford convertible, start flirting ineptly and inappropriately with the staff in coffee shops.

No – your husband doesn't die in any of those ways, but now, tonight, on a slow, cold, rainy Thursday at the end of November, when he's twenty-nine years old.

He dies in London, a city he never liked, and very far from home.

He dies on a bus, of all places, at ten-thirty-four p.m.

He dies because he loves you. He dies because he's brave, or maybe insecure – sometimes it's hard to tell. He dies because he doesn't want to see you hurt, or scared. He dies because he's stupid. He dies because he doesn't think. He dies because he believes it's his job to protect you. He dies because maybe you believe this too, and expect it of him.

You don't know why he dies.

You know the how, but not the why.

This is the how: after a film, at the cinema. Tod didn't particularly want to go (he'd spent the afternoon teaching Tolstoy to hungover first years), but he could tell you did, and so he had a cup of coffee and you caught the tube down to Trafalgar Square. A thirty-one-minute trip. The film turns out to be a British kitchen-sink drama, as dreary as the weather. Tod's going to be polite about it, but you can feel his scepticism, his resistance to it: the shifting in his seat, the moving of his elbow on and off the armrest.

Then the rolling of credits, the filtering of audience members towards the exit, all of them glum, listless, their faces drawn and grey from the glare of the projector, like extras in the film that's just ended. Outside, there's construction at the entrance to the Tube. But a bus is coming, looming large, streaked with rain and grime: should we take the bus? His idea. You trot together across the street, the headlights of passing cars carving funnels through the rain. A big puddle by the curb. He jumps over first, stops to extend his hand to you, which you take, not because you need it but out of the same courtesy that made him offer.

Inside the bus, the heat is up, the windows are steamed, the aisle is slick with rain dripping off passengers' coats and boots. You can't see the city beyond the glass, just a rapid blur of darkness and light. Something about running in the rain, the cold, the impulsive movement, has loosened you both up. The gloom of the cinema has fallen away like a cloak. The two of you talk about the movie like you might have when you first met, rather than simply viewing it together and digesting it separately, agreeing to disagree. Instead, the chat is animated, with you stubbornly defending the film, and him trying to convince you what was wrong with it, with the whole genre – the lack of structure, the dismal stoicism, the working-class stereotypes. If he's talking too loudly, you don't notice. If he's coming across as 'American' – loud, brash, knowing, confident – it's almost a relief, a release. This is what he is, or once was. Your American husband with his American name. Tod. Before living in Britain made him small.

You'll remember thinking: Tod looks good. He looks happy.

And then, the shouting: 'Shut up, shut up!'

There's a man at the front end of the bus. It's unclear who he's talking to, if anybody. But he's up now, out of his seat. A pale, wired, skin-headed man. Dressed in a hoody, torn jeans.

'Shut the hell up,' he says again. He's glaring around, skittishly.

Other passengers look down, away, in that instinctive manner. Avoiding eye contact. But you don't. Later, you'll wonder why. The man spots you, fixates on you, begins to advance, coming down the aisle, repeating it like a mantra: shut up, shut the hell up, shut up. Then you do look away, at the window next to you, but it's too late: you can still see him reflected in the foggy glass, his features distorted, his face strange and twisted.

And then he is there, by you, over you. Shouting down at you. 'Shut the hell up, you stupid bitch.' And you feel flecks of his spit on your hair, your scalp. Like he's frothing at the mouth, rabid.

5

And that's when Tod, your husband, stands up. He's smiling, in that uncomfortable way he does when he's nervous. He's nervous. He holds up his hands, palms out, like you would to placate a wild dog. 'All right, man,' he says, 'take it easy, okay?'

The man takes a step back, surprised (he hadn't connected the two of you) and for a moment seems confused, dazed. Then his eyes refocus. On Tod.

'What the hell are you going to do, mate?' he says. 'I'll mess you up.'

Tod laughs, shakes his head. 'Buddy, we don't want any trouble.'

The man has his hands in the pouch of his hoody. You notice this. You don't think Tod has noticed. You want to tell him, 'Don't, Tod. Don't.' You want to tell him to let it go, sit down. But you're afraid to say anything. You're afraid to move, to breathe. Frozen fear. Later, you will detest this reaction. You'll wonder about all the things you could have said, or done, to divert the outcome to anything else.

'Just leave her alone,' Tod is saying. 'Just back off, okay?'

The man looks from him to you, as if he can visibly see the relationship between you, the bond. It seems to anger him. He spits in your direction, deliberately this time – a gob that hits your cheek. Hot, wet, rank. And Tod reaches for him, grabs him, and they are both shouting at each other, and other people are moving, getting out of the way. There is no space to fight, in the aisle of a bus. It is awkward and clumsy and almost juvenile. Tod is much bigger than the man and overpowers him. The air is hot, snapping with a kind of violent energy. You never thought of Tod as strong, physically strong, until then. Not in that way. He pins the man with a forearm and punches down at him, into his face. Tod is not swearing but focused and intent, furious.

6

Tod sits back abruptly, as if he has decided the fight is finished. He has won. The man slithers out from under him, begins to crawl away, getting to his feet, staggering. Down the aisle, down the stairs. A banging noise, as he smashes at the doors. He either forces them open or the bus driver prudently opens them for him, setting the man loose.

All those faces in the aisle, peering towards you and Tod. Tod is still sitting there. He is looking down. That's when you see the handle. You don't even know it's a knife, at first. It is just this handle, black, gleaming, protruding from his chest. He is cupping his hands around it, as if afraid to touch it, as if afraid touching it will make it real, will make happen what has already happened.

There is blood now, soaking through his T-shirt. So dark, staining the white cotton like blotting paper. His T-shirt has the image of a Mustang on it, and the word *Medusa*. A movie car. You've always liked it, liked him in it. A macho car, but a strong woman – the creature who can turn people to stone. Tod now looks as if he's turning to stone, solidifying. You're kneeling by him, saying his name, pressing your palm to the bloody T-shirt. You don't pull out the knife. You know you're not supposed to do that. You shout for help. You tell somebody to get out their fucking phone. Actually, several people already have their phones out – filming your panic. Others are yelling, having seen the blood. Maybe one of them calls for help. One of them must.

A woman kneels down opposite, but doesn't know what to do either. Tod is looking at you, helplessly. All the breath knocked out of his lungs, punctured, emptying. A slow burble of pink froth at his lips. No last words. No 'I love you'. No apologies. No regrets. No movie moments. But at the end – seemingly aware – he takes hold of your hand, both of you slippery with blood now, and grips it fiercely. So hot.

7

The heat of his life pumping between you, squeezed between your palms. And then the slow stopping, the relaxation, the glazing of the eyes.

By the time you let go, by the time they *make* you let go, his fingers have gone cold. Just a matter of minutes. You are guided off the bus, into the rain. A blanket, draped over your shoulders. Your hand is still ripe with his blood. You are still cupping your palm as if it is holding his. You can still feel it tingling with the pressure of his grip. You are not crying. People are around you, holding up more camera phones, taking pictures, recording. Some clips will be played on the news, others will creep on to YouTube. You can go back to this moment at any time, forever. The sound of rain, the smell of the dirty city: smoke diesel rain sweat hate fear. These things will always remind you of this night, here, when the man you loved was stabbed in the heart and died and went still and cold and some part of you went cold too, like a bit of that blade had stabbed through him into you. A shard of ice, a fleck of death. It will prove vital for all that lies ahead of you.

newton's cradle

After. After you opted for a cremation, not a coffin; after you chose the silver and black urn to hold the ashes, which in turn got tucked into a wall niche behind a plaque, among dozens of other plaques, with names and dates on them; after the funeral ceremony, held in a clean, newly carpeted room that smelled like lemon air freshener and looked like a conference centre; after you listened to the amusing anecdotes told by colleagues, friends, family from America; after you hugged and held each of them and accepted, alternately, their condolences or their compliments on how well you seemed to be 'holding up'; after the trial, which was swift, efficient, an 'open-and-shut' case, so obvious to everybody from the start that he was guilty – the whole thing was on CCTV – just a drugged-up junkie, paranoid, probably schizophrenic, *downright dangerous*, stabbing a young man, a caring husband, a promising scholar, in a frenzied attack; after the interest faded and the articles dwindled to a trickle, the media eye roaming elsewhere; after the Christmas holidays arrived and you visited your mother and received things wrapped in shiny paper and cards scribbled with season's greetings; after clocks struck midnight and a digit changed and one year became another; after all of that you return to work, as if nothing has happened, as if now your life will carry on in the same way as it did before, only without him, without your husband, without Tod.

Death and loss and grief does not exempt you from banality.

You work in a law firm, as a legal secretary. Not a lifelong dream but what you ended up doing, temporarily, when Tod got the postdoc position and the two of you moved to London from Wales, your home, where you'd met at university (Tod studying literature, you studying theatre). The job agency asked you to fill in a basic questionnaire and because you could type – fast and accurate – and because somebody, somewhere, was on maternity leave, you took up a temporary post at Bradley & Bradley, a mid-sized firm of twenty or so lawyers, based in Hackney, and the temp work kept getting extended, seemed to go on indefinitely, until eventually – two years in – you had a permanent job.

The lawyer you work for is middle-aged, wears plain blue suits, gives you holiday bonuses, is primarily an inheritance and estate solicitor, has never said or done anything inappropriate. You sit at your desk and greet clients, arrange appointments and meetings, type up memos, photocopy legal documents, scan birth certificates, marriage certificates, death certificates, amend wills and annulments, arrange and organise his files, having grown to like the work, the sense of order. It has always given you an impression of control, of there being some master plan. This whole business of birth and life and marriage and death and inheritance. There are laws pertaining to all of it, answers for every question, and your boss knows them, or, if not, he can look them up. Of course, Tod's death has changed all that.

Not long after your return – only three or four days, maybe – you are called into your boss's office. It is as big as yours and Tod's living room (you still think in this way, in terms of you and Tod, Tod and you) and seven storeys up, with a view of the Thames, the Shard, London. A mahogany desk, long and oblong, like a billiard table. On the desk, pictures of your boss's wife and kids. Studio portraits, in black and white. The kids all grown up now. Attending university, well-adjusted, diligent, destined for modest levels of success.

On the left side of the desk, one of those sets of steel spheres suspended from wires – a Newton's cradle – making clicking sounds as the spheres swing from one end, then the other. Counting time. Click. Click. Click.

Behind the desk, your boss smiles kindly, sympathetically. He has a mole in the centre of his forehead, and receding, thinning hair that he keeps short, dyes blonde to hide it. He asks you how you're doing, how you're 'getting on'. This is a phrase people use, have been using with you, lately. He says he knows how difficult it must be for you.

While he talks, he twirls a pen between his thumb and forefinger, the motion constant, endless, dizzying.

You look away, out the window. See an aeroplane scudding across the sky, which is grey as slate, a monotone colour, no definition at all. The plane scraping a chalk mark of jet stream. When you turn back your boss is talking about receiving complaints. Appointments that have been scheduled incorrectly, clients who have shown up at the

11

wrong time, or have been given misinformation. You know this is true, don't bother to explain, deny, or justify it. Only nod, affirming.

'Do you need more time?' he asks you.

When you don't answer, he hurries on, explaining that he's happy to give you as much time as you need. The phrase strikes you as absurd, ridiculous. How can you give somebody time? As if time is an object, a little package, or parcel. You imagine a black-and-white cartoon like the ones they run in newspapers: one character handing a bag to another, labelled 'time'. *Here, have some more of this.* Your boss is in earnest though, means well. You have used up your bereavement leave, and all your holidays for the year. But he would be happy to give you unpaid leave, save your position for you.

'Until you're ready to come back,' he says, and smiles again.

The spheres in the Newton's cradle continue to bash uselessly against each other. Your boss checks his watch, discreetly. Just a twist of the wrist, a flick of the eyes. Well-practiced. It is nine-forty-five, and he has an appointment at ten. One of the meetings you haven't got wrong or mixed up through carelessness. You know that's the real problem: carelessness. Lack of care. It's not that you're distracted, or scatter-brained from shock. You simply don't care enough any more to do your job thoroughly. All these people who seem to come and go. *Talking of Michelangelo.* You can't recall where the quote is from. Just that it's meant to signify meaninglessness.

You tell your boss that it's probably best if you just give notice, and not come back. He sits up straighter, reaches for a pile of papers and shuffles them together, like a giant deck of cards, before laying them flat. 'I didn't mean that,' he says.

'I'm not trying to get rid of you. It's just, there are things that need doing. Maybe you could go down to part-time, do a few days a week for a while?' He scratches his mole, looks at you hopefully.

You shake your head, as if it's already decided. And it is. You ask him if he has ever lost somebody. Not in an accusatory way, but merely a curious one. He deals so much in the aftermath of death – who gets how much money, or what part of the estate – and you haven't had cause to truly consider it before. It was simply part of the everyday duties you were given, which you undertook on behalf of other people.

Your boss has to think about it. He scratches at his mole. 'Well, my parents are both dead,' he says. Then, as if realising that sounds trite, he adds, 'Though that's different, of course. They lived full lives, passed on in old age.' He checks his watch again. 'You shouldn't act hastily,' he says. 'Take some time, think it over. I can hold a place for you. I can contact the agency.'

You wonder if he has already done this, asked about the possibility of another temp. Probably. He is kind, but also efficient. You don't feel hard done by at the thought he is already planning your replacement. You don't feel anything about it, one way or the other.

'No,' you say, 'it's fine. I'm all done here.'

The finality of it rings true to you. You don't just mean this job, but this city, this country, this life. It was never really yours, anyway. You yawn – you can't help it – and arch your back. The chairs in his office are hard-backed and your tailbone is sore from sitting there. You're weary of the situation and, you know, he is too. But there is etiquette. There are social graces.

'What will you do?' he asks.

A good question. And a good way of drawing the conversation to a close, of leading you out the door.

'I'm going away,' you say. You are looking at where the plane was. It's gone now, but the jet stream still lingers against the sky, melting into the cloud layer. 'To Prague.'

He says 'ah' as if he understands, though he is frowning, now, uncertain. He says, hesitantly, that he's heard it's beautiful. Hoping for an explanation. You tell him Prague is where Tod proposed to you, which is true. But that's not the reason you've had the impulse, just now, to go back. The sky, the plane. The flat greyness. You remember Prague in monochrome, a charcoal sketch. Cold and colourless. The way you feel.

'That could be good,' he says. 'To go away, get away. I can't imagine...' He stops, trails off. He is looking at the photo of his wife. Perhaps trying to picture it – the swift and sudden loss, being the one left behind. You stare at the Newton's cradle. Each collision of the steel spheres seems to grow louder, filling up the room, deafening as cannons. Boom. Boom. Boom. Pounding in your skull, making it resonate. You lean forward, touch the last sphere with a finger, stopping it. Your boss looks at you, startled, and down at the Newton's cradle. The spheres hanging vacantly in stasis. Motionless. Silent.

'I always hated that thing,' you say.

transit

The proposed trip provides purpose, things to do: handing in formal notice at the law firm, booking a flight, finding your passport, terminating the rental agreement on the flat, packing, deciding what to keep (books, trinkets, a few photographs) and what to leave or throw away (everything else). This is what they call 'putting your affairs in order'. And soon it is done, and you are travelling, in transit, en route.

And then this: on the plane to Prague, the woman next to you has an episode in the middle of the flight. It seems serious, maybe even a stroke, or heart attack.

Later, you'll wonder if this is now to be your curse, after allowing Tod to die – if you are to be surrounded by death wherever you go. Delirious, skittish thoughts. Fate and curses are for fairy tales, not real life, right?

Before it happens, there is the usual safety video, flight attendant demonstration, take-off, and small-talk – the woman asking you questions at a time when you don't want to be asked anything: *Where are you going? How long will you be staying?* You reply vaguely, evasively, while holding up the earbuds of your MP3 player, implying the desire for peace, for privacy – a hint she fails to take. Eventually, to avoid further chit-chat, when she pauses for breath you simply put in your earbuds, smile insincerely by way of apology.

She folds her arms, looks ahead, clearly affronted.

The MP3 player is still laden with Tod's music; his tastes were tyrannically alternative, and you couldn't be bothered to open a personal account, download tracks and albums of your own. It would have meant enduring his sarcasm and ridicule, so you yielded instead. These small parts of ourselves we forfeit, these concessions we make when we're in a relationship, when we purport to love somebody.

You did love him. You're sure of that. As sure as you are of anything, these days.

Every so often, the woman stirs, restless. She has the window seat, but is not content to gaze out into the dark, and has no book, no magazine, no distractions. She's old, but not ancient. Maybe sixty, or so. The age of your mother, who seems to you very far from any signs of ill health – always walking, hiking, running half-marathons. Joining new clubs and groups, all of them fitness orientated. Shortly after the funeral, she recommended Tai-Chi, her latest passion. She said it would help you cope, deal with it. Referring to your grief as 'it' seemed to turn 'it' into a thing, a creature, an incubus. You tried to imagine yourself performing slow karate chops to defend yourself against 'it' and ward 'it' off. That was hard to imagine.

When you phoned your mother to tell her about Prague, she sighed loudly, flapping her lips like a horse, and said, 'You always had a tendency to wallow in your miseries.'

Her own husband – your father – died ten years ago. By that time, they had already split up. Your mother didn't take a day off work, organised a university scholarship in his name for youths from underprivileged backgrounds, got drunk on gin gimlets and admitted privately to you that she thought your father might have been abused as a child. His uncle, she said. The one with the goatee, and delicate hands. Never trust a man with delicate hands, she'd declared grandly – an odd, and oddly affecting, piece of maternal advice.

This woman doesn't look anything like your mother, but doesn't look unwell at all either. Her limbs are lean, her movements vigorous. You can faintly smell her perfume and moisturiser. She abstains from the single complimentary alcoholic beverage, opts for tomato juice. There are no meals on the flight – it's only a couple of hours – but when the in-flight snacks are delivered, she receives one in advance of everyone else: the vegetarian or gluten-free option. She makes a big event of opening it – a salad pot – and drizzling the sachet of dressing. Before taking a bite she smiles politely, unable to help appearing a touch triumphant.

The window behind the woman is glowing with daylight, bright and hazy as a screen of diffusion, like you might see in a photographer's studio. Against it the woman's profile is dark, shaded, a partial silhouette. You don't watch her eat, but from the corner of your eye you are aware of this shadow, nibbling bites off her fork, pursing her lips around the tines.

When your own snack arrives – a ham and cheese panini – it feels awkward to keep your earbuds in, to continue to shut her out. So you remove them, carefully wind them up, and take a few bites, which is all you can manage. It's

17

not only that the bread is hard and stale, the cheese oily cool – you haven't had much of an appetite for days, weeks, months. Since it happened.

Soon, predictably, the woman is talking to you, buzzing away on your right. It's apparent, very quickly, that your answers don't matter. She is simply one of those people who needs to talk. Buzz, buzz, buzz. She is going to visit her son, who is in the electrical supply industry. He is doing well, has made a success of himself – Prague is a good place to be, for businesses.

'And you?' she asks. 'Do you have any family in the Czech Republic?'

No, you say, which is true. Though it's also true (and you neglect to tell her this) that your grandfather was born there, that he immigrated to Wales when he was one year old, a fact that you and your mother tend to forget, since he was not the kind to speak of his past, or of anything at all, really. So, though you have no family that you know of, you have ancestral roots. You have some shared past with the country.

The woman is saying something else. She is talking of the mother of cities, the golden city, and the city of a hundred spires. You're baffled, trying to picture all these fairy-tale places, until you understand she is listing all the alternate names for Prague. The tourist names. Then she stops, checks herself, glances at you shrewdly.

She asks, 'Where are you staying?'

You explain that you've rented a little bedsit, not a hotel. Something inexpensive, practical. Out of the tourist districts, over in Praha Two. You found it online. It's a mistake, the way you go on – she notes the confidence, your familiarity with the city's layout, and asks if you've been there before. Only twice, you tell her, and leave it at that. But she is peering at you expectantly. Waiting. You are half-turned in your seat,

18

your spine all twisted. Squinting at her against the glare of the window hurts your eyes, makes them physically sting – as if you're going snow-blind. So eventually you give in. She has won.

'It's where my husband proposed.'

You leave out that it was also the place you and Tod first travelled together, back when you were students. Your hope being that the curt declaration will staunch her curiosity.

'Oh,' she says, leaning backwards and forwards, craning her neck, checking the nearby rows. 'Where is he sitting? Would he like to switch seats with me?'

And so you have to explain, he's not with you. He's dead. And – since you feel she deserves it, feel she's somehow wheedled this information out of you – you add, casually and cuttingly, 'He was stabbed in the heart.'

The woman makes a small, strange sound and puts her hand to her mouth, as if she's burped and wants to politely cover it up, take it back. Only she can't. She is very still for a time, and (this must be a trick of the light) you have the impression that the glare of the window is shining *right through her head*, out the front of her eye sockets. As if her face is a mask, and behind it there is nothing.

She reaches for her glass of juice, which is empty, and raises it to her lips, mimes the act of drinking. Puts it down. Then she begins to fan herself, quite frantically, seemingly forgetting your conversation entirely. 'These planes. The air-conditioning. They get so hot.' Even though it isn't hot at all: it's chilly, frigid. Stuffy, yes, but not hot. She asks if she can borrow your water and then – without waiting for an answer – reaches for it, gulps and gulps, spilling it all down her chin, on her blouse.

When she's done, she crunches the cup, makes a croaking sound, leans forward and puts her forehead against the seat in front of her. You watch all this, perplexed, without any sense yet that something is seriously wrong. She is breathing – you can hear her breathing. Ragged and thin. Then, a strange gurgle. You've never witnessed this kind of thing before. That's part of it, why you're slow to react. But also you feel removed from it, as if you're observing dispassionately. As if your seat is empty and you have simply dropped in on this scene, to watch it, without being able to engage or partake.

It's possible you'd continue to sit like that, except a young man across the aisle leans over, touches your shoulder, asks if the woman's okay. You look at him, baffled, admit you don't know. 'We better call the attendant,' he says. And he presses a button on his arm rest, causing a little light to come on directly above him – a glowing bulb in the shape of a person. Head and arms. When they don't come immediately, he shouts, demands attention – 'We've got a sick woman here.' Other people are standing up, turning around, trying to get a look. Some of them have their camera phones out already, filming, snapping photos – each picture emitting that little electronic click. It reminds you of the Newtown's cradle: click, click, click. Or the night Tod died. Click, click, click. All those eager, greedy lenses.

Then a flight attendant is there; you are asked to move, which you do. Slipping out of your seat and withdrawing, retreating. Not just a few feet away, but to the tail of the plane, into that alcove near the toilets. From there you have a view of the commotion in the aisles: a clump of people, somebody announcing they're a doctor, in the way they often do in films. You watch this for maybe five or six minutes. They lay the woman in the aisle, kneel over her, put an oxygen mask on her face. It goes on for so long people lose interest. They sit back down, put their phones away, pick up their magazines,

20

continue eating their snacks. She's not dying, it seems. You assume there would be more interest if she were dying.

You are remembering the bus, the faces turned towards you. In your memory they are not sympathetic, caring, or overly concerned. Rather, they seem captivated, riveted, and even relieved. That certain pleasure people get, from seeing misfortune befall others. Like escaping a game of Russian roulette.

You slide open the door to the toilet, step in there. You splash water on your face, pad it dry with paper towel, clean and scented and very soft. A small pleasure. You are shocked, but not in shock. What you are shocked by is how utterly prosaic you found it. The kind of thing that might have shaken you considerably before. Haunted you even. You would have needed to tell people, gotten it off your chest. *Did you hear what happened on my flight to Prague?* Not now. Now, what seems surprising to you is that this kind of thing doesn't happen more often. Our soft and flawed and yielding bodies, running on air and water and food, charged by a single organ in the centre of our chest, the fluttering rhythm as delicate as a hummingbird's wings. Each of us so terrifyingly vulnerable as we move through space and time. Leading our bewildering lives. All it takes is a little push, a shove, a wrong turn, a bad move, a lapse in judgement. Or, in the woman's case, a slight emotional jolt. Was it your fault? No. Not in any deliberate way. But still. You took pleasure in proclaiming it – *stabbed in the heart* – as if you could pass on the wound, somehow. And, apparently, you did.

When you come back out, they have moved the woman closer to you, to that area at the rear of the plane, beside the toilets and by the flight attendant's seats. She's strapped to a padded folding stretcher. Grey and practical. She still has the oxygen mask on her face, and now a cannula and drip in her arm as well. But she is alert, lucid. Drawn by your movement, she turns her head, fixes her eyes on you. Her mouth is hidden. Is she looking at you angrily, accusingly? You can't tell. You consider bending over, saying something kind. Making some token gesture. Or asking the attendants about her. But you don't. It doesn't matter. She'll live. For all you know this could be a frequent occurrence – perhaps she's one of those people who have fainting spells, dizzy fits, 'bad turns'. It may not have been anything so serious as a heart attack, after all.

Eventually, the flight attendant notices you hovering there, and asks you to take your seat. Again, you're struck by the strangeness of language. Take your seat. Take it where? Pick it up and carry it elsewhere, or throw it from the plane. Jettison it like ballast. Jump out after it, maybe. At these cartoon-like thoughts you begin to smile to yourself, but alter it into a sympathetic grimace: the infirm woman is still staring at you with baleful eyes.

customs

It looks the same here as anywhere, everywhere: a vast concrete cave. The ceiling built low (if you jumped and reached up you could touch it) with square panels and dull fluorescent lighting. No windows. Linoleum floors streaked with scuff marks from boots, shoes, suitcases. Signs hanging from wires, in several languages, designating different areas for Czech and EU citizens and international travellers. Beneath each, people stand in queues, shuffling from foot to foot, blinking uncertainly in the harsh light, each line like one long creature with hundreds of heads and feet. When the front takes a step forward, the movement ripples all the way down, winding back and forth between the ropes and stanchions.

You join the EEA line. It is by far the slowest, with the most people, and not enough booths open. The officials are all diligent, thorough, meticulous. Checking passports, asking the odd question, and occasionally telling people to wait – or directing them to another area. The whole business, the sluggish churnings of bureaucracy, would have aggravated Tod. He would have spent long sections of the wait muttering to you about how inefficient the process was, pointing to the other lines, where at times the officials seemingly have nothing to do. And you would have agreed, not because you necessarily did, but to placate him. Really you view minor ordeals like this in more resigned terms than Tod ever did – something to be endured, like bad weather, or delayed trains.

When your turn comes, you don't feel the flutter of anxiety you can recall from previous trips, the sense you might have done something wrong. You simply smile at the official, hand over your passport. It's about eight years old, and the golden lettering on the front has faded. It feels like a worn wallet. He accepts it, flicks it open expertly, smiles back at you. There is something leering about it. He has a crooked tooth, a well-groomed moustache. He asks you how long you're staying for, and it sounds like a pick-up line. Three months, you say. You're taking a Czech language course. Both lies. You have no idea how long you're staying, or what you'll be doing. But he grunts, as if in approval, and asks no more questions. He hands back the passport, winks, tells you to enjoy your stay, that you're *the good kind of traveller*.

You thank him, automatically, though in truth you're startled: by the inept attempt at flirtation, the lack of professional polish. These officials are usually so neutral, so neutered. Emotionless and expressionless as robots.

The good kind of traveller. You consider the phrase as you stand at baggage claim, watching suitcases emerge from a dark hole, skitter on to the conveyer belt, then crawl around and around, aimlessly, like beetles. The official was speaking off the cuff – a misguided compliment – and you can't be certain what he meant, but you can guess. He meant that you're white, and British, and female. He meant that you're not loud, brash, drunk, like the women who come for hen parties. He meant that you're pleasant, and nice, but not too striking, not *provocative*. You dress down: casual jeans and T-shirts, walking shoes. You seem modest, co-operative, compliant. And, of course, you're exempt from the racial profiling that is not meant to go on, but often does. You don't have dark skin. You don't wear a burka, or a hijab, or traditional dress. You don't come from a country riven with strife, civil war, crisis. You aren't a refugee or a political activist. You aren't going to be a problem.

The good kind of traveller. A seemingly innocuous comment. But one that stays with you, and one that you'll remember when *they* approach you, and you'll understand at once why you're perfect for the job they have in mind. Or seemingly so. Perfect in a very superficial way. A painting, a veneer. They will underestimate the rest of you, the depths of you. They will fail to realise – until it's too late – that appearing compliant and obedient is merely a persona, a mask that you happen to wear particularly well. When it suits you.

Your luggage arrives, eventually. A big blue duffel bag, full of books. You expect to get some reading done, but don't expect much else. You sling it over your shoulder, carry it towards the exit – glass doors that slice open and closed on automatic sensors – and step through into the Arrivals hall of Václav Havel Airport. On your immediate left is a kiosk selling snacks and drinks. It's nearly eleven o'clock at night, Czech time, and having hardly eaten on the flight you should be hungry, but you aren't.

From a nearby cashpoint you get some money, as much as your bank allows in a single withdrawal: three hundred pounds, or nearly nine thousand koruny. About a quarter of what you have left, after the funeral expenses, the flight, booking the bedsit. Tod didn't have any life insurance – the idea of dying so young simply unfeasible – and living in London didn't allow you to put away any real savings. Still, you have enough to get by, for now.

Your first purchase in Prague is a pack of cigarettes, a European brand chosen at random: Smart cigarettes. The name pleasingly oxymoronic. Outside, by one of the dozens of bus shelters, you light a Smart and blow smoke into the cold winter air. As with your taste in music, the smoking was a side of you that Tod disapproved of, managed to change. Or encouraged you to subdue. The two of you were thinking of trying, or starting to try, for a baby, and he'd been adamant the smoking had to stop, which it did. But there's no Tod to stop you now, and no need. The nicotine rush feels fresh and virgin – a dizzying high.

You wish you'd been more honest with him, about your wants and needs, your likes and dislikes. He was always so vocal, so communicative. The teacher in him, perhaps. During your arguments he would speak very calmly and make big, repetitive gestures with his hands, as if explaining a lesson plan. Even if you didn't agree with him, you tended to defer, acquiesce, simply for the sake of ease. You thought you were doing it for him – the little compromises everybody talks about, when they speak in general terms about relationships – but see now it was insulting, duplicitous. If you'd cared enough, you would have fought more, fought harder, to convey your point of view, retain some sense of self. It might have made your relationship stronger, somehow. More solid. And, right now, you wouldn't be feeling this twinge of relief and satisfaction at the taste of cigarette smoke, instead of what you know you *should* be feeling: remorse, melancholy, grief. You miss him, yes. That's a given. But finally, you can smoke again. Finally, you can do whatever the hell you want.

trouble will find you

The landlady of the bedsit said she would meet you at seven in the morning, and because of the late flight you have several hours to kill. So you catch one of the last airport buses to Wenceslas Square, which – like Times Square, or Piccadilly Circus – is always bright, always bustling, always noisy. You remember that, from the time Tod proposed. The square isn't actually a square. It's more of a boulevard. About a kilometre long. Maybe fifty metres across. Lined with a series of impressive buildings – art nouveau, or neo-Renaissance, or some other classic style. All five or six storeys high. Most now refashioned for tourism: retail outlets and souvenir shops and cafés and bars and restaurants and hotels with revolving doors and casinos offering slots, poker, roulette. You don't bother with any of it, settle on a bench near Můstek Metro, beneath a building topped by a modern-looking clock, the

28

golden hands slow-ticking around. The people who are out now are clubbers, bar-hoppers, groups here for hen or stag parties. All drunk, loud, energetic. Some glance your way. Sitting there, blowing smoke into the cold, your feet kicked up on your duffel bag, huddled in your coat, your headphones in, listening to Tod's playlists. You don't look like a mark, a tourist. Nobody has bothered you, bothered with you. Nobody has even talked to you.

Not until Mario.

He finds you at two in the morning: as if he has been waiting for that clock to hit the hour. A short man, dressed in a beige linen suit. Dark brown leather shoes. Maybe alligator skin. Polished to glossiness, reflecting the lights of the square. A black shirt, unbuttoned to show his chest, which is shaved and smooth. He has well-oiled hair and teeth so clean and white they look false. He doesn't speak immediately, but smiles, staring at you curiously, without malice. As if you are a cat that has adopted this perch for the night.

He reminds you of one of the characters in *Casablanca*. Some kind of hustler, or conman, or petty crook. When he appears (and he really does seem to appear, like a magic trick) you happen to be listening to that song – a favourite on Tod's playlist – about trouble finding you. And it feels like it has. But you're not worried about it. You don't seem to be worried about much, since Tod's death.

He says something, inaudible over the music. You remove your earbuds, and without you prompting him he repeats himself: asking for a cigarette, patting at his jacket as if to emphasise that normally he would have one – he would have numerous cigarettes – but he's forgotten them. He has used English for your sake. You fish the pack of Smart out of your pocket, toss it to him. He extracts a cigarette slowly, presents the pack back to you, and he does it so graciously, so reverently, it feels like a proposal. Not very different, at all, from the way Tod held out the ring, only a few blocks from here.

That's when the man tells you his name, and sits down on the bench. He explains that he often comes here, to this bench. That he likes to watch the people. His accent is distinct, crisp, but not heavy. He is sitting on the opposite end of the bench, separate from you. There is no sign of a come-on, no oily impropriety. After that brief introduction, he merely sits, and smokes, and watches, and soon you relax and return to doing the same. You're still aware of him, but his presence has faded into the background – like any other part of the street scene – until he speaks again, asks what you're doing here. There's no reason to lie, so you explain about the bedsit, your morning meeting with the landlady. That it didn't seem worth getting a hotel for just a few hours.

Ah, he says, though he sounds a bit disappointed. As if the answer is more ordinary than he expected. More ordinary than he wanted.

Calmly, still smoking, and looking straight ahead, he tells you that he lives in Prague, has done for several years, but it isn't home to him, either. It never will be. Then he glances sideways at you, puts his hand to his face, as if placing a mask there. 'Because of my face,' he says. 'Because of the colour of my face.' The colour of his face is not white. He would not be classified as a 'good traveller' according to that customs official. Mario shrugs, as if resigned to this, and carefully bends down and stubs the cigarette on the ground. Then he stands, goes to drop it in the bin next to the bench. He tells you it's cold, and that he knows of a bar nearby – not a tourist place. A good spot to warm up, to kill some time. If you'd like to go, he could show you, take you there.

The obvious answer is no, of course. How foolish and naïve to accept – to go with a stranger, in a pale suit and

30

alligator skin shoes, to some bar he claims to know about. We're all taught – we're all trained – to do the safe thing, the *smart* thing, in these situations. And there is safety in the lights and noise and bustle of the square. But the bus, too, was supposed to be safe. Full of people. And all they did was turn and stare and gape and watch Tod die.

You ask Mario, 'What do you get out of it?'

He smiles, appreciating the directness. 'You will buy me a drink, of course.' The way he says this makes it sound like a simple transaction. And maybe it is.

You stand, pick up your bag, sling it over your shoulder. You're nervous, and it's a good feeling. Like putting your hand to an electric wire, feeling the shock. It's nice to feel something, anything. Besides, the bench was hard and the novelty of Wenceslas Square was wearing off. Five more hours is a long time, to be sitting alone in the cold through the night.

As you walk with him, out of the lights of the square and towards a darker side street, you feel a twinge of doubt. The old instincts. You ask, with that same directness, if he plans to mug you, if he intends any harm. He laughs, his teeth shining in the shadows. 'Not me. Others, maybe. But I will do my best to protect you.' He sounds half-serious, half-joking.

It's hard to tell, with Mario.

slippage

All of the possibilities you discussed actually happen: Mario
shows you the bar, you buy him a drink, and you are almost
mugged. Not by him, but a man who seems to be his friend,
or acquaintance. This doesn't take place immediately. At first,
the bar is exactly what Mario promised: a place to have a
beer, keep warm. It's two blocks north and four blocks west
of Wenceslas Square. You kept track, in your head, as you
walked with him. Your sense of direction has always been
spot-on, unerring, *ridiculously good*, as Tod used to say. And
it seemed prudent, to know where you were going, to know
where Mario was leading you.

The bar is packed – mostly men, mostly Czech, mostly
middle-aged or older, mostly standing. A few of them glance
at you – openly, brazenly, and yes, lecherously – but none say
anything. No insinuating comments, no boozy come-ons, no

quick feels as you worm your way between them, awkward with your duffel bag. You can't see any free tables, but Mario finds you one, somehow, pulling back a chair with a flourish. Mario the magician. You sit, fitting your foot through the strap of your duffel bag, so the bag can't be ferreted away, carried off. Not unless you're carried off with it. An old travelling trick, but useful.

Mario motions to you, says something – hard to hear over the raised voices and raucous laughter – but you figure out he's asking for money, asking you to hold up your end of the bargain. You have to get out your wallet – a mistake, since it's stuffed with fresh notes – and fumble through it, trying to remember the exchange rate, the worth of koruny, the numbers so high. You hand him a two hundred koruna note, about a fiver, and this seems to please him. You know he's clocked the rest of the cash, nestling in there, but you don't know yet if that's worrying. You think of your cigarettes, the ironic brand name, *Smart*. It wasn't very smart to withdraw so much money at once, or reveal it. You will need to be smarter, watch yourself.

Mario is gone for a time and returns with two beers in the pint-sized glasses they call *půllitr*. He is smiling, satisfied; it's the smile of the salesman, when the contract is signed, when the handshake seals the deal. Your small transaction has gone exactly according to plan. You both hold up your glasses, crack them together. *Na zdraví*, you say. The beer is pils, and cold, and good. Sitting back, wiping his lips, Mario asks if you know Czech – and you tell him not much. Only the basics. *Na zdraví. Prosím. Děkuji. Jak se máš.*

'And so,' he says, '*jak se máš*? How are you?'

The expected tourist answer is *dobře*. Good. But Czechs don't say that, and you certainly don't feel it. Instead you say, '*Jde to*.' It goes. Like *ça va*, in French. You've always appreciated such phrases, the stoic fatalism embedded within them. Whether you're feeling well or ill, whether things are going good or bad, is meaningless. Foul is fair, and fair is foul. It is all one and the same. It goes.

Mario seems to appreciate it, too. Or your use of it. He nods, leans back, looks at you anew. You have the feeling that he's done all this before – many times, perhaps – but that it's not unfolding in the same way, with the same lines. You're off-script, already. Out of character. Not playing the role he expected you to play.

You aren't playing any role, really.

Mario can talk. That much becomes evident. He unrolls a smooth, casual flow of conversation, like a cowboy uncoiling rope. His English is proper and impeccable, as if he has taken great pains to learn the language correctly, not colloquially. He has a tendency to make precise gestures with his hands to emphasise points: pinning his forefinger on the table top, swiping sideways with his palm, or pinching all five fingers together and holding them up, as if offering you a jewel, to be considered carefully, from various angles. He's doing most of the talking, but also – every so often – teasing a bit of information out of you. That you're British, a Welsh woman who's been living in London. That you're recently widowed. That your husband was an American scholar. That you've come here seeking something. Only you can't say what, or why. You tell him what you told the customs official, that you're going to take a language course. Mario accepts this, but warns you Czech is not an easy language to learn.

More beers appear, at certain intervals. The bar doesn't show any signs of closing, even though it must be well past traditional closing times. You don't actually know what time it is, and that's a good feeling, to be off-clock, out of time. You're drunk, of course, but not as drunk as Mario –

he is a good-natured lightweight, laughing giddily at his own idiosyncratic stories – and you feel very lucid, calm, controlled.

It's when you're feeling like this that Mario's friend shows up, looming over you both before taking a chair at your table. He does actually *take* it, too, without asking – turning it around and forcibly putting it down backwards, then straddling it. So different from Mario, in appearance and demeanour. About the same height, but twice as wide. A shaved head and blunt, brutish features. His eyes unnaturally protruding, bulging. As if constantly glaring at things. Glaring at you, from the moment he sits down. You are instantly wary; you know this type of man. We all know his type. Not wild, hopped-up, feral, like the addict who stabbed Tod – who didn't even remember it, *didn't know what he was doing*, as his lawyer claimed – but, rather, bristling with a natural capacity for violence. An inclination for it, even. A predisposition.

He smiles at you, his teeth small and yellow and uneven. 'Hi,' he says, pursing his lips into a threatening kiss. 'Hi, pretty lady.'

You look to Mario, who sighs as if he was expecting this, but still finds it wearisome. He gestures jadedly, introduces the man as Denis, explaining that he and Denis work together, sometimes.

'What kind of work?' you ask.

This and that, Mario says, and Denis laughs.

Denis is here to stay. He shows that in his posture, hunched over the chair like a gargoyle, in the obvious and belligerent way he is staring at you. He's drinking from a battered metal stein and when not taking a swig he keeps his fingers wrapped around the handle, holding it on the table as if gripping a mallet. His knuckles are red, swollen.

A small star tattooed on each. At first you and Mario keep up pretences, continue talking, as if Denis's presence isn't disruptive, hasn't completely changed the dynamic of the situation. Denis speaks very little – only commenting when Mario tries to include him, tries to loosen him up, and even then doing so aggressively. At regular intervals, Denis checks his watch, barks something short and sharp at Mario in another language. Not Czech. You don't think it's Czech. To these queries, Mario merely shrugs, responds demurely.

You ask Denis if he is Slovakian – an innocent question, meant to show him you're not scared of him. Not intimidated. He looks at you as if you've slapped him, so startled to hear you speak *to* him, rather than around him. Rather than adopt that policy of avoidance. Then his lips twist into a smile and a sneer. 'I am not Slovak, pretty lady.'

Mario laughs, a little too loudly. 'No, Denis is not Slovak. He is just crazy. He is like your British comic, no? Dennis the Menace.'

As if to prove the point, Denis picks up Mario's glass, brings it to his mouth, fits the rim in his teeth, and bites it off, cleanly. The glass cracking in a perfect crescent, which he then removes from his mouth, places delicately on the table. 'I am out of beer,' he says.

Mario looks to you, somewhat apologetically. For more money, presumably. You reach for your wallet again. You keep it under the table, trying to conceal from Denis the amount in there, and slide another two hundred over to Mario. He palms it discretely, and assures you he will be right back.

You're left with Denis. The piece of glass in the shape of his mouth glinting on the table. Shining in the murk of the bar like the Cheshire Cat's grin. Mirroring the one on his face. He's staring at you, in his deliberately menacing way.

You stare back. You feel something in you that isn't fear, and isn't even aversion, but a kind of cold, hard hate. It surprises you to find it there. Hidden like a pearl, growing around the shrapnel of bitterness left by Tod's death. Maybe some of that is reflected in your gaze. You wait till Denis breaks eye contact, reaching for a cigarette, and then tell him you're going to the bathroom.

You head for the back of the bar, not knowing if it's the right direction. There's a door and you push through it. It opens into an alleyway: cold, frosty, the cobblestones glittering with ice like flecks of mica. Against the walls, dumpsters and bin bags. A few fire escapes, frozen drain pipes. One end of the alley is solid brick. The other is a main road – you can see traffic down there. You consider walking away, simply leaving. But you left your bag inside, tucked under the table.

As you hesitate, trying to decide, the door opens. And, of course, it's Denis. Having followed you, to make sure you don't do exactly what you're considering doing. He doesn't ask, doesn't even pretend to want an explanation. He grabs you by the shoulders and shoves you against the wall. He tells you to give him your wallet, and passport. It strikes you as slightly comical – the ease with which those things can be taken. He doesn't even need to threaten you. He just has to say it, and expects it to happen, to be obeyed. This is how such scenarios must always play out, for him.

Then Mario is there, too. He sees what's happening, shakes his head remorsefully. 'Ah, Denis.' Then, to you, he adds, 'I am sorry about this.' But he doesn't make a move to stop it, to intervene on your behalf. He merely acts as if it's unlucky, this turn of events, this situation you've gotten yourself into. As if you've fallen into a pit of quicksand, or a pool of piranhas. Unfortunate, yes. But what's to be done?

Except: you tell Denis that you won't give him any money, anything.

Denis blinks, startled – that same look he gave you when you spoke to him inside.

'You have none?'

He knows you do, so you admit it – but explain that you won't give him any. Mario finds this very funny. He laughs, impressed, content to observe the show. He is so nonchalant he actually still has his drink in hand – a fresh *půllitr* of beer. He sips at it, wipes foam from his lips.

Denis doesn't laugh. As before, you're not playing along, not reciting your lines according to your script. You wonder how many times they've done this, or something similar. To tourists, travellers. Performing their double-act – a vaudeville routine that allows room for improvisation but generally unfolds along pre-established lines. A few drinks, a little scare, and the mark will cough up some cash. It's so blatant, in such a public location. You can hear the sounds of the bar, see the lights of the main street. And you simply can't bring yourself to feel the fear and intimidation Denis is demanding, and Mario expecting.

Denis shakes you, as if you're a doll that isn't working.

'The money, you stupid English.' He puts one forearm across your chest, leaning hard against you, and begins to paw at you with his other hand, feeling for your wallet in a forceful, practical way. Impersonal and roughly invasive, like a body search. That makes it feel serious. That makes it real. You grab his forearm, wrench at it, kick out at his shin. Struggle furiously, viciously, violently. All this catches him off-guard. He tries to adjust, react, and in doing so suddenly falls – slipping on the ice underfoot, his cheap trainers giving him no traction at all. His arms windmilling, his feet flying out from under him. Landing hard and heavy on his back.

The dull, hollow sound as his skull hits frozen stone. It is quick, awkward, and comical – fitting to his namesake. Denis the Menace brought low.

For a second, everything is still: Denis at your feet, Mario paused mid-drink, you standing tense and charged, dominant. Then Denis moans and rolls over and curls up and clutches at his skull. He tries to stand, slips again, goes down again. You and Mario watch this for a time, and then look at each other. Now should be the time to run, call the police – but the impulse simply isn't there. Instead, when Mario moves to help Denis, you instinctively join him: one of you on each side, supporting Denis in gaining his feet. He is weak-kneed, wobbly. Even once up he can't support himself. He is half-conscious, punch-drunk as a boxer after a knock-out blow. You have to drag him between you back to your table. This draws a few looks. Some of the men must have known, or suspected, what was going on. And now this – not the usual outcome.

At the table, Denis sinks into his chair and folds his arms and rests his head on them, drifting into a concussed daze. Mario takes Denis's new beer and pours half into your glass, half into his own: an olive branch. You drink deeply, savouring the taste, feeling giddy from your triumph – the downfall of Denis. Did all that really just happen?

Mario apologises, seemingly genuine, and tells you that Denis misunderstood the point of your being there in the bar with him. It is something they do, he explains. But it wasn't supposed to be that way with you.

You tell him you appreciate that, but that you'll be leaving, given the circumstances.

Mario sinks in his chair, crestfallen, and seeks to delay your departure by lighting a cigarette (his own, this time, which he had all along) and holding out the pack to offer one to you. Another peace offering. You accept it, but not a light. You tuck it in your own pack, for safekeeping, like a business card. After a few drags, Mario seems to cheer up and smiles, saying he can't wait to tell people about this. About the English woman who knocked out Denis. You remind him that you're Welsh, and he concedes this. He smiles reminiscently, thinking back, and then guffaws. He holds up his beer to you in a toast.

'If you ever need work, come to me. I will pay. I could use a person like you.'

You ask him what he means, a person like what? He considers, rubs his jaw. Explains that there is work, for certain types of people, certain travellers. And you know he means *the good kind of traveller*. The ones with the right look. But there's more: it is also that you did not panic, he says. You did not seem afraid at all. Did not lose your cool. Then he moves his cigarette in a circle, tracing a pattern around your head, weaving a wreath of smoke. 'You are so cool, almost ice cold. Like that fairy tale, yes? You are the real-life snow queen.'

He declares this proudly, with a flourish. The magician's last act of the night. It makes you smile. He doesn't know just how apt it sounds.

marta

When you booked your bedsit, the landlady emailed a set of directions. It's near Náměstí Míru Metro – five blocks over and one block down from the station. Except the Metro still isn't open yet, and won't be for another half hour. Rather than wait for further trouble to find you, you decide to walk, and clear your head. Carrying the duffel bag slung over one shoulder, weaving your way beneath its weight. The layout of the city comes back to you: southeast past Národní Museum, down to Anglická, and towards the square with that church – Saint Ludmila, or Ludmily – to the Metro. From there, it's easy to follow the landlady's instructions, to reach thirty-five Moravská – a crumbling neoclassical building that might have been an impressive home, a century ago. Now divided up into single rooms and flats – too budget to even be listed on regular sites. The cast iron gate opens, but the front door doesn't.

You allow your bag to drop. Slump down beside it. Feeling like a sack of books yourself. The landlady said she could meet you by seven. You light a cigarette, let it trickle smoke without taking many drags. Feel your eyes go heavy. Lean up against a faux-doric column. Drift and doze. Waiting for her, and for dawn.

Then there is somebody there with you. Squatting on the steps, smoking, gazing into the middle distance. An older woman, with a birthmark on her left cheek. Her hair is short, coarse, black, bristly. Cut close to her scalp. Patchy in places, mottled in others, going grey. She has a solid, muscular build. She's dressed in jeans and boots, a flannel shirt and fisherman's slicker. This must be your landlady. Marta.

Seeing you're awake, she lets her cigarette drop, stamps it out. Extends her hand – the fingers tawny, yellowed from a lifetime of smoke and nicotine, the nails blunt and brittle.

'You are Eira.'

The curt declaration startles you – makes you doubt the accuracy of the statement. Are you still Eira, still yourself? You say that you are, because it's expected. She asks you about the journey from Wales, which confuses you, until you remember your credit card billing address is still the old house in Llandinam, where you and Tod lived before he got the postdoc in London. You don't correct her, tell her the journey was uneventful.

With this formality out of the way, Marta stands and unlocks the door to the property, leading you inside. What would have once been an entrance hall is now a shared foyer for all the tenants, the wainscoting stained, the lino-leum peeling. A central staircase, carpeted in brown, winds upwards in rectangles, allowing you to see to the roof, four or five floors above. Your room, Marta explains, is at the top.

It takes a while to climb the stairs. Marta stops frequently to turn back and talk, as if she cannot walk and talk at the same time. She tells you that she recently had cancer, that this (motioning to her hair, holding a hand above it) is because of the treatment: it did not grow back the same. She tells you she owns a boat, kept on the Vltava. Her husband was a fisherman, but he died. A heart attack. Now she runs tours on the river, but business is not good. You listen to all this dreamily. You are drunk, and sleep deprived, and near exhaustion. The morning has a hazy, hallucinatory feel, and Marta's words – blunt and clipped as her hair – come to you from a distance.

You murmur apologies, for the cancer, the dead husband, the failing business. You tell her you are a widow, too, and she grunts. It sounds somehow approving, or at least respectful. As if you are set apart, the two of you, and made closer by the fact of your widowhood. She tells you she will take you on a boat tour, show you the city from the river. Any time. Just let her know the day before. You say that you're interested, that you will.

Your apartment is cramped, even smaller than the photos on the website made it look. A single room, with a single bed, a single chair at a small desk, a single hotplate, the metal burner rusted and bubbled. A single window, overlooking the street. Lime-green walls, the paint cracked and flaking. In one corner, a shower cubicle has been installed, but the toilet is outside in the hall, accessed by another door. Marta doesn't attempt to explain or justify any of this. She simply opens the door, steps in, and the two of you stare at it in silence.

You tell her it's fine, and she says, '*Dobře.*'

She needs the first month's rent up front. Once you count it out in cash – five thousand koruny, or about one hundred and sixty pounds – she gives you the keys. Tells you there's a shared fridge on the first-floor landing. She turns to go, then seems to remember something, and glances back. 'You can have guests. Men, women. Is fine. But if they stay long, is extra.'

She doesn't specify what she means by 'long'. A few hours? A few days? You don't ask. It doesn't seem to matter, to her or to you. When she's gone you shut the door, drop your duffel bag, lie back on the bed, fully dressed, atop the covers. So this is your home. So this is where you are. A widow like Marta, but at the age of thirty-one. You still feel too young to be a widow. You still feel as young as you did ten years ago, when you and Tod met at university. You feel that you could roll over, reach for him, palm his chest, feel the heat of his body, the beating of his heart.

But, of course, such feelings are self-indulgent, inane. His heart was stopped by a slim metal blade; his body and organs incinerated, reduced to ash that was grey and pebbled and reminded you of gravel, of cat litter. Most of it went into that nook in the wall behind his plaque – but some his parents had insisted on taking home, to America, to be kept on their mantel in Boston next to a photo of the real, smiling, handsome, happy Tod. It struck you as strange, to divide the remains – to divide Tod – in this way (who ended up with which parts, you wondered?), but you didn't argue: apparently it was not uncommon, and it didn't matter to you. But it mattered to them. They wanted him home, implicitly blamed you for his death, held you responsible. Unfair, but also undeniably true: if he'd never moved to Britain, if he'd stayed in America, he most likely would still be alive. Or if he hadn't gone to the cinema that night, at your request. All the little choices that lead to one night, one moment, one action.

The sad, senseless, absurd, pitiable ending of a life.

You think these things and stare at the ceiling, which is spider-webbed with cracks. Only the patterns are not nearly as symmetrical or purposeful as a spider's web. They are haphazard, random, inscrutable. Meaningless.

time

You quickly come to understand that you have nothing to do, here in Prague. You unpack, of course. Go through all the books you have brought and stack them on the small desk. Some are about grief, about bereavement, about coping. Those optimistic self-help guides, mostly by American authors. They were given to you as gifts, by your mother, your friends, and it was for their sakes, not yours, that you accepted them. At that time, you were still adhering to social graces, doing what was expected of you.

No more. They go in a pile near the bin, as if in anticipation of that next step.

You have also brought some of Tod's books: the ones he studied and wrote about, and encouraged you to read. To give you common ground. To understand his work. You always put off or ignored his recommendations, and have only brought them now out of a residual guilt. Your desire to read them has not increased since his death (if anything it has diminished), so you stack them next to the bereavement books.

Clothes go in the small chest of drawers, a battered antique painted cream-white. A few tops go on hangers, hooked to the back of the door. In the cupboard beneath the hotplate you find tea bags, half a pack of penne, and a near-empty bottle of vegetable oil.

You have a cup of tea, shower, and fall asleep, travel-weary, still half-way between drunk and hungover. Wake up in the early evening, having missed the day, having managed to jetlag yourself, despite it being only a one-hour time difference. You feel jittery, hyper-alert. You watch headlight beams strafe across the ceiling, the movement alarming and intrusive, like a frantically turning lighthouse beacon. Warning you away.

In the morning, you eat plain pasta for breakfast and then sit on the edge of the bed for a long time, staring at the floor, your hair hanging on either side of your face, creating a tunnel-effect. You have not come with any real plans or itinerary. You do not have a checklist of tourist destinations you'd like to see, things you'd like to do. You and Tod saw them all, did them all, during your previous trips. The Žižkov TV Tower. Prague Castle. The Old Town. Charles Bridge. The Jewish Cemetery. The Astronomical Clock. You have no need, and no desire, to revisit them.

Instead you wander, in the cold. First up and down the streets of your neighbourhood, and then, in the following days, further – moving out towards the suburbs, where communist-era tower blocks loom like concrete monoliths, or inwards towards the city centre, the bent and winding streets, avoiding the tourist areas whenever possible. The pavements are pebbled with grit, the gutters glazed with ice. No real snow, at the moment. Just this slowly deepening freeze.

From a market down the street you buy some basic staples that can be cooked on a single hob: eggs, rice, potatoes, canned soup. And the other essentials: coffee, beer, wine, cigarettes. Sticking with Smart, again. When you're hungry, which isn't often, you boil something on the hot plate, eat it without pleasure or satisfaction. Breakfast is coffee and a cigarette, breathed out the window to avoid setting off the smoke detector. Then, after you see Marta smoking in her own room, which is one floor down, you simply remove the battery from the detector. The room is saturated with stale smoke anyway – that particular scent that never leaves the carpets, the bed, the walls.

The books sit on your desk, untouched.

Days pass. You have no calendar, no watch, and your phone has long since run out of battery. You vaguely intended to get a charger, but, in your wanderings, you have passed several phone kiosks and shops and never felt the impulse to pick one up. There will be texts and messages – from friends, relatives, your mother. And it's a relief not to have to deal with them. Just as, you imagine, it must be a relief to them when they get your voicemail, are able to leave a supportive message and feel good about helping you, rather than get mired in an actual conversation, with the potential for messy emotional outpouring. This way, they can offer you the verbal equivalent of a pat on the back: *There, there. Time heals all wounds. This too shall pass. He would want you to move on.* You've heard those maxims already, or variations on them. Condensed versions of the wisdom in the bereavement books. You do email your mother, so as not to worry her. A way of making contact, without connecting. To tell her you are fine, that this is helping. *It was the right thing to do.* She

48

writes back, briefly, saying she is so pleased for you. A short note, tapped on her phone.

Despite the cold, Prague is hazy, murky. An inversion layer has settled over the streets. You heard of this, last time you visited, but never witnessed it. A coalescence of smog and pollution. As if some giant silk worm has taken up residence, spun a cocoon over the city. You can see to the end of a block ahead of you; after that, the buildings become vague shapes, the cars and people just shadows.

You understand that painting now – the one of the watches dripping and melting in the heat of some nameless, aimless desert. Something similar seems to be happening here, in Prague. Or perhaps it's the opposite. Instead of becoming malleable, drawn out, extended, time is congealing, slowly solidifying, coming to a halt. Either way, time is revealed to be arbitrary, meaningless. A human construct about as tangible as shadows on a cave wall.

On one of your morning wanderings, you find yourself in the Old Town. It's nearing nine o'clock, even though you've been walking for hours (you're often awake long before daylight). It's not yet busy or bustling. No A-frame signs advertising puppet theatre, or live jazz, or mask shops. No tourists, craning their necks, pointing and clicking with cameras and phones. No stag or hen parties. Just cobbled streets, empty doorways, shuttered windows. Your feet lead you, by chance or a faint recollection – embedded muscle memory – around a corner, down a narrow alley and out into a small square dominated by the front of a church, and the Astronomical Clock. You stood here – in this exact spot – years before, with Tod. Along with dozens of other tourists, on a hot June day. All of you smelling of sweat and sunscreen and anticipation. The clock is renowned, astonishingly intricate – centuries old but still functioning, with numerous dials and cogs set within its face. A kind of elaborate cuckoo clock that performs a pantomime play when it strikes the hour. You wait for the hour, as you did then, only alone, this time – in the cold of winter rather than the heat of summer.

The hands on the clock face creep around slowly, each tick a momentous effort. At times it seems as if they aren't moving at all. But eventually, finally, the clock strikes nine. Two shutters open. Mechanical figures appear within, passing by the windows: the twelve apostles, each carved individually. And, either side, figures representing human vice lurch to life. A man holding a money pouch, signifying greed. Another with a mirror, for vanity. A third playing a lute, to show lust and decadence. While close at hand a skeleton shakes his hourglass, rings a little bell, his rigid grin gleeful and indifferent. Serving as a reminder of what awaits each of these characters, and each of us. Like a grand version of those sculptures and paintings – *memento mori* – the Victorians kept on their mantles. Featuring flowers, skulls, hourglasses. Cheerful and eerie reminders that time is passing, that life is fleeting, that death is coming. Sooner than you think.

An obvious message, so easily ignored amid the fray of life. You're sure that's what you would have done, the last time you were here. You would have watched the little display and taken a few photos and then gone for a drink with Tod and forgotten. Now, these wooden figures stuck on their rails and ruts and perches seem a simple and profound representation of what you know from experience to be true.

the bridge

One morning your walk takes you to the Vltava, the major river that meanders through the centre of Prague, divides Praha One and Praha Two. Looking down at the blackened water, smooth and free from waves, sleek as obsidian, you know it must be flowing but the only signs of movement are the oiling currents that seem to shimmer across the surface, and even those are so subtle and delicate that they could be a trick of the light – just a reflection or refraction. It's hard to tell if the river is actually in motion, or if it has somehow slowed, hardened, fallen under the spell of stasis that has settled over the rest of the city. Possibly the surface is coated with a very thin layer of black ice, not yet thick enough to turn opaque. You've seen that before, on canals back in Britain. Just a millimetre of ice, like a veneer.

But no: it is flowing. There, at the base of the bridge, you can make out a rippling of current where the waters part around the pillar. This bridge is known, renowned – it is *a thing to see* when in Prague – dating from the fifteenth century. So old its brickwork is soot-blackened, the stones dark and speckled like pieces of charcoal fitted together. Underfoot it is cobbled. Vehicles don't go over it. Every few metres, on either side, there's a statue of some dignitary, some luminary, from Prague's past. All these traits make it an iconic spot – *Charles Bridge!* A location that has been used in famous films. A place where significant meetings occur. Where innumerable photos have been snapped, countless poses struck by earnest tourists.

But, of course, that's not why you came here. You've been here, done all that. You could probably find the photos, if you wanted. Of you and Tod in summer clothes: shorts and tees, walking shoes, a small-ish backpack for snacks, for water. You were that kind of couple. Respectful, capable, inquisitive. Learning just enough language to get by, to show you were trying. And the photos you took seemed to capture that, prove it. No outrageous poses, no silly stunts or pranks. No excessive drinking. Just two young people, in love, seeing the sights, sharing their lives.

Your return here was by accident rather than by design – a wrong turn, or a right one, on one of your daily wanderings. It's still quite early, with the sun low in the sky, though it's hard to tell through the cloud layer and smog. You don't have the bridge to yourself, but the other people on it cross in both directions with quick, efficient strides. No time or inclination to take photographs, play tourist – they are locals on set schedules, with trams to catch, offices to reach, desks to sit at, shops to open, meetings to make.

You have the time, though. Or rather, you have stepped out of time. Since you have no deadlines, no appointments, no place to be, nothing to do, the days are passing unnoticed, in a glaze of repetition that has oozed into weeks. Time so languid it may as well be stopped. It feels as if it has. An illusion, like the river that looks still and frozen yet is moving. You stare into the enigmatic water-mirage, flat and featureless as a black mirror, reflecting nothing. You can't even see a version of yourself down there, just the darkness.

As ever, when looking down from a height, you feel that perverse but natural desire to lean too far, to fall. An impulse that's stronger in some people than others, but that we all recognise. For you it's strong enough to trigger the rush of vertigo, the exhilaration that would accompany it, the sense in your body *that you are actually falling,* that the river surface is rushing up to meet you, and in a matter of seconds you'll feel the icy shock of water, devastatingly cold. Come up gasping, or let yourself sink, your clothes heavy as chainmail, your boots breezeblocks, dragging you down.

The thought of it gives you a thrill, like running the side of your thumb along a knife blade, evoking that shiver, that frisson.

Tod hated your love of heights, hated to go near ledges himself, and couldn't stand how you acted around them. So careless, so confident. Like that cliff face in Capri – right to the crumbling edge, staring down hundreds of feet, higher than the seabirds, which were white specks below you, swirling round and round like scraps of paper in a whirlpool. And Tod standing maybe three metres behind, beckoning to you, urging you to be careful, to step back.

This height is nothing compared to that. But still, the familiar tingle makes you think, maybe you always had it in you. A fascination with oblivion, with falling into the void. Not only now, during what would be described as a time of shock and trauma – *such a tragic loss, that poor woman, her and her broken heart* – but before Tod's death. Maybe your penchant for vertigo thrills, the allure of heights, is in-built, genetic; a natural aberration.

Maybe it sets you apart. Maybe it makes you different from most people.

These are the kinds of things you think while standing on the bridge. These, you are confident, are not truly suicidal thoughts. You don't actually *want* to jump, to hit the ice-cold water fully clothed, to soak and sink. It seems too melodramatic, and also too obvious – a sad fate more suited to the jilted or betrayed or abused heroines in Tod's Russian novels. Those books stacked on your desk. There's a reason you've left them untouched: the ones you did try reading at Tod's behest you found unbearably frustrating, the characters too dreary or moping or fatalistic. Too resigned.

Nobody would think that of you, you hope. You are reasonably sure you would have the reader's sympathy, despite your emotional detachment.

As if to confirm this, you notice that somebody is trying to get your attention. A figure down at the river's edge is waving, using both arms in a scissoring motion over their head, like a traffic control worker directing planes on the runway. The person is standing at the bottom of some stone steps, which lead to a wooden jetty. On the jetty, a dark green sign – the print too small to read from a distance. And, at the end, a boat. A fishing boat. Something about the figure is familiar, and after a few seconds you clock that it's Marta. She must have recognised you, too. She said something about this – about her boat, and launch. Every day she must be here, and this day you're here too. You wave back, acknowledging her, and begin to walk towards her side of the bridge. She invited you, after all. And it would seem rude to simply walk away now.

a boat ride

Marta's boat is called, appropriately, Marta. It has a deep, carvel hull – the long wooden planks painted pale blue – and a wheelhouse at the front, with a hatch leading to the cabin below deck. It's a sturdy trawler, a good boat. Her husband built it and christened it. When the boat passed to her, she didn't change the name. Even though it seemed odd to pilot a boat with her own name, she didn't want the bad luck that changing it might bring.

She tells you this as you stand on the dock, handing her the gear and supplies she's brought along for the day's trip: tackle box, fishing rods, packed lunches, a red plastic cooler marked with scuffs and rimmed with grime. Her sign at the end of the dock is just a chalkboard, propped up, scribbled on with white lettering, Czech at the top, and English beneath it: *Fishing trips and boat tours. See the city from the water. Two trips per day. Morning and afternoon.* At the bottom is Marta's phone number.

Once the boat is loaded, the two of you wait on the dock to see if any other customers might show up. You sit in folding lawn chairs – the seats and backrests made of nylon strips, beginning to fray in places. You smoke and watch the water, talk only occasionally. From this close you can more clearly see the slow-moving surface, gently turning with eddies and back currents, so sluggish it seems to be congealing. You ask Marta if it ever freezes, the Vltava. She nods, *ano*. Sometimes. Not as often as when she was growing up. Back then, she tells you, the young people would come here to skate, even play hockey. But there were accidents. Every so often a child would take a risk, skate on thin ice, go through. She doesn't elaborate; she leaves it at that, leaves you with the image of children sinking, unable to swim with skates on their feet.

After a certain amount of time – about an hour – Marta claps her hands to her knees and stands up.

'No customers this morning. Is fine. Is usual. I still fish. You come.'

It isn't a question, or an offer – more of an order. And you obey, waiting as Marta hops back aboard, ducks into the wheelhouse, and fires up the engine. It chortles to life in the morning cold, coughing a few times, emitting an initial backfire of billowing exhaust from the smokestack, jutting up above the roof. Poking her head back out, she tells you to undo the lines. You manage, after some fiddling.

Letting the lines drop, you stand complacently and watch the boat drift away from the dock, carried by the current. Marta motions impatiently, urging you to *jump, jump*, and you do – straining to make the gap, slipping on the water-slick deck, landing hard on your hip. Laughing, Marta comes out of the wheelhouse to help you up, and you find that you're laughing too. A strange sensation, to laugh, after so long.

'Bring in the ropes, the buoys,' Marta tells you, pointing, and returns to the wheel.

You follow orders, and in a way it is quite pleasant – to be instructed, to have purpose. To be active. The ropes are cold and slick as you pull them in, hand over hand, coiling them inexpertly on deck. The buoys are large but light, like thick-skinned balloons, red and rubbery. By the time this is done, Marta has steered the craft to the centre of the river, and turned it upstream. You pass under Charles Bridge – the ancient stonework forming an arch overhead, glistening wet, thick with moss and algae. For a moment the reverberations of the engine are enclosed, echoing, amplified, until you drift out the other side.

The back of the wheelhouse is extended with a fibreglass canopy, with a bench seat on either side to accommodate clients. You go in to sit near Marta, and, for a time, as you float south through the city, she points out various sights to you: the distant spires of St. Vitus Cathedral, the rooftops of Prague castle, and the fourteenth-century bathhouse that's been converted into a five-storey nightclub. And, further upriver, Žofín Palace, on Slovansky Island. She does not elaborate as to the significance of these sites. She merely gestures, and states the names. You wonder if this is the extent of her usual riverboat tours. The thought pleases, and amuses. You appreciate the brevity, the concision. What more do tourists need, really? This is this, and that is that.

A day cruiser approaches, large and garishly painted, flags flapping off the stern, and Marta steers closer to shore to give it a wide berth. Tourists wave at you from the upper deck. Neither of you waves back. Within half an hour, the buildings of central Prague have fallen away and the surroundings become more industrial: first low warehouses, then some kind of chemical refinery, with thin chimneys leaking dark smoke, like a whole pack of cigarettes burning at once. Marta no longer points out landmarks. Nothing here is worth noting.

The industrial area gives way to woodland – the transition abrupt, nearly instantaneous. The banks are dense with trees, mostly willow and poplar. After another quarter hour, Marta eases up on the throttle, lets the trawler lose its momentum. You think she intends to turn around, head back, but she lets out the anchor instead, and tells you it's time to fish.

That is what you do – drifting in the slow current, the bow pointed upstream, the two of you sitting in the back, each of you cradling a rod. Fishing. You know as much about fishing as you do about boats, but, when you ask, Marta only shakes her head and laughs and says, 'If you get a bite, don't let go.' It sounds like a proverb, the way she says it.

Downstream, beyond the river bends, you can see Prague, the buildings dim and shadowy, obscured by the smog. It makes the cityscape look ominous, menacing. Out here the air is cleaner, fresher, though a glaze of clouds still coats the sky. The woods are silent and calm, the only sound the faint, endless slap of water against the hull. A cold wind is blowing steadily, cutting through your coat, causing your eyes to water.

Marta must notice it too. She says something about a north wind from the Baltic Sea. You ask how far along the river you can travel. She gestures vaguely over her shoulder, further upriver. 'Very far. Almost to Austria, to the Lipno Dam.' Turning back towards Prague, she adds, 'And that way even further. At Mělník it becomes Elbe, and Elbe goes to Germany, to Dresden.' From beneath her seat she pulls out a battered Thermos. She unscrews the lid and pours you both a mug of coffee, tops it up with liberal splashes of something that must be liquor, even though the bottle is not labelled. It tastes strong and herbal, medicinal, and warms you from within.

For the most part you sit in silence, staring at the black water, at the thin threads of fishing line running like spider webs off the stern, glistening with water drops. Between cups of Marta's special coffee you smoke – another way to keep warm. You consider possible topics of conversation: asking Marta about her husband, about whether they had any children; telling her about Tod, about the stabbing, the loss. But you don't give voice to these ideas. Such prying and confiding would feel pointless. Your husbands, your pasts, your histories, none of those things matter. You're here, in a boat, in the Czech Republic, fishing. Two widows, sharing coffee and cigarettes. Even that word – widow – defines you in terms of what you once were, a wife, not what you are. Two *women*, sharing coffee and cigarettes.

All you say, instead, is *děkuji*. Thank you.

'We have not caught anything yet,' Marta says.

You explain it doesn't matter; it's enough to be out here. She grunts, unconvinced, and secures her rod in one of the holders on the stern, then gets out her fishing knife – a slim, curved blade about six-inches long – and begins to whittle a piece of wood. Within a few minutes she's carved out a rough-looking duck, and holds it up – as if she needs to impress you, or leave an impression, due to the failure of the fishing. You smile politely, compliment her on her skill. Not knowing what else you should say, when it comes to wood whittling.

She says the knife was her husband's, has outlasted him by several years. Then, looking bashful, she ends her little demonstration. Puts both knife and duck away. She sits back down. Makes a general comment about it being hard, the loss of a husband. And you expect her to leave it at that. You *want* her to leave it at that. But unfortunately she goes on, awkwardly. She says she sees you, coming and going. Always alone. It is not good to be alone, she says. You take a long drag on your cigarette, looking straight ahead. There is a tension in your jaw – an ache. It feels like a betrayal, or a trap. The whole thing a set-up. As if she's brought you out here to help you, save you. Play surrogate mother.

'You should do social things,' she says, in the same way she told you to hop aboard, to pull in the ropes. 'Be around people. I know what it is like, you see.'

You nod, stiffly, and tap ash over the side. Tell her you'll think about it. She says you can come out with her, on the boat, whenever you like.

You smile bitterly. 'I'll keep that in mind,' you say, in a way that makes it clear you won't be taking her up on the offer.

After that she goes quiet, perhaps sensing that something has changed. The warmth of the coffee and liquor leaking away, the warmth of your camaraderie leeching out of you, the wind picking up, the cold turning that much sharper, its edge cutting.

You have both been stubbing out finished cigarettes in an old tin, stained and ashy, where the butts are entwined together like a nest of worms. Now, you flick yours overboard, into the water, where it lands with a deflating hiss. Seconds later, a fish snaps at it – the flash of gullet, the quick flick of tail. You both look in that direction, surprised. A few seconds later the butt floats back up again, the fish having realised it's been duped.

Marta looks quizzically at her rod, pulls on the line a few times, and releases it. 'My bait is not working,' she says, and sighs, then settles back into her chair. After a few minutes of further pretence, you suggest that it's time to head back.

lessons

Walking down Vinohradská, in the drizzling sleet, you see the sign: *Czech For You!* Accompanied by a cartoon line drawing, the smiling teeth spilling off the side of the man's face, like one of those pictures done by children for charitable causes. It stops you, that sign. Perhaps because you've told a number of people that you're intending to learn Czech.

Until now, you've had no real intention of pursuing it. But it has a powerful pull, that silly, slightly unhinged ad. Maybe it's fated; maybe a language course is something you should try. Maybe Marta was right, and being around people is a good idea, healthy. All those grief guides – which you've left by the bin – would recommend the same, you're sure. And what's the alternative? More wandering. Or Mario. As of late you've been walking down to Wenceslas Square. Not to take him up on his offer of some work. Not specifically. But out of curiosity. That night – the strangeness, the sense of threat and newness – was the only moment of this trip that hasn't felt as if you've been stuck in stasis, time frozen, nothing happening.

Better, surely, to try something else, even as clichéd as a language course, than set loose that part of yourself. Let it have more reign. To do something deliberately risky, dangerous. To take that step, to let yourself fall. So, you go inside, sign up for a month-long course in beginner's Czech. There are forms to fill, and payment up front. More than you can afford – most of your remaining money – but you pay all the same.

The administrator tells you the current course started on Monday (it's now Wednesday), but you're welcome to join the class tomorrow morning, which you do. Sitting at the back, with a fresh blank notebook in front of you, and a set of photocopied pages handed out by the teacher – a tall, slim Czech who is handsome and accommodating, his English impeccable. He looks as if he could be a waiter in a five-star restaurant (which he is in the evenings, you learn later).

Back in school – a student again. The feeling disturbingly familiar, the seats just as rigid, the classrooms just as cheerily drab. The lighting high-key, the air so cold you can see your breath some mornings (the teacher apologises constantly about the lack of heat, assures you repeatedly it is getting fixed). Yet somehow comforting, comfortable, despite that. If nothing else, you know your role here. You simply have to sit and listen and jot down notes. Every so often you fill in a quiz, or are paired up with another student to practice your speaking skills, memorising and repeating set conversations: how to order food, how to ask for directions to the library, the museum, the police. *Víš kde jsem? Můžeš me pomoci?*

With the other students you make an effort, are polite, attentive, engaged. You know there is a degree of superficiality to this – it's merely a persona, worn to fit the classroom environment – but they don't seem to notice, or care. No doubt they have problems of their own, are wearing masks of their own. We all do this, constantly. Engage in these forms of play-acting.

Your fellow students are all mildly interesting, in their own ways. There is the Australian woman who worked on films, as a set designer – all the blockbusters by one big-name director – but is now living here, with her husband, who's a hedge-fund broker. There is the Bangladeshi woman who also came here for a man, who met her husband on the day of her arranged marriage and has only been married two months. When you ask her how it's going, she says, wryly, 'So far, so good.' Along with them there's the Dutch student, already fluent in German, English, and Dutch, learning Czech as a way of talking to his girlfriend in her own language. Then there is the American woman who attends the class for the first week, but after that opts out, saying she can't commit: it was just something her partner thought would be good for her. And the Canadian boy (he really does look like a boy) who is so painfully, obviously alone, and lonely. Who admits to you, between dialogues one day, that he came out to Prague on a one-way ticket, wanting to a be a writer, get some life experience, meet new people, maybe fall in love.

For so many others, it's apparent their presence in Prague – and the class – is connected to another person. A husband, a partner, a potential partner. As if we need that other to define ourselves, our *self*. In a way, you're still doing the same, or pretending to: you've come to Prague since it meant something to you and Tod. Though you're beginning to wonder how true that is. It was the place you first travelled together, and the place he proposed. That's enough to explain your visit to anybody who knew the two of you, as a couple, an item. It has a sentimental and romantic ring to it, a way of going back, of coming to terms, of dealing with grief. But, in truth, Prague doesn't mean more to you than any other place you visited with Tod. The reason the two of you first came, no doubt, was simply due to images, anecdotes, marketing posters. It seemed a romantic city to visit, like Venice, or Barcelona (places you also visited with him). He didn't have any true connection to the country, and your faint link through your grandfather hasn't made you feel any more at home here, either.

You don't tell any of this to your fellow students, of course. You don't need to justify your visit to them in the way you did to people back home. You merely say you're interested in the language, the culture. You visited Prague before and fell in love with the place. Using these convenient, acceptable lies.

You realise within a few days that the class isn't what you hoped it would be: it may be what you need, but it isn't what you want. You find it hard to concentrate. You make token notes, engage in the dialogues and group discussions, play along with the others, but outside of class you retain little, never revise or memorise. By the end of the first week, you find you are tuning out, gazing at the frost on the window, the hazy streets beyond, listening to the rattle of rain and sleet on the pane. This, too, is a familiar feeling, and still comforting – just like being back in school. You don't need to pay attention unless called on directly, and your tutor is far more understanding, patient, and supportive than your school teachers ever were. This is only his day job, a way to top-up his tips. He has no investment in his students. He will smile tolerantly, is always quick to repeat his question, or coach you through the answer.

In between, you feel as if you are still wandering the streets, still adrift in the cold, still trying to figure out this city and why you are in it, as if the buildings are puzzle blocks, one giant concrete Rubik's cube.

In the second week, you skip a morning or two. This doesn't seem to affect your performance in class. There is no real sense of progression, and some of the other students – aside from the Dutch polyglot – are just as hapless as you. You don't fall behind, even attending irregularly. But eventually the impulse to attend at all dwindles, and unlike school you feel no obligation to keep up the pretence. You walk in at the start of the fourth week, when the class is in session, but instead of joining the others in the classroom you head to the office. You explain to the administrator (the same red-haired young woman who signed you up) that you appreciated the tutor, got on with your classmates, but would like to drop out. She expresses surprise, disappointment, but it's as feigned as your student persona: she's used to this. People coming and going, entering and exiting. All with their own reasons. She says the school can refund you for the remaining week of your tuition, but not for the classes you've already skipped.

So that is the extent of your experience as a Czech learner – seemingly unimportant, mostly forgettable. Except for the fact that, as you're having this discussion – checking out, as it were – the Canadian boy is making a cup of tea, using the kettle in the kitchenette across the corridor, which students are allowed and encouraged to do. You noticed him when you first entered, thought little of it. But when you finish – taking cash for your tuition refund – and leave the office, he's waiting for you, looking concerned. He says he overheard, is sorry to learn you're quitting. He asks, hesitantly, if you're okay, and you tell him you are. It sounds straightforward enough, and he smiles shyly, says you should keep in touch – that maybe you could get a cup of coffee sometime? The two of you, or with the other students? You look at him curiously, wondering if this is an awkward, juvenile attempt at a pick-up. But no, he's simply being friendly, sociable, maudlin. Unwilling to let even a passing acquaintance go. The sentimentality of youth.

'Sure,' you say, 'why not?' Then, putting him to the test, you ask, 'Now?'

He looks at the cup of coffee he has just made, laughs, and puts it down on the windowsill. 'I guess so,' he says. 'We're just doing the same dialogues again today.'

A seemingly innocuous exchange, which will lead to no long-term friendship, no amorous liaison, no platonic indie-film relationship. This boy means nothing to you, and never will. He is only a minor player, exempt from the real drama to come. His is a walk-on role, a bit part, with a few token scenes. But his presence is important, nonetheless. It's vital, actually, since he is the one telling this story.

He is me.

beginnings

That's how I heard some of this, how I heard the start of it. Until the day you and I went out for coffee and started drinking, we hadn't actually talked much, aside from the few times we were paired up in class: the repetitive droning of language dialogues, with short intervals in which we chatted about the city, the weather, while waiting for other students to finish and catch up. I had noticed you, or had taken note of you. But then, I'd taken note of everybody – had taken notes on them, actually. I'd told you I wanted to be a writer, that I'd joined the class for the experience. It was also for research. I recorded mannerisms, jotted down dialogue, observed and described, trying to capture everybody in that class as potential characters. I had several pages dedicated to you, the enigmatic woman with the Welsh name. Eira.

The day you quit the class, you and I went to that tourist bar a few blocks away from the language school. It had been a keep or a dungeon at one time and all the drinking areas were underground, in vaulted cellars, like something out of Poe. We tried to order coffee, but they didn't serve it, so we got beers instead. It was a good place to drink at eleven o'clock in the morning – there were no windows and it was impossible to tell the time of day. We had our own nook, with a rough-hewn oak table. They were going for a kind of mediaeval atmosphere, and served their *tuplák* beers in big steel tankards. At first, we didn't do much except sit, and sip. The place was almost empty, with only a handful of other customers, but lively Czech rock leaked from the speakers – a sly attempt on the part of management to make it seem as if it was a normal time to be sitting around drinking.

You got out your pack of Smart, and lit up. You offered me one and I accepted it because I was embarrassed not to. It has to be said, I was intimidated by you. You just had this look that seemed to say, *I don't care any more. About anything.*

There was nothing extraordinary about the meeting, no sense of instant connection or potential friendship. But I got the feeling you were okay with me, and I was okay with you. I've always liked people who can just sit, and think, and be around somebody, without feeling obligated to talk about things that don't matter.

After the first *tuplák*, I asked you what you were doing in Prague, and you told me the real story. Very succinctly, and straightforwardly: that your husband had been killed, stabbed in a confrontation on a bus in London, and that you had been at loose ends ever since. You'd originally decided to come because it was a city that meant something, to you and to him, but that was more of an excuse than anything else.

Then you said, 'What about you?'

I think I said 'Jesus' or something like that, and told you how sorry I was.

My reaction had an odd effect: it made you laugh. I was doing this thing, where I raise my eyebrows and stare straight ahead, as if I've been lobotomised, sent into a state of total shock. You waved your cigarette, brushing your tragic backstory aside, said not to worry about it. I took a long pull from my tankard and plonked it down hard. I said I'd known there was something about you – something that was different, or not quite typical.

You looked at me curiously, and I admitted I'd been watching the other students, observing them, in the hopes of mining some material. I'd already told you about wanting to be a writer. Now I explained I didn't know how to go about it. I was just living in Prague, messing around, blowing all the money I'd saved up doing odd jobs back home. I hadn't written much, and knew enough about literature to tell what I had written wasn't any good.

You listened tolerantly. You'd just told me your husband had been stabbed in the heart and here I was, moaning about my artistic struggles. But you took it at face value. You said, even-handedly, that these things take time. That I was young. That I had to stick with it. You said you'd been a decent actress once, that you'd had aspirations along those lines, after university, but had given them up. They'd seemed too impractical, too unrealistic. You were getting older, and had gotten married. You weren't earning and you and your husband wanted a nicer place, space to start a family. London was expensive.

'But now,' you said. 'I wish I'd kept up my acting. It meant more than I realised. And the rest didn't amount to much. Besides, Tod's dead anyway.'

Because his death had come up again, I asked you about it – about how it happened. So, you me told the details, with that air of resignation: the bus, the aggro junkie, the scuffle, the knife. I was enthralled, and in response all I could think to say were the kinds of things you'd no doubt heard countless times already: that it was such a tragedy, him being so young. That it wasn't fair. That you were doing amazingly well. That you were 'holding up' better than most people would have, including me. You accepted these trite comments without resentment. You were very polite, very patient.

A lot of the things I said, I wouldn't say now, obviously.

We drank through lunch, finished your pack of cigarettes. I was pretty wobbly by then. I wasn't used to drinking at that time of day. At some point, I asked you what you planned to do, now that you'd quit the language class. You looked off, to the left, stared at the rest of the bar. A few more people had come in by then, and some were eating – we could smell the fried food, hear the incomprehensible murmuring of several Czech conversations.

Turning back to me, you said you'd met a guy – a guy called Mario – on the night you'd arrived. In Wenceslas Square. A kind of street hustler. He said he might be able to find work for you, if you wanted it. You were running out of money, so had to do something.

I was in awe. I sensed, in you, all the things I'd come to Prague wanting to do, and hoping to experience – but was too young, timid, and scared to undertake. Not you.

Shortly after, you stood up, stretched, said you were going to walk off your buzz. I stammered something about keeping in touch, scribbled my number and address on the back of a napkin. I rose with you. I wanted to follow you. But, of course, I didn't. You shook my hand and took my napkin and pulled on your jacket and left.

I finished my beer, hurried back to my flat, got out my notebook, and in a drunken blaze jotted down everything we'd discussed, everything you said. I thought I'd had some kind of epiphany; I thought you were the key to something. And then, once you reappeared, contacted me again, I was convinced of it. By then you were in deep, involved in something dangerous, and potentially deadly. A matter of life and death. I didn't know the full story, but I trusted you enough to believe you were doing what was right. That you were on the side of good.

I tried to help, as best I could. Now, of course, I wish I could have done better.

Maybe that's why I've felt compelled to get this down, write out your story. I wanted people to know. What you did, the risks you took. This great act of generosity. And though I couldn't do anything else, couldn't do nearly enough, I could at least do this. As a form of personal penance, and a way of discovering, and recovering, the truth. Or, at least, something *closer* to the truth. And, of course, as a way of getting closer to you. Understanding you.

That's part of it too. That can't be denied.

part two

looking for trouble

You find him where he found you: in the square, in the cold, in the night. But earlier, at a respectable hour, when there are far more locals and tourists about, far fewer drunks. A fresh dusting of snow on the ground, the crystals hard and crusted, like sand. Where pedestrians have stepped it's been crushed into greyish grit that reminds you of Tod's cremated remains.

You see Mario before he sees you – from afar. He's lounging in the doorway of one of the twenty-four-hour electronic casinos, dressed immaculately in his beige linen suit. This time, it's complemented by a green dress shirt. A leather overcoat. A cigarillo scissored between the fingers of his right hand. The lights of the roulette wheel in the window beside him washing over his face, casting it blue, then red, then yellow. Mario the magician. Already on the hustle, ready to work his magic.

You have time, as you approach, to wonder how you have arrived at this, or, more specifically, what has drawn you back here. Maybe the fact that you feel, in doing so, you're taking a step off the clockwork tracks, breaking not just routine but character. You're doing something nobody would expect of you, or suspect you were capable of: wilfully seeking out trouble. It's a thrill, sure. But, more than that, it amounts to a kind of freedom. Like you can peel off your skin, step out of it, kick your old self into the gutter, become somebody else.

Or maybe you're just bored, dulled. You feel so *bloody numb*, all the time. And this seems like it could alleviate it. You can't wander around Prague forever, seeking nothing.

Or maybe it's simply that you need money. There's always that. You wonder if that was partly the purpose of the language classes: to use up the last of your cash, to push yourself to this point. To see what happens next.

Regardless, Mario doesn't seem surprised to see you. Pleased, yes. But not surprised. He notices you and straightens and smiles, widely, letting smoke leak from the sides of his mouth.

'The snow queen,' he says, affectionately. 'I hoped I'd be seeing you.'

He transfers his cigarillo, extends his hand, which you take. His palm smooth and cool as porcelain. You ask him firstly how his friend is – Denis. The one who received the knock on the head. At that, Mario laughs, mimes rapping on his own skull, like people do to demonstrate that it's empty. He says Denis is fine. He was a little concussed for a few days, but recovered quickly. He hardly remembers anything, bears no ill will.

This strikes you as funny, that your attacker and would-be mugger might be the one who feels mistreated, or hard done by.

'And you?' Mario says. 'You are the same?'

You tell him you're getting by, but that money is running out. You're wondering about his proposal, the work he mentioned.

'Ah,' he says, as if he's been waiting for you to broach the subject. 'Yes, we all need money. We should talk. There is work, definitely. A job coming up, in fact. For the right person.' He looks at you, as if honestly trying to judge, and tells you he thinks you might be the right person.

You ask him what kind of work it is, but he shakes his head, quick and professional. Here is not the place to talk. He makes a circular motion with his cigarillo, adopting that showman's air.

'Let's go for a walk,' he tells you, and stoops to stub out the cigarillo. 'A *procházka*, yes?'

So that's what you do, the two of you. You wander together down the boulevard, along the eastern side of Wenceslas Square. Like old friends. Or a couple out for a stroll. It's crowded, but the noise of footsteps, the constant stir of other conversations, creates a kind of privacy – nobody can overhear anybody else because they're all talking, laughing, walking.

Mario saunters along with his collar turned up, his hands buried in the pockets of his overcoat, which you see now is not real leather – the plastic material creased, splitting. He looks straight ahead as he talks to you. He asks firstly if you have a passport, which confuses you – it's the kind of thing you would expect from a formal employer, not a hustler. You tell him you do.

'And you can drive?' he asks. 'You have a licence?'

'A British licence, sure.'

'And you have never been in trouble? No criminal record?'

'No.'

After each of your answers, he nods. Satisfied. You follow him to the northern end of Wenceslas Square, and continue on into the Old Town, among the jazz bars and puppet theatres, all the tourist shops. In front of one theatre a man in dark clothing works a knee-high marionette, making it dance and kick, hoping to attract punters. Mario walks by, nearly stepping on the puppet, which hops back out of reach, waving a fist in mock-irritation.

Mario tells you the work is simple and straightforward. It's not dangerous or risky at all, provided you do as you're told. You will make very good money. But, he adds, it is not legal. He asks if you understand, and you say yes. He asks if you have a problem with that, and you say no. Good, he says. *Dobrý*. He claps his hands – the sound echoing loudly – and rubs them together, as if warming them. It gives him a gleeful air.

Again, you ask him what it is he wants you to do, and he waves vaguely. Says that it usually involves crossing the border into Ukraine, out of Europe. Picking something up, and coming back. Just once. Only ever once.

Under your breath, almost to yourself, you mutter one word, 'Drugs.'

'Sometimes drugs, yes. Sometimes goods, other things.' He thinks a minute, and then adds, 'Products.' He seems pleased with the all-encompassing nature of the term.

You point out that he said there was no risk, no danger. Drug smuggling is risky. Mario laughs, a tight, high sound – not his usual laugh. A nervous laugh. Like he's had a blast of helium. He explains it is only risky if you screw it up. If you do the wrong thing. There are rarely problems. They have people at the border.

They. It's the first time he's used that word. You ask him – to be sure – whether you're working for him, or somebody else. He admits he is just the middleman. He finds people. People like you. People who look innocent, who *are* innocent. People who can cross borders. People who, for whatever reason, are willing to do this thing. For money, mainly. Then he sets up a meeting. That's the next step. After that, you are committed.

You just have to keep your cool, he says, and glances sidelong at you. He says that's why he thought you'd be perfect. The way you were with Denis. Your lack of panic, fear.

'You are the snow queen, right?'

You've come out in a small square, still in the Old Town, but away from the areas popular with tourists at night. No one is around; the only sound the echo of your footsteps on frozen cobblestones. Mario stops and turns to you, and you stand facing each other, your breath mingling in the cold. You notice that his nose is slightly crooked, from being broken and healing wrong.

He says this is as much as he can tell you, at this stage. There is no pressure, but if you agree to it, if you go ahead, then you must fulfil your side of the bargain. He shakes his head, wryly. 'These people, they do not like – how do you say – *to be trifled with*? If you want the work, you must be serious. You do it, you get paid, you walk away. That's it.'

You ask him how much, and he names a sum, in dollars. Five figures. More than you need, even more than you expected. But hearing it doesn't give you any thrill, and confirms what you already suspected: you're not really doing this for the money. Any amount of money.

You tell him you're interested. You tell him you'll do it.

He touches you, lightly, on the shoulder. He is pleased by your decisiveness, you can tell. It seems to confirm for him his instincts are correct, in using you. He says he will phone you,

79

that the next stage is the meeting. When you admit that you don't have a mobile that works, he looks at you, puzzled and possibly irritated by this small inconvenience.

'That will have to be sorted out,' he says, 'and quickly.'

He jots down his number, tells you to contact him as soon as you can. Having established that, you're ready to part ways, for now: Mario pulls up his coat collar and turns to go, raising his hand in a casual wave. You glance around to get your bearings, and head in the opposite direction.

On the walk back, you skirt the edge of Old Town Square, near the Astronomical Clock, now still and silent, hovering between strikes. But all the characters are up there, in their places, ready for things to begin unwinding, ready to be put in motion. Like chess pieces at the start of a game. Passing beneath them, you wonder if you've been wrong all along, if this isn't about breaking free at all. Maybe it's simply fated, inevitable, already irrevocable. The stabbing on the bus, Tod's death, your odd decision to come to Prague, the chance meeting with Mario. It all happened the way it had to, and everything else that occurs from here on in will unfold in the same way. As it must.

the meeting

The woman pours water from a decanter into a small glass tumbler, picks up the glass and considers it, holding it at the base, pinched between her thumb and fingers. She drinks it swiftly, all at once, and puts it down on the low table between you. The table is laid with an assortment of snacks: dark bread, sardines in oil, pickles, cucumbers – other foods you don't recognise. She selects a slice of pickle, and square of bread. Like the water, these snacks are presented but not offered to you, or Mario. Yet.

At the back of the room, an ornate stained-glass window depicting a biblical scene: the beheading of John the Baptist, orchestrated by Salome. His head on a plate, seemingly still conscious or aware, looking anxious. Beyond, visible through the panes, a kaleidoscope view of Prague, broken into shards of colour.

To one side, an open fireplace – the logs damp and smoky, hissing faintly. The firelight and windows provide the only illumination – no lamps or overheads – so that the corners and sides of the room dissolve into shadow, making it hard to gauge the size of the space. It feels cavernous. This is where the meeting is to take place, in the heart of an old mansion in Praha Seven, on a hill facing back towards the castle, St. Vitus Cathedral, the Vltava. You have travelled here with Mario, who's beside you, to meet your new employers. After your conversation, you picked up a cheap mobile from a phone kiosk – it seemed safer and easier than buying a charger for your own phone – and texted him your new number. His call came the next day: they wanted to meet you. He drove you out, coaching you along the way on how to conduct yourself. Mostly, he said, it would be best to keep quiet, to let them do the talking.

At that point, you didn't know what to expect. Men in suits, maybe. Muscled and wedge-like. Their eyes hidden by Ray-Bans. Their pockets bulging with weaponry. Gruff mannerisms, and theatrical accents.

Instead, there is this woman. Middle-aged, lean and elegant, in a black gown, with a patterned shawl wrapped round her upper body. Dark auburn hair, wound into a single braid, thick as a rope, which hangs over one shoulder. As she considers you, her mouth remains pursed, puckered, as if she can taste the lingering tartness of the pickle.

There is a man, too, sitting at a harpsichord opposite the fire. The instrument is as large as a grand piano, but with two tiers of keys. A haunting string-sound emanating from it. He is entirely focused on his music. He is wearing wire-rimmed glasses with tinted yellow lenses, despite the low lighting. It gives him an owlish appearance, makes him difficult to read. He hasn't been introduced, and you don't know if he is hired help – an entertainer of some sort – or an associate. Either way, it's clear the woman is in charge. It's clear you will be dealing with her, or she with you.

The woman says her name is Valerie.

Valerie settles into her sofa, adjusts her shawl, and says your full name as if announcing you at a ball: 'Welcome, Eira.' She says that Mario has told her about you, that you are here for an extended stay, that you have never had trouble with the law, that you are British. From Aberystwyth, in Wales. That startles you. Not just that she knows all this – it's in your passport – but that she bothers to remind you she knows. Deliberate. They can find you, is what she is saying.

'I was born there,' you tell her, 'but live in London now.'

Then, to show you're not intimidated, you ask her about herself: where is she from? It's a smokescreen, but you are curious, too – her English is crisp and clear as ice, but laced with a faint accent. Unplaceable.

She smiles at your presumptuousness. 'We are from here and there,' she tells you. 'Here and there and everywhere.' She gestures back and forth, to demonstrate. Her arm movements fluid, like a tentacle. 'We have business all over. Like our Danish friend says, many irons in the fire.'

Her smile falls away. She strokes her braid, as if it's some kind of pet, perched there. She says it is an aspect of their business they wanted to see you about. Mario believes you are the right kind of person for a particular job they have coming up. She asks you, outright, if you think he is correct: are you the right kind of person? You tell her you know hardly anything about it. How can you be sure, until you know more?

'Ah,' she says, looking significantly at Mario. 'That is very reasonable. I like that you are prudent. Not reckless. We cannot risk recklessness. Everything must go smoothly – on this job most of all.'

She clasps her hands, rests them on her knees. She says that the job involves a pick up. You will need a car. You will need to rent it, in your own name. You will drive east through Slovakia, and at Ubl'a you will cross the border out of Europe into Ukraine, telling them that you are doing some sightseeing. When you cross over doesn't matter – but when you come back is crucial. You must remember that. Before you go, Mario will give you an address, and a suitcase to take with you.

You ask what will be in the suitcase, cutting Valerie off. She looks at Mario, who pats at his brow with a handkerchief, and then she looks over at the musician, who adjusts his posture and strikes a loud chord, ominously off-key. She laughs at this – as if he has done it on purpose, to provide musical accompaniment. Then she sobers, suddenly, and smooths out her skirt with a palm, causing the fabric to rasp. She says that it is not your concern, the contents of the suitcase. You will know what you need to know. That is for the best.

You shrug, reach instinctively for your pack of cigarettes, and once they're in hand you pause. Ask Valerie whether she minds if you smoke. She says that she does mind. She says that smoking will kill you. What she needs you to do is listen. Not smoke.

You put the cigarettes away, tell her the job sounds straightforward enough.

'It is,' she says, 'if everything is done correctly.'

She explains the return journey is more complicated. You must spend the night at an inn, near the border, on the Ukrainian side. You must cross back at Ubl'a the next morning, at a specified time. You must get in the correct lane; they will tell you which one. You know better than to ask why these details are important.

She says you will be bringing somebody back with you.

84

That startles you, and it must show on your face. Valerie lets it sink in, takes a sip of her water. Sits back and rests one elbow on the armrest of the sofa. She asks if that is a problem, and you shake your head, tell her no. It's just that Mario said you would most likely be transporting goods or merchandise or a product. Some*thing*, not some*body*.

Valerie's head turns, swivelling from you to Mario. The motion is theatrical, deliberate. She says Mario should not have told you any such thing. She says that Mario does not know enough to speculate, and that just because their business has involved those types of things in the past does not mean it will again – this time or any other time.

Mario assures her he didn't mean anything by it, that he was just trying to give you a general idea. Then, withering under her glare, he looks down, his excuses taper off, dwindle to nothing, and he merely mumbles an apology, which seems to satisfy her.

Besides, she says, this job won't be any more complicated. It is the same as if you were transporting products. You can think of it as a product, if that makes it easier for you.

She turns to the harpsichordist, asks something in their language. Not Czech. Maybe Russian, or Ukrainian? Or something else? Without interrupting his song, he looks over and replies, his voice high and falsetto soft. Then he smiles, as if at a private joke. His gums are pulled back, receding. The teeth square, yellow, perhaps even dentures. A skeleton's grin.

His fingers keep moving, stroking the keys.

You ask who it is you'll be picking up, and she says you don't need to know that, yet. You have to get there first. You have to prove your commitment and capability for success. You could still walk away now. Nothing about the conversation is incriminating, or illegal. It is just a simple favour, really, they are asking. And since they are friends with Mario, and you are his friend also, you seem the right person for the favour. A friend of a friend. And, of course, favours are repaid. She's smiling as she says all this, happy to have laid it out in such a clean-cut, straightforward way.

You shift on the sofa. The heat from the fire makes the leather feel as if it's melting, turning tacky. Under your shirt you can feel a worm of sweat, slow-crawling down your spine. You look sideways at Mario. He is smiling encouragingly at you, but his posture is rigid, his features fixed. You understand that he's scared, terrified that he has gotten it wrong, that you will back out now. The fire pops like a gunshot.

You tell them that it all seems clear, that you'll do it.

Something goes out of the room, then. A crystalline tension cracks, breaks apart, and melts away. Mario nods over and over, as if in meditation. The harpsichordist resumes his tune (you hadn't noticed him stopping) and Valerie pours herself another water. Then, as if to confirm you've passed her test, she pours you one. She holds hers up, and you touch glasses.

When you drink, the water burns and stings. The water is not water. The water is pure vodka. She watches you keenly, waiting for a reaction. You do not balk, do not make a face or choke. You swallow that sip nonchalantly, take another, comment on its smoothness.

'Yes,' she says, seemingly pleased, 'it is very good. The best.'

Before you go, she pours you both another and offers you the snacks – to soak up the vodka, she says – and fills you in on a few other practicalities: that after you have picked up the rental car, Mario will provide you with some cash for the journey, along with the suitcase. That you are to check in with him, and them, once you have made the exchange and are back at the inn. They will provide further information on crossing the border then.

And, of course, she says, you must go through with it. You are committed now. No backing out. If you do not hold up your side, there will be consequences.

'I could let Pavel tell you about those,' she says.

Pavel finishes his song, as if on cue. Then murmurs something demurely to her. Barely audible, even if you could understand their language.

'*Da*,' she says, agreeing. Then, to you, 'He's modest, but I can show you. Come.'

She stands, and motions for you to do the same. Vodka in hand, she leads you casually over to Pavel and his harpsichord. 'Show us your hands, Pavel,' she says. He removes them from the keys, holds them up, as if accustomed to humouring her. The first thing you notice is that his fingers are slim and long – almost unnaturally so. The skin milky, smooth, free of calluses. Delicate. You remember, absurdly, your mother's maternal advice: *never trust a man with delicate hands*. Like all maxims, it is quite useless, redundant; you don't need such wisdom to know Pavel is not to be trusted.

'Pavel has many talents,' Valerie says. 'Not just music. He was a surgeon, too. So he knows everything about the body. Now he is not a surgeon any more. Now he works for me. You might say that he is the opposite of a surgeon, even though he still uses his skills. And you do not want him using them on you. You understand.' It is a statement, not a question.

You look into Pavel's eyes, partially veiled behind those yellow lenses, hold his gaze until you see him blink, as if startled. Then you stare at Valerie, right *at* her. You can feel the kick of the vodka, the way it makes you burn, emboldens you. You tell her that there's no use trying to threaten or intimidate you. It won't work. It sounds simple and true, the way you say it.

The room is incredibly quiet. The sun has passed behind a pane of red glass in the window, tainting the light burgundy. You can hear the fire crackling, and your own pulse resonating in your skull. You know you have shocked them – all of them – and it's a good feeling.

Mario laughs, suddenly and uproariously. A desperate bid to break the tension. 'I told you. Didn't I tell you?' he says, coming over, patting you on the back. 'She is one cool customer. A snow queen. She knocked out Denis. Did I mention that? He tried to mug her, and ended up flat on his back.'

Valerie's smile is thin and brittle. She looks you up and down, as if reassessing you. As if wondering if you might present an entirely different kind of problem from which she is accustomed. She says that, so long as you do what they've discussed, you won't have to worry at all about Pavel. You raise your glass, as if mock-toasting Pavel and his hands, and knock back the last of your vodka, relishing the sheer searing thrill of it.

octavia

Committed. This the word they used, the word Mario used.
You are committed now. As in a relationship, as in a marriage.
Even if you don't know quite what you have committed to,
a bond has been formed. A pact has been made. The gravity
of this pact is apparent in the way everything proceeds –
swift, focused, efficient. Two days after your meeting with
Valerie and Pavel, Mario phones with details of the rental
car they want you to reserve: the make and model (Vauxhall
Corsa) and location (an agency at the airport). It has to go
on your credit card, in your name, and subsequently you
must forward the confirmation email to them. Mario will
compensate you in cash when you pick up the suitcase and
travel money.

It makes sense, of course. This way the booking cannot be
traced to them.

But this also occurs to you once you've made the reservation: they were specific about the details, the make and model (not just anything from the 'small car' category), so they know what car you'll be driving.

It's a precaution, you assume. A way for them to track their homing pigeon.

In case you fly off course.

On the given day, at six in the morning, you catch a bus out to the airport, retracing the route you took when you arrived in Prague, several weeks ago. Except it is near dawn now, not late at night. From the window of the bus you see a series of brick warehouses with corrugated tin roofs. A cluster of concrete tower blocks, abandoned, the windows boarded up or broken or gaping, vacant. A decrepit truck stop. Nothing looks familiar. The city isn't the same city you arrived in. You don't feel the same either.

It's only when you get to the airport that you feel a twinge of déjà vu. A stirring of recognition as you wind your way among bus shelters. The car rental agencies are grouped in a building opposite Arrivals. Most of the companies are the same here as anywhere – Hertz, Avis, Europcar – but Valerie has specified one you don't recognise: Czecho-go. You wonder if this is the company they always use, if they have some kind of understanding with the manager, or owners. Maybe they *are* the owners. *Many irons in the fire*, was what Valerie said.

The Czecho-go service desk is near the end of the row. A red counter and glowing lightbox sign, displaying their black and white logo. Behind it, two employees in matching uniforms. There's a queue of three people, so you wait. Not patiently but resignedly. Watching the clock on the wall – a round analogue clock. The face pale yellow and numberless, the gleaming circle eerily reminiscent of Pavel's tinted glasses. The hour hand seemingly still, the minute hand quivering, moving slowly forward. Barely perceptible. But moving nonetheless. Time is real again for you. You have a deadline, a destination. First to meet Mario, then to the border, and then to a town in Ukraine, by a certain time on a certain day.

You have stepped out of stasis, got back on a track. Not a track you would have expected, not even necessarily a track of your own choosing. But on a track, all the same, with a job to do, and a role to play. The pretence, the need for performance, brings back recollections of your theatre days. It even feels as if there is a script of sorts, which you're required to stick to. Valerie is directing; you merely need to follow her vision, her designs. Easy enough.

And yet. In considering that, while awaiting your turn, already you feel the desire to improvise, to do something unexpected, go off-script. Something you were prone to doing, on stage – to the exasperation of directors, and fellow actors. A natural contrariness, maybe. An inclination towards deviance (the same that led you back to Mario in the first place?). Feelings best kept in check. Lest they get you in trouble. Or rather, get you in *more* trouble.

The queue is moving. First one customer, then another, pays their fee, signs the requisite forms, and is handed a set of keys. A strange exchange, when viewed from a distance. These odd rituals we adhere to. Afterwards, each customer wanders out towards the parking lot, looking anxious and confused, one towing a suitcase, another pushing a luggage trolley.

Your turn. The clerk is a young Czech woman, who of course speaks fluent English. For you she adopts it smoothly, seamlessly, not even needing to ask. Instead, she asks if you have a reservation, and you tell her you do. You slide the print-out across the counter to her. She looks at it critically, professionally, like an art dealer assessing a painting, and then types the reservation number into her keyboard, calling up your file.

'A Vauxhall Corsa, three-door?'

'That's the one.'

Only, as she is about to confirm the booking, you spontaneously ask if they have any upgrades available. You wouldn't mind a larger car. A five-door saloon, if possible. Or an estate. If it's not too much more. It shouldn't be a problem, she tells you, and types in a quick search. You imagine this isn't uncommon: customers changing their minds, or reassessing their needs. For you, it isn't just a whim, or your innate waywardness – though that maybe factors into it – but a matter of instinct, of self-preservation. *Be smart.*

Valerie and Pavel won't know about the switch. And, if they find out, you'll simply say the car originally reserved turned out not to be available, so the agency offered a free upgrade. That kind of thing happens; it has happened to you before.

A small deception. Possibly a dangerous one. But it also seems prudent. You don't like being watched, monitored, assessed. Not in school and not at work and not in public. You've always been wary of CCTV cameras, hated the compulsive snapping of camera phones, even before the night of Tod's death, the bystanders. This was something that he found exasperating: the way you could grow tense, uncomfortable, when aware of being observed, being recorded. You found it hard to explain, and after a while didn't bother.

Smile – You're on Camera!

Those light-hearted posters that you always find so menacing, ominous – as perhaps you're meant to, the happy-face logo heightening rather than diminishing the implicit threat.

The woman taps the return key triumphantly, tells you they *do* have an upgrade, and a discount on the upgrade, trying her best up-sell on you, not understanding that you're already sold, decided. The new vehicle is a Škoda Octavia. A good Czech car, the clerk jokes. And you smile. You tell her, idly, that Octavia is also a character from Shakespeare.

'Oh,' she says, sliding the form across the counter. 'How nice.'

You don't bother to mention that you played Octavia once. You just sign where you're supposed to sign, tick where you're supposed to tick. While you finish, she takes your credit card and swipes it, holds out the keypad for you to punch in your pin. All of this is done in near-silence – no need to talk or coach you through it. The routine so second nature it occurs subliminally, almost unconsciously.

A receipt is torn, the form is folded, filed. She holds the keys out to you, tells you the Octavia is at the back of the lot. If you have any problems on the trip, she says, you can call the number on the back of the receipt. She smiles, letting you know this is just a formality – of course you won't have any problems.

On the clock behind her, the minute hand quivers, like the needle on a lie detector.

the suitcase

On the way to meet Mario you drive by the language school. You catch a glimpse, in passing, of the room, your old classmates. Through the windows, each of them in profile, just their shoulders and heads. Like Roman busts, all directed towards the front of the room, the teacher. It's like driving by a train carriage, or overtaking a bus. Seeing all these people who don't see you, and who don't have any real connection to you. A glimpse and they're gone, the language school falling away behind you, passing into your past.

You cross over some tram tracks – the shuddering bump as your wheels hit it – and turn left. The satnav on the dash dictates directions, and shows your driving as it occurs – a video version of your movements, your motion. When you come to a roundabout, the blue arrow traces a circle, except instead of clockwise it's anti-clockwise. The direction feels unfamiliar, distinctly odd. They drive on the right here, and roundabouts go backwards.

Time is moving, yes. But in which direction?

It would be useful, for your sake, if it *was* moving backwards: the wait at the rental agency, and the morning traffic on the drive from Praha Six to Praha One, has put you behind, according to the schedule you were given. The schedule you were *assigned*, and expected to stick to. Just by a quarter of an hour, but you get the sense your new employers value punctuality, precision. Everything working like clockwork. Nothing askew, nothing amiss. Valerie said something to this effect: no detours, no surprises. That's how they ensure these jobs, these transactions, are always a success. Still. There are some things that can't be helped. Even they must accept that, and be understanding of such slight delays.

Whether they'd be understanding of the change in vehicles is another matter.

You've been given an address, where you're to meet Mario, but it isn't a house. You wonder if that's for his own safety – to hide his address, where he lives. For a moment, you try to imagine Mario's house, and can't. It seems to you he must exist on the street, not truly homeless but simply without need of a home. Maybe never sleeping, or sleeping on his feet, in his beige suit, always so miraculously clean. You know this isn't so, but it seems like it should be.

In any event, you won't be meeting him at his house. You're meeting him in the outdoor car park of a large supermarket. Possibly that's a convention: public spaces are safe spaces. That's where the satnav is leading you, one street, one turn, at a time. Like playing a video game. Just follow the digital arrows, avoid obstacles, don't crash. And, like in those video games, the end point is marked by a chequered flag.

Though in this case, in reality, it will also be marked by a man holding a suitcase and some cash.

When the store comes into view, you switch off the satnav, strangling the chirrupy, encouraging voice in mid-flow. The car park is sprawling – spaces for hundreds of vehicles, with half of them full. People trudging, dragging children, laboriously pushing trolleys filled with bags of groceries. All that motion. A good place to hide a handoff, and better than a multistorey or a ticketed car park – many of which have surveillance cameras, these days.

Amid all that movement, that chaos, it should be impossible to spot Mario, but it isn't. As you slow at a crossing he walks right in front of your vehicle, without noticing that it's you. In one hand, the suitcase. Modest-sized, grey and rectangular, slightly shabby. It goes well with his suit, his look. He glances at his watch, continues towards the supermarket's petrol station and snack bar. Near it are two picnic benches. A rubbish bin. Gulls circling, scrounging for scraps. That's where you're supposed to meet him. You don't know if he is late as well, or if he has been doing a circuit of the car park, trying to find you.

You raise a hand to honk, signal to him, but then think better of it. No need to draw attention to yourself. Or let him know about your new car.

You drive to the far side and park, get out. Calmly walk back across. Mario has settled on one of the concrete benches, and is sucking hard at a cigarette. The magician looks anxious. Not nearly so cool as when you met him. Still worried, perhaps, that he has made a mistake, that things are already going awry.

When he looks up and sees you, his smile is genuine, as wide as his face. 'Ah,' he says, rising to his feet, brushing off his knees. 'You are here. Good.' You explain about the traffic, the queue. He waves it away with a swirl of smoke. Tells you not to worry, that he hasn't phoned them, that they don't have to know. A response that is revealing in itself.

'Where are you parked?' he asks.

'Over there.'

You gesture vaguely, but he doesn't seem too interested. You are here, that's what matters. He lifts up the suitcase and holds it out, abruptly, as if eager to be rid of it. As if it might contain uranium, bio-weapons, chemical waste, a bomb. Something hazardous. You accept it, of course. You have already accepted it. It is as if the suitcase is already yours for safekeeping, not his. That is what you have agreed to, even if you don't know what, exactly, it will entail.

The outside of the case is a hard shell covered in fake leather. In your hand it feels heavy, loaded. But with drugs, or money, or something else?

'It is locked,' Mario says, as if he, too, has speculated. 'And you are not to open it.'

You wonder how the person you're giving the case to will open it, but know better than to ask. The key must be going separately. By post, maybe. Or by another person.

Wind blows between you, pushing Mario's smoke sideways. A hatchback circles the island, swings in to fill up. Mario idly looks around, dips into his jacket pocket, and passes you something else: an envelope. Doing this very casually. He murmurs that it contains the directions for the next stage of your journey, your destination in Ukraine, and the travel money Valerie mentioned. For petrol, food, whatever. Some koruny, and also some Ukrainian hryvnia. The real money – your payment – will be waiting for you on your return.

That done, to seal the deal, he offers you a cigarette, but you refuse – polite but firm. You're behind their schedule already. You should get going.

'Yes,' he says, 'of course.'

Only he seems reluctant to let you go, to say goodbye outright. He explains that, after this is all done, and you are paid, you are not to come looking for him again. That is how it works. You can stay in Prague, or go. Use the money any way you like. But they never ask the same people again. It is best that way. If one person crossed the border again and again, they would be noticed, eventually. 'After this,' he says, 'I do not know you, and you do not know me.' You nod, thank him awkwardly for this opportunity – you even use that word, which sounds laughable. You shake his hand. He holds on a moment longer than is necessary, gripping it firmly while studying you.

He says he is counting on you. That this is a risk for him, too. Every time, it's a risk. He makes a recommendation, sets up the meeting, and it must go well. If he vouches for you, and it doesn't, it comes back to him. 'The stakes,' he says, 'are very high.'

He doesn't use the term 'life and death' but you assume that's what he means. You tell him not to worry, and he says he isn't, laughs heartily, calls you his snow queen. Trying to convince himself, it sounds like. Of this role he has cast you in. A role you are ready to play.

You are still standing there, shaking hands, the gesture elongated into a strange pose, when something hits the ground between you. Landing partly on Mario's foot, in fact – on the toe of his alligator-skin shoe. You both look down. It's a white dollop of bird shit, from one of the gulls. The mess appearing so incongruous against the polished leather.

Mario lets go of your hand, staring dismally at the mess.

'That,' he says, 'is very unfortunate.'

gyrru gyrru gyrru

In the Octavia you bore through the smog enclosing Prague, before abruptly tearing free of it, emerging into the surrounding countryside. The transition is startling, striking; something you recall from your boat ride. Though the inversion layer seems so pervasive, so all-encompassing, it's not everywhere – just restricted to the city centre, a product of the heat generated by bodies, lights, engines, space heaters, furnaces, radiators, chimneys, fireplaces: the warm air causing the cold to coalesce, creating a stifling bubble of life. Escape is a relief. Like a wasp bursting out of its nest, taking flight – the sense of space vast, the sense of freedom overwhelming, the sense of possibility alluring.

Here, the air is clear, the winter sky a hard, marbled blue, glinting with sunlight – like the ceiling of an ice cavern. And the sun: bright, brutal, blinding. Sitting low in the sky, even at midday. So strange, but not unpleasant, to feel the heat of it through the car windows – on your forearm, your lap – when you know the world outside is cold, the temperature well below freezing. The surrounding fields crusted with frost. The birch trees at the roadside barren and leafless, their grey bark sculpted smooth, standing staunch and still as stone. Frozen angels. Feathers of hoarfrost sprouting from the outstretched branches.

You head southeast, towards Slovakia. There's no formal border between the Czech and Slovak Republics. Both are part of the EU. The border – the real border – will be at the eastern edge of Slovakia, in the town Valerie specified in her note to you. Ubl'a. You've punched in the coordinates on your satnav. The route is straightforward enough – mostly dual carriageways or *dálnice*, the Czech motorways. The blue line on the screen representing your path stretches straight as a spear, and the mileage counter in the bottom right-hand corner signifies that you'll be on this motorway, the D1, for hours, until you reach Slovakia. Another three hundred kilometres. Every so often, the voice pipes up, reminding you. It has defaulted to Czech. You're sure there must be a setting to change to English – it's for tourists, after all – but numbers and directions aren't hard to understand; you retained that much, from your language class. *Zůstaňte na této silnici dvacet devadesát kilometrů.* The voice of your satnav sounds just like the voice coach from the dialogues your teacher used. Perhaps the producers even hired the same person, his soothing, encouraging tones being in high demand.

You can put up with the Czech satnav voice, but not the Czech radio. The stations you find are filled with frantic, intense hard dance and house tracks, often imitating or using English language hits, but cut up and remixed, a roaring blender of multi-lingual noise. You switch it off, put in your earbuds instead, listen to your MP3 player shuffle through a 'travel' playlist Tod had put together for the two of you. Already the music on it seems dated, capturing an obsolete period in your life. Without Tod's constant updates, his monitoring and tinkering and purchasing, the music has become a time capsule of before, of the period you have begun to think of as 'then' rather than 'now'. When you were a wife, not a widow. Part of a couple, not a person.

You have told Marta that you are going on a trip for a few days, to clear your head, find some perspective. It seemed sensible to tell her something, to provide yourself with an alibi of sorts, rather than have her notice your absence, begin to worry, and perhaps ask around. She grunted, nodded, told you she thought it a good idea. Said the countryside around Prague is very beautiful.

It was easy to lie to her; you have always been a skilled dissembler. Seamlessly stitching over fabrications with patches of truth. Maybe that's why you were a good actor, since dissembling isn't just part of the job criteria, it *is* the job. To convince the audience that the scripted dialogue is natural, the rehearsed actions spontaneous, the simulated emotions authentic. All through pretence and fakery. Making lies feel real. Then again, sometimes that's the case in life, as well. You lied to Tod. No more so than anybody in a long-term relationship. But lies, all the same. Little white lies, the lies that get us through the day. Lies about how money had been spent (on groceries, not a night out; bills, not a new top). Lies about the wing mirror you'd smashed on the car – somebody else had done it. Or lies about being held late at work, when really you wanted a drink, to be alone. Lies about getting stuck in traffic, or being late to pick him up, drop him off. So many lies based around time, and timings. He was fixated on scheduling, to such an extent that if one of you wasn't on time you needed a reason, an excuse. You couldn't just say: I'm late because I couldn't be bothered to get here on time.

Little lies like that. And bigger lies. About being happy in London. About being content in your job. About not regretting giving up acting. Lies about all those aspects of your life, which you pretended were okay. You were lying even when you weren't lying.

You were lying to yourself.

And, of course, you lied about cheating on him. About getting near black-out drunk with your girlfriends and picking up some guy and going back to his place and fucking him, or letting him fuck you – slobbering, quick, raw, hungry, hot, rough, clutching – while Tod was away at some academic conference, presenting a paper on one of his Russian novelists. Talking so knowledgeably about those tragic heroines, engaged in extramarital affairs, not knowing what his own wife was up to. Irony suited to the books themselves.

Of course, you lied about that. Not about doing it. You did tell him, eventually. Part of the point of *doing* it was to tell him, to blast things wide open. An ultimatum. Let's make this relationship work or end it, *put it down like a dog*. And so, you 'talked things through' and 'worked it out' and took all the steps couples are supposed to take: you made more time for each other, left your work in the office, scheduled date nights, bought expensive wines and tried new things in the bedroom. You pretended it got better, was getting better.

So you didn't lie to him about the fling. You lied about when it happened, and how far it went, and you lied about how much you enjoyed it – claiming that you hadn't, that it was terrible, hideous, *repellent*. Only it wasn't. It was a thrill, an intoxication. Even now, thinking back, you feel something like lust, or the echo of it. A shiver.

All these thoughts, skimming through your head as you drive.

You light a cigarette, as if the memories of sex have triggered that after-sex instinct. Smoking is definitely against rental car policy, but you can't be the first to do it. You press the button on the armrest to roll down your window. The blast of cold is shocking, exhilarating. The air screaming by like a jet stream. You hold your hand out in it, feeling the pressure of wind, spreading your fingers until they're numb.

When you pull your hand back in, put it on the steering wheel, your fingers are frozen, cramped. A tingling sting as the sensation comes back into them. Both pleasant and painful.

Despite all the lies, big and small, you still believe you and Tod had something worth keeping. Or maybe worth maintaining is the better phrase. Maintaining a relationship, like you might a cooker or a washing machine. Another vital, domestic appliance. A mod con.

Cooker not working? Call the repair man.

Marriage not working? Call the marriage counsellor.

You tried that too, in the wake of 'what happened' – as Tod referred to it.

On your MP3 player, the track ends, and another kicks in. It's one of yours – a rarity, on Tod's playlists. A Welsh song, a driving song. The words *Gyrru Gyrru Gyrru* simple enough: it means *Driving Driving Driving*. Tod hated it, hated anything that left him out, left him feeling alienated. But he'd put it on your travel list because you'd insisted. You remember driving with him, singing it again and again until finally, grudgingly, you got him to sing too.

Gyrru Gyrru Gyrru. Driving Driving Driving.

You pass a small group of magpies, perched on the fence at the roadside. Huddled together against the cold. You're moving too fast to count them, and can't remember what they mean. Something about sorrow and joy, a girl and a boy. You've never put much stock in maxims, proverbs, and old wives' tales. That was Tod's territory. He was endearingly superstitious.

There. You feel it then: a flicker of longing, something like love. What you were hoping for, trying to cultivate in yourself. Like cupping a match, breathing on the flame.

Gyrru Gyrru Gyrru. Driving Driving Driving.

Gently, regretfully, you lower your foot on the accelerator. Stamping that feeling out. Leaving it behind. Making the cold world blur.

borders

Just before noon you cross the Slovakian border, though it doesn't seem like much of a border. Marked only by a small white road sign, with a crest of some sort – perhaps the same as on the national flag – and the words *Slovenská republika*. As innocuous as the signs marking the crossing between England and Wales, and vice versa. No check points, no guards – just a truck stop, off to the left. The motorway you're on continues right into Slovakia, a route that runs east-west across Europe. A 'soft' border between EU countries. A term you've always accepted, but which now strikes you as odd. As if a border can be spongy, malleable, semi-permeable: more like a cell membrane, or Alice's looking glass. You can pass through by osmosis.

And, as in a looking-glass world, on the other side differences aren't immediately apparent. The road signs look similar, the nuances between the languages too subtle for you to pick up, and the landscape and scenery are unchanged. Near the highway, a perpetual series of telephone poles, the occasional cottage or farmhouse. Beyond, low hills covered with deciduous forest, the trees all bare and stark and unrecognisable – merging into a tangled mass. And, ahead, a long banner of grey tarmac that endlessly unfurls. It carries you to the outskirts of Trenčín, where you loop north on the D1, now – confusingly – also part of the E50 and the E75 at the same time, and shortly after you spot a turning for a services and petrol station.

Your instructions were explicit on this aspect of the trip: stops are only allowed when necessary. Is it necessary? You have enough fuel to drive another hour or two. But Prague and the menace of Valerie and Pavel seem far off, and after a morning of driving you want a break. You pull in, to grab a coffee, use the toilet, fill up the fuel. Do all the things people do on long trips. And it's now you notice some slight differences between here and there, where you've been and where you are. The license plates have changed – different layout and demarcation – and petrol prices are in Euros, not koruny. The envelope of cash Mario gave you contains both, as well as Ukrainian hryvnia, so you have no issues paying, but the changes do generate a subtle feeling of dislocation. At the counter, you're overly relieved to see they still sell Smart here, having invested in your choice of brand with a bias that verges on superstition.

You buy a fresh pack, light one for comfort, and keep driving. For the most part, you travel on various sections of the E50, as it heads northeast towards Žilina, then southeast, first in the guise of route 18, then on to the D1 again. Regardless of name, the road remains unvaried, the journey monotonous. You follow the satnav, tune out, switch off. The sense of having a destination and new purpose breaks apart, and time reverts to its crystalline state for minutes, hours, the only sign of its passage the ticking digits on your dash.

Even if it doesn't feel like it, you still must be making progress, going somewhere.

And then you are there. The border.

Arriving at it, you are underwhelmed. The international borders you have seen, the borders you are used to, are seemingly indomitable: the border on either side of the English Channel, or the one between Canada and the States, which you and Tod crossed by car, during your trip to visit his family. It had been near Niagara: half a dozen lanes, hour-long queues, armed guards with sniffer dogs roaming between the vehicles, looking at drivers, at vehicles, at number plates. Maybe it had been a critical day. Maybe there'd been a fugitive. Or a terrorist alert. The atmosphere tense, edgy. The border marked by what looked like a military compound, through which all traffic had to pass. As solid and permanent as a part of the landscape.

And perhaps since the border between the Czech and Slovak Republics was so underwhelming – practically negligible – you expected something more intimidating or impressive at Ubl'a. The first indication that this may not be the case is the town itself, which you drive through en route. It consists of a hairdressers, a boarded-up petrol station, a café with the words *Vyprážaný Sýr* scrawled on the awning, and a fishing and hunting store – rods and reels and rifles hanging in the windows, alongside a large mounted carp and a stuffed bear rearing up on its hind legs, wearing a hunting cap of its own. You wonder where they shot the bear, and if there are even any bears left in Eastern Europe. You wonder, too, who had the idea of dressing the bear up like his own killer, adding insult to its demise.

All in all, the town of Ubl'a is not particularly memorable, or impressive. The border, even less so. Passing through forests beyond Ubl'a you round a bend and see what looks like a pair of shacks, one on either side of the road. They're about the size of log cabins, but layered with clapboard, painted white. From a distance they look like ice cubes. It's only when you spot the flag poles atop them that you're certain this is the border, an actual 'hard' border. The flags aren't flapping, and as a result aren't recognisable. They hang limply like dish cloths, barely twitching in the scant wind. To either side, empty fields stretch far away. The fields, like the roadside, are crusted with frost, but it hasn't begun to snow properly yet. There is no fencing across the fields and you wonder if they're barren or fallow, if somebody owns them and uses them. To farm livestock, or for growing wheat, hay, barley. The government must own them. It would be too odd for a farmer to be ploughing or tilling the fields, crossing from one country to the other on one row, then back again on the next. It would undermine the whole concept of the border if a farmer were to do that, in plain view of people waiting to cross.

As you get closer, you see that the huts do have barriers. Those yellow and black booms that extend across the road, and can be raised and lowered. The sight inevitably reminds you of a film you saw as a child – watching late-night TV with your father – in which a motorcyclist tried to duck beneath such a barrier and smashed his head into it. The helmet shattering, the wooden bar snapping, the splintered remnants hanging, dripping blood. You can't remember if the scene was set at a border. Only the image has stayed with you. As a reminder of attempted transgressions, of the consequence of stepping outside designated boundaries. Of crossing over.

You, of course, are not going to attempt anything so dramatic. This is supposed to be the straightforward part.

You don't even have your cargo yet. Your real cargo. Your flesh-and-blood cargo. Just the suitcase you were given, tucked in the boot. You've placed your duffel bag on top of it, though not in such a way that it might seem as if you were deliberately trying to hide or conceal it, should they ask to check the boot. Which they won't. You are almost positive they won't. You *believe* they won't.

As you pull up to the queue on the eastbound side – which is only half a dozen cars long – you idly consider what you would say or do if they did. The guard, who in your mind is a man, a burly Eastern European with a dark beard, might ask you what the locked suitcase contains, and at that point you would either have to admit you don't know, or you would have to lie, inventing something that seems plausible. Something that needs to be locked away, kept discrete. Your personal effects. Private files. Bondage gear. By that point it probably wouldn't matter. You doubt they would ask and then not check, anyway. No, if it reaches that stage you'll be caught out, for sure.

Still. You wonder at the fact that your employers didn't seem concerned about this part of the journey. They didn't give you specific guidance or instructions. Not like the return crossing, about which they were very particular. And wondering that makes you wonder more, about what might be in the suitcase, about why it isn't worth protecting.

The car in front of you is a rental, like yours. You can tell because it has the same Czecho-go logo in the bottom left-hand corner of the back window. It's not an Octavia, but a Corsa – the make that you were originally meant to acquire. For a minute you consider the fanciful idea that this is the exact car you almost had. How surreal that it has ended up out here, waiting to cross in front of you. You imagine getting out, walking up to the driver's side door, knocking on the window, which rolls down to reveal a woman with your face. Oh, it's only you, she might say, or you might say. Both of you relieved to meet your double, your doppelganger, in this looking-glass realm.

But no. The car has two people in it. The driver has her arm looped behind the passenger's headrest. A couple, on a little vacation, or a romantic getaway. Ghosts of your past.

You smoke to kill time, the smoke slipping away through the barely open window in slow ribbons. You don't flick your ash outside, on to the tarmac. You don't want to offend the guards, by acting too casually. They might decide to search you, just to put you in your place. Just to show that they can. *Who do these Westerners think they are?*

By the roadside, a raven is pecking repeatedly at something frozen and dead and flat, and as limp and unrecognisable as the flags. Whatever it is, the raven seems grateful to have found it. A gift from the roadkill gods. The raven continues pecking away – tick, tick, tick – as you move past it, to the front of the queue.

Shortly after, the Corsa is let through and the guard in the booth beckons you forward.

You stub out your cigarette, roll down your window the rest of the way, and take your foot off the brake, easing forward. The guard is not burly but young, clean-shaven, with a blonde crew cut, the short hairs glinting like a wire comb on top of his head. You smile at him and he smiles back. He asks for your passport and you hand it to him, open to the photo page: a younger you, the you from years ago. Your hair longer, hanging loose to your shoulders. Your face smoother, your eyes wider, larger, more hopeful. He looks at her and then looks at you. You wonder if he is struck by the difference, comparing the two of you. If he sits and wonders about the changes in people, the way time works away at them. Or if he is simply clinical, doing his job, making sure that, at one point, you could realistically have been that girl.

He asks you the purpose of your trip. You already have your answer prepared: that you are staying in Prague, that you wanted to see some of Ukraine, and that your grandfather was from the region. Another small deceit that comes to you readily, convincingly. You've prepared a fake itinerary in case he asks, but he doesn't. He just stamps the passport, snaps it shut, and hands it back to you. 'Enjoy your trip,' he says. 'Welcome to Ukraine.' Giving you no hassle, no trouble at all. Here, as at the airport, you are the good kind of traveller.

Which, of course, is why Mario recommended you, why Valerie chose you.

Then, before you pull away – emboldened by your success – you gesture out your window, and ask him if the field next to the border is used for farming.

He blinks, caught by surprise, and turns to look at it, considering. The fumes from your engine are rising around the two of you like mist. That distinct exhaust scent.

'I think so,' he says. 'Yes, I think they grow hops in it.'

You don't comment on the strangeness of it – that would be pushing it – but you think about it, after you thank him and drive on. Perhaps it isn't so strange, after all. Perhaps it is your definition, or conception, of borders that is strange: permanent, rigid, insurmountable. But what is the difference between a 'hard' border and a 'soft' border, between this one and the other, between the Czech and Slovak Republics, between Europe and Ukraine? They're all just lines on a map, which can change, which have changed. You crossed over so easily – the checkpoint might as well not have been there. Perhaps the act of crossing, of transgression, isn't so risky, or dangerous, as we're taught. No need to jump barricades or scoot under barriers. No smashed head or crashed vehicles.

Still, the very ease of this crossing makes you decidedly *uneasy*. In theatre, a poor dress rehearsal makes for a good opening night. A smooth, trouble-free dress rehearsal is a terrible omen. And this, of course, was merely a dress rehearsal for tomorrow.

do not open

Despite your musings on the permeability of borders, after crossing you are very aware that you are somewhere else, or elsewhere – though at first it's hard to say what creates this impression, why it feels different from crossing into Slovakia. The countryside looks largely the same. Low hills and desolate fields. Rows of stunted, frost-covered trees. A cobalt sky. A sun simmering low on the horizon. So what has changed? What's different?

Not the landscape, but the atmosphere. The milieu. It's evident in the road signs, and place names – no longer in the Western alphabet, but Ukrainian, in Cyrillic script. Some of the letters stand out as familiar: T, R, P. But others look so foreign they may as well be hieroglyphs. Blocky and chunky and indecipherable. It's evident, too, in the roads themselves, the infrastructure. As you progress, the tarmac becomes rougher, rippled with cracks and tiger-stripes of tar. A noticeable lack of upkeep. You feel the bumps through your seat, the vibrations travelling up your tail bone, along your spine.

You should feel more exposed here, more vulnerable, but you don't. If anything, you have a greater sense of freedom, a stronger sense of autonomy. You're alone, secure, encased in your Octavia, accelerating through this foreign space, both part of the landscape, and apart from it.

According to the satnav, you still have another hour to go. You see very few other vehicles. Occasionally you pass a crossroads, a cluster of farm buildings, a rusted-out tractor, but mostly it's seemingly limitless stretches of tarmac. You spend much of the time thinking about the suitcase you have in the back. Until the border, you hadn't given its contents much thought. Any thought, really. It had been forgotten, in the boot. But the fact Valerie seemed so unconcerned about you crossing with it both intrigues and irritates you. What are you going to exchange, for this person you're picking up? If it's drugs, or money, then they've put you at risk. If it isn't, you want to know what it is. You deserve to know. You are, after all, the courier. You are more than that, actually. You are the messenger, the harbinger.

Back in Prague, even on the other side of the border, you wouldn't have considered opening it, going against Valerie's instructions. But out here, alone in this bleak, blasted landscape, it seems not just an option, but a genuine possibility. Why not? What could happen? Who else is there? It would be a transgression, but not a risk. Not an immediate risk, anyway. The threats they levelled at you back in their house seem insubstantial, far removed. Buffered by distance and borders.

Curiosity killed the cat, sure. But how many cats were killed from *lack* of curiosity, from ignorance, naïvety, timidity?

You pass an open gate, giving access into a field. At the centre of the field, a single tree, bent and twisted and gnarled. Its branches dotted with birds, blackly still. Crows or ravens. The same as the one at the border, but not pecking away. These ones just sit. Watching. Waiting. For you? A mile further along, you slow to a halt. You swing wide, easing on to the hard shoulder, and circle around casually, heading back the way you came. This time, at the gate, you turn in. Twin ruts lead through the frosted grass, guiding you towards the tree. Rolling to a halt underneath it, you get out. Stand for a time in the cold, breathing. You can see every horizon. The late afternoon light dimming, shadows stretching across the ground. You feel small, isolated as the tree, insignificant as the ravens. Your car, the case in it. All of it transitory, empty of meaning. Shapes against a void.

Meaning comes from within. We give things meaning. Nothing means anything without human knowledge, and perspective. So thinking, you walk around to the back of the car, insert your key in the lock, and twist. The lid of the box-like boot pops open. You raise it, letting the hydraulic struts ease it up, hold it, and reach in to move your duffel bag aside.

The suitcase sits there, clamped shut like a clamshell.

You lift it, feeling its weight again. You look around. There is nobody. Kneeling, you lay it in the snow and examine the latches. They are locked, yes, but they don't seem to be particularly secure. It's not an attaché case, not a government briefcase. Not even metal. The body is plastic, coated in a layer of faux-leather. Shoddy hinges, spray-painted chrome. Just the kind of case you could buy at any discount market stall, which you imagine is exactly what they did.

You know a trick. Not a particularly good one. Something your mother taught you. One of the many uses of a hairpin. Pulling one from your duffel bag, you straighten it into a thin stem of wire. Stiff enough to act as a makeshift lock-pick. You remember your mother using it against you, when you'd locked yourself in your bathroom. A petulant teen, pulling a strop. Your bathroom had one of those ineffective locks, built into the door knob. Easily picked.

The suitcase is even easier. You fit the safety pin into the keyhole of one latch, and wiggle till you hear the click. It opens. Satisfied, you move on to the other latch. You have more trouble with it, but not too much. Soon both are open. Valerie is either overconfident, or careless. You sit there, savouring the sense of defiance, disobedience. Of crossing her. Knowing this is a turning point. You could re-latch it, put the case away, stash it back under your duffel bag, and leave it at that. Like sneaking out of the house and returning without getting caught.

But you want to know. Need to know. What are they exchanging for a person? It must be money, or even gold. A lot of it, judging by the weight. The thought doesn't occur to you that you might covet it, take it and run away with it. There's no appeal at all in that. It's just the knowing. Just the knowledge. That's all you want.

You open the case.

You are unsure about what you're seeing, at first. It is so unexpected. So bizarre. You reach inside, pull one out to make sure. Rough-hewn, grey, heavy. Hard. A rock. It's just a rock. Inside, there are mostly rocks. All about the same shape. All chosen to fit in, to give the case some weight, some heft. Underneath, as if as an afterthought, there are some notes, cash – more along the lines of what you expected. But not in cool, sleek bundles tied by elastic bands, as you see in films. These are loose, scattered. Grimy and crumpled. The denominations aren't even consistent, and at least some appear to be old Czechoslovakian koruna, from when

116

the two were one country. The currency now long-since outdated, defunct.

No wonder they didn't worry about you crossing the border, or bother with a proper lock. They are not careless or overconfident at all. They are cynical, clinical. Ruthless.

You feel cheated. Tricked. Even though the trick is obviously meant for someone else, the person you're paying. Above you, one of the ravens croaks, curious. You look up. A dozen or so glinting beaks are pointed down at you, like daggers. And black, inscrutable eyes. An unkindness. You remember that a flock of ravens is called an unkindness. You lean back, raise your arm, consider throwing the rock at them. But you don't.

It is not the ravens who have been playing tricks.

arriving

Brown water running along the gutters. A dried-up fountain, with a statue in the middle, missing its head and arms. Just a torso. Buildings that are concrete boxes – square or rectangular, grey or brown. Broken windows. Fallen archways. Collapsed roofs. Facades crumbling like chalk, to reveal girders, pinions. Roads without curbs or sidewalks or lane markings, or even paving. These are your first impressions of your destination. The place you have driven almost a thousand kilometres to reach. The town sign defaced, illegible, as if somebody wanted it smeared out of existence.

Out in the countryside the poverty was less noticeable, particularly as it's winter – how to tell if those fields you drove through were fertile, plentiful, rich and rewarding, or barren, hard, and impossible to scrape a living out of? The fences were untended, falling down in places, but that's not uncommon, in your experience of the countryside. And the distant farmhouses? Hard to judge anything from afar. But here, in this urban area, the sense of poverty is stark, shocking. The genteel words you have been trained to use – rundown, underprivileged, impoverished – hold no sway here. This place is devastated, wrecked, ruined. That is the word: *ruined*. It feels as if you are driving through a ruin – the remnants of what's been left behind after a war. The desolation accentuated by the winter weather, by the slurries of brown snow on the ground, the emptiness of the streets. Only a few people are about, wrapped up in layers of clothing, peering from beneath hoods, scarves, caps. They see you from the side, in quick glances. Then scurry on rather than stop to stare. The car must stand out: new, expensive, with Czech plates. You intuit their suspicion, their hostility towards you – the foreigner – but that could be paranoia, fed by the fading light. You know other parts of Ukraine are not like this. Not the major cities. Kiev. You've seen pictures of Kiev. You've seen it on TV, on Eurovision. *Hello, from Kiev!* The shrill greeting of the presenter. But this place, away from those cosmopolitan centres, has been left to wither. Too far from the tree. Then again, you know there are places back in Wales almost like this. In America, too. Tod told you about Detroit, the blight. And mining towns in Northern England. Here, it is heightened by the foreignness, the unfamiliar look and feel. That sense of otherness.

You have limited knowledge of the situation in Ukraine, a vague understanding of its history. Just a few facts picked up in school, or from the news. The Chernobyl disaster. The country was once a territory of the USSR. At the edge of the Eastern Bloc, and a front line in the Cold War. A history of trouble: economic, social, political. Maybe the condition of this town is a result of that turmoil. Maybe it's typical of the towns in the region, or maybe it's an anomaly.

You don't know for certain. What you do know is that this is where you're meant to be, today, to make the exchange.

You have the address on a piece of paper, in your wallet. Fortunately, the satnav still functions here. It's more nonchalant than you: the Czech guide sounds just as calm, placid, and soothing as ever. *Odbočit vlevo.* Turn left. Turn right. Go across the next roundabout – even when the roundabout is a broken circle of old cobblestones, with a section of steel truss work blocking one of the exits. Not your exit, luckily.

You carry on. You seem to be in a residential area. Here, at least, the buildings show some signs of life, of inhabitation: balconies with laundry racks, or rusted kettle barbecues. The occasional flag, hung from a window. The yellow and blue of Ukraine. Perhaps in defiance of Russia. Or perhaps some sporting contest is currently going on. Down one alley, three children dressed in winter coats play a game with sticks and a ball. Street hockey. They stop to glance up at the sound of your vehicle, and then you have passed by.

On the satnav, beyond three more turns, you can see the little chequered flag that marks the end of this journey, and the next stage in your errand. You manoeuvre around a burnt-out Jeep and turn into a cul-de-sac. A five-storey horseshoe of tiny apartments. Each with an iron-railed balcony. Sliding glass doors. You see more laundry racks, lawn chairs. Potted plants, withered and frosted.

You pull over beside a street bin, overflowing with black bags. Your wheels grind down to stillness. You have the sense of being watched, which, of course, you are. Curtains twitch at some windows. The shadows of heads peering out. It's a menacing spot. You don't just feel hemmed in – you *are* hemmed in. Blocked on three sides, with the only exit the narrow alley you entered by. You don't even think you have room to turn around. You'll have to back out. When the time comes.

Your satnav is telling you, repeatedly, *Dorazil jsi*. You have arrived. You switch it off. Kill the engine. Sit for a minute, hoping that somebody will appear, come out. You were given no instructions about the actual meeting. Just that you were to go to this address.

After a few minutes, you get out of the car. You shut the door, and the noise of it resonates in the confined space, bouncing hollowly off the concrete walls. Echoing up, up, dissipating eventually over the rooftops. From the backseat you get your jacket and beanie, pull these on. More for the false sense of protection they provide than as barrier against the cold. A faint stink lingers in the air. Refuse and other human rot.

You take a few steps forward. Stop. Look around. You see a man. He is not more than twenty metres away, previously shielded from view by the large bin. He is standing in an open archway – tunnel-like, an exterior walkway of some sort. And staring at you. Drinking from a bottle tucked in a paper bag. Thick wool mitts on his hands, fingerless to allow for grip. Looking at you, he tilts back the bottle and takes a long, deliberate swig.

You walk over to him, confident that this is who you are here to see. He watches you approach. He is older than you. Around fifty, fifty-five. Aged further by alcohol. His nose a mass of veins, his cheeks ruddy, his eyes rheumy and bloodshot. You can smell the drink on him. Vodka, or some kind of moonshine – maybe even methyl alcohol. He doesn't say anything, and neither do you. Just stop in front of him, at a safe distance. Several paces back.

He sneers, showing blackened teeth. Mutters something in another language – you assume Ukrainian. You tell him you don't understand. You tell him that you're here to meet somebody. You try it in English first, and then Czech. You can't tell if he registers this. But he seems to get something from it. He spits at your feet, and says something shocking, and oddly striking.

He calls you an evil witch, in English.

Then he withdraws into his corridor, like some kind of subterranean creature, and all you hear are his footsteps padding away, slopping in puddles. Such a strange insult – almost comical. Not a bitch but an evil witch. Why evil? Doesn't he understand its meaning? Was it muddled in translation? You can't remember a single time, in your entire life, that anybody has accused you of being evil. You would laugh it off, if you weren't so puzzled.

You're considering getting back in the car, reversing out of there. Maybe calling Mario, for clearer instructions. But, as you turn away from the man's hallway, you see that a figure has come out on one of the third-storey balconies: a short, squat woman. Her hair loose and scraggly around her face. She is holding up a piece of cloth – a dishrag, or a dirty old shirt – and waving it forlornly. Less like somebody trying to get your attention, and more like somebody giving up, offering to surrender.

the trade

A criminal on the run, some member of their organisation who needs to cross the border. Or a refugee, somebody who has made it here, this far, and is willing to pay extra to get into Europe. Or a smuggler. Or a slave. Somebody who has been sold, or sold themselves, into slavery. To be used, possibly abused, on the other side. To be auctioned out to a wealthy family, or a brothel owner. A pimp.

You've had plenty of time to consider who you might be picking up. Long hours in the car, when you puzzled over what you've been told – which isn't much. But you know that it is illegal, and in light of that all these various possibilities have occurred to you. You have discounted none of them. You assess and reassess your expectations while you wait for the woman who signalled to you. She pointed and called something that might have been 'stay'.

So you stay. You get the suitcase out of the boot, and stand by the car. Waiting.

After several minutes she emerges from one of the corridors at the base of the horseshoe-shaped tower-block. You cross to her. She's in her mid-forties, dressed in clothes that aren't much more than rags. A tattered apron. Torn stockings. A pair of battered trainers, one sole held on with duct tape. A grey bun on top of her head. Her face is grey as well, and granular. Her eyes are skittish, frenetic. Looking around you, past you, as if she thinks there might be other people with you, nearby, in hiding. A trap of some sort.

She is still holding that dirty cloth in her hand – the one she waved to attract your attention. Rather than exchange any form of greeting, she signals with it again, whipping it in a quick, jerking motion: back the way she came. You are to follow. This woman, apparently, is not the one you're picking up.

Her movements are surprisingly quick, darting. Moving down the corridor and along two side passages, mostly in the dark. Subterranean scurrying. The corridor smells of sweat and rankness and gasoline. Every so often, the woman holds her rag to her face, as if in defence against the stench.

You feel you're being naïve, just following, just going along with her. Leaving your expensive rental car exposed, and entering this den, this hovel. All on your own. But then, you're not all on your own. You're a representative. And it must be known who you represent. Should this woman, or anybody else, try something, your employers would not be happy. There would be repercussions. There would be retribution. That must have been made clear. Or perhaps it is simply assumed.

Now she is leading you past a broken elevator – the doors half open, the shaft empty, vacant, foul-smelling – and up a stairwell, which doubles back on itself twice. Then out into a hall on the third floor. You see nobody else, but you sense there are other occupants, behind the doors. Aware of you, your presence and your passing and your purpose. As if you truly are an emissary, a delegate. Bestowed with authoritative power. As if you could stop at any one of their doors and call them out, take them with you.

The walls are water-stained, sloughing plaster like snakeskin. The carpeting is mildewed, spongy underfoot. Smelling faintly of urine.

Her door – or the door she brings you to – is at the end. By this point she is in what you would call an agitated state. Muttering to herself, her body making jerky, disjointed motions. Like those marionettes near Wenceslas Square. She paws at the door, forces it open. It swings inwards, revealing a living area of some sort – mattresses on the floor – and a kitchenette. All just quick impressions. Cupboard doors hanging off. Piles of dishes, paper plates, empty food tins. A nest. And the people. Half a dozen of them. At first you think they are all young children, and all boys: they are dressed in soiled shirts and trousers, and have the pale, thin, undefined bodies of the permanently malnourished. But, as your eyes adjust to the dimness, the murk, you see that some are probably older – teenagers – and some are adolescent girls. But so thin – their physiques underdeveloped – that it's hard to tell; there is little difference. As a group they hang back from the door, watching you warily but without any real sense of animosity. They are worried only of what *you* might do to them.

Somewhere, a baby is wailing.

The woman enters the room and goes to one of the boys and snatches something from his hand. A canister. She splashes its contents on to the rag and holds it to her face and takes a long, soothing inhale. This seems to steady her.

Removing it, she stares at you defiantly, almost proudly, and passes the canister back to the boy.

You understand that this is why you are here. Why the trade couldn't be done downstairs. She needed you to bear witness. To see. To understand.

She moves along the line of youths and children. Whether they are hers, or simply ones that have ended up in her care, you don't know. You never will know. She stops and puts both her hands on the shoulder of one and guides him forward, pushing him towards you. He is small, and does not walk properly. He has a limp of some kind. A bad foot, or leg. His face hidden in a hoody. The features poking out are pointed, elfin. He could be six or seven, or he could be older, afflicted by stunted growth.

He is holding something in his hands. Slips of paper.

The woman stops him in front of you and nods, curtly. Her eyes glazed with fumes, seeming to look just beyond you. She is waiting for something, and for a few moments you don't comprehend that she is waiting for you. You are too overcome. Too overwhelmed. But you still have enough of your faculties to recall this is a two-sided transaction.

You hold up the suitcase.

The woman looks at it. Lets go of his shoulders. Takes it.

That is all. The trade has taken place. She either doesn't think to check the contents, or doesn't have the courage to question you about it, or is too high, or too far gone, to consider it rationally, properly.

The boy is looking up at you. He has skin so pale it's practically translucent. Blue veins threaded beneath the surface. Big eyes that blink, birdlike. Not knowing what else to do, you reach out and take him by the hand, tell him to come. He allows you to hold it, but doesn't grip it back. In the other hand he is still clutching his papers.

At the door you look back at the woman, once. Her expression is indescribable and unforgettable. In the days ahead you will look back on this moment, and that expression. You will understand it to be a look beyond misery and anguish and despair, beyond having lost heart and hope. Beyond, even, the realm of human emotion. Rather, a sense of soullessness. A desolation.

Then you are going, walking down the corridor, leading this boy in the hoody by the hand. At the stairs it occurs to you that you should hurry. You don't know what this woman was promised in payment, but it must have been more than rocks and soiled, obsolete notes. So old that banks likely wouldn't even exchange them. The locks on the suitcase only took you a few minutes to pick. You suspect now that no key has been sent, even if one had been promised, but it won't take long for her to open the locks, or break them open.

This happens when you reach the ground floor, the forecourt, now far darker than when you went up – twilight comes early to the tenement, the sides of the building blocking out the remaining daylight. In this new gloom you hear the sound, echoing down through the building. A terrible, high-pitched keening. A wailing. You pull the boy's arm, shift into a run. He has trouble, limping along at your side. But he doesn't resist. He is trying to keep up, to keep pace with you. He wants to go, to get away too. With you.

This is the beginning. Of the two of you. Of being on the run, together.

From the very start, he places his faith in you.

Something lands by your feet, cracks on the concrete. Goes skittering off across gravel and ice. A rock. One of the rocks. Glancing back, you see the woman on the balcony, shaking the suitcase at the sky, screaming, pulling at her hair. The kids and youths are the ones throwing the rocks. Raining

127

them down on you in punishment. None hit you, but one hits the bonnet of the rental car, bounces off, leaving a deep dent, chips in the paint.

You unlock the car with the key-fob while running. Yank open the passenger's door, guide the boy inside. Hurry around behind, using the car for shelter, and get in the driver's side. It all seems to occur in jump cuts, short flashes of experience, that stuttery sense of panic, alarm. No room to turn the car around. Just shoving the key in the ignition, throwing the gearstick into reverse, stomping on the accelerator and running it backwards down the alley, half-turned in your seat to steer. Just missing the burnt-out Jeep.

When you glance back, forward, you can still see the woman – on her knees now, her fists wrapped around the bars of her balcony, shaking at it in her fury, as if trapped in a cage, and all the others, all her children, howling and dancing around her in aggravation, but just as impotent and helpless and entombed.

gogol

You glance at the boy watching the world go by outside his window. He sits in his seat clutching his pieces of paper. He isn't wearing his seatbelt, and you don't ask him to. He is alert and tense as a stray cat. He smells like a cat, too: a sour stench that emanates from his clothes, his hair, his skin. Oily and malign. His hood is still up and he remains hidden in it. His pale nose poking out. A tangle of black hair hanging in front of his eyes. His feet just touching the floor of the car.

You drive with focussed determination, navigating from memory, not having yet reprogrammed the satnav. The buildings of the town seeming to fall away around you: first becoming half-collapsed structures, then crumbling into piles of brick and rubble, and finally dissolving into the landscape. It's only once you are outside the town limits that you're freed from the anxiety of the alley – the feeling that you could be caught at any minute, trapped in purgatory with the inhabitants, their nightmare life-in-death. Surely you can't trade a suitcase full of rocks and worthless notes for a child without consequences. Surely there must be repercussions.

This feeling – of guilt, remorse, wrongdoing – coupled with the realisation that you have got away with it – *evil witch* – compels you to explain, to the boy, that it's not really your fault; that you're just making the exchange, and delivering him. That you had no idea what was in the suitcase, until it was too late. That it's a terrible thing that has been done, to his mother, or whoever that woman was. You go on like this for some time, a confession of sorts, seeking to absolve yourself. Telling him what's been building up inside you. Except, when you glance over, you see the lack of understanding in his eyes. The utter incomprehension, mingled with caution. Like a pet regarding its owner – having no idea what any of it means, only that you are upset, a strange lady speaking so adamantly, defensively.

'You don't understand English.'

It's not a question, and his look is confirmation enough. It comes as something of a relief, to know that whatever you've said hasn't registered, that whatever you say is merely sound to him. Vowels and consonants floating in the air between you. Totally meaningless. But your outburst, your monologue, has made you feel calmer. You roll down your window, light up a Smart. The boy doesn't seem at all bothered by this. You remember his mother, the rag, try to imagine all the things he's seen, but can't. There's a disconnect in your capacity to understand. The phrase 'worlds apart' doesn't begin to account for it.

As if to accentuate this, he holds out a trembling hand, like a beggar asking for alms. You look at the hand – the nails rimmed with grime, the palm lined with dirt, cuts, scrapes.

It takes a moment to clock that he's asking for a drag. You hesitate, hand over the smoke. He puffs at it offhandedly, casually, like another child – a typical child – might suck idly on a lollipop. When he's done, he hands it back. Accustomed to sharing. A seasoned smoker. You don't immediately take a drag. You have a brief, shameful, flutter of concern – about what ailment this boy might be suffering from, what illnesses he might be infected with. You immediately regret these thoughts, despise yourself for thinking them, and suck defiantly on the filter to dispel them.

For the next few miles, the two of you pass the cigarette back and forth, sharing the comfort of nicotine. It makes him look older, the act of smoking. It may well be that he's seven or eight. You've always found it difficult to judge the ages of children, and his state – begrimed, enfeebled, undernourished – makes it all the harder.

When the cigarette is finished, you carefully stub it out in the car's ashtray. The first time you have done so. As if you are teaching him one good habit – not to litter – out of guilt for irresponsibly allowing him to smoke. When you finish, he opens and shuts the ashtray a few times, testing its function. A newness. Then he plays with his window, again imitating your action. Using the electric button to scroll it down, letting in blasts of cold air, and then rolling it back up. He's likely never been in a vehicle this new, this luxurious.

You cross a bridge over a river, the surface glazed with ice, ghost-pale and glowing against the growing dark. It has begun to snow lightly – thick, delicate flakes that twirl through your headlight beams like confetti – but it isn't sticking to the roads yet.

In the passenger seat, you notice the boy peering sideways at you, while pretending not to. You catch his eye, put a palm on your chest, and introduce yourself. Saying your name, sounding out the syllables for him, in a slow and simple way that reminds you of your Czech language class. Ei-ra. That's me, you say. Then you point to him, tap his sternum, ask him what he's called. He understands enough to get your meaning. He says something that sounds like Go-goal. Gogol. You repeat it aloud, to make sure you've got it right: Gogol. And he nods – your pronunciation, at least, is correct. Such an odd name. An ugly name, for an ugly boy. And something familiar about it, though at first you can't recall what.

It's only later, after minutes of silence, when you've stopped thinking about it, that the memory resurfaces: a famous author. One of Tod's dead Russians. You know nothing about him, except a phrase Tod was fond of quoting, with ironic relish: *we have all emerged from Gogol's overcoat.* It didn't mean anything to you then, and doesn't mean anything now.

This particular Gogol doesn't have an overcoat. He doesn't have any coat. Just a dirty, torn hoody. He is still huddled in it, even though you have the heater on high, as if the chill in him runs too deep, can't be warmed by ordinary means. You know that feeling. That sense of being bitterly cold, benumbed. Emotionless.

Maybe the two of you have more in common than you think.

disneyland

Your instructions are to drive straight to the inn on this side of the border. But you haven't eaten since morning, and the boy, Gogol, looks as if he may not have eaten for days, weeks. His entire life. Not eaten properly, anyway.

At the roadside, a cluster of buildings rises up, takes shape. A truck stop, petrol station, and café – the same trio of structures you'd find back home. You put the indicator on, turn in. Parked in the fuel bay is a beat-up lorry, the hubcaps rusting, the canvas sides streaked with oil. Only a handful of cars parked at the café, beneath its blue awning. A glowing neon sign with Cyrillic script, which you assume says *Open*. The lights are on, at least. People move about inside.

You park beside a pile of ploughed snow, waist-high, the contours melted like slag, and refrozen into ice. You turn to Gogol, who is regarding you apprehensively. You mime the act of eating, as if biting an invisible sandwich. 'Food,' you say. 'Time for food.'

He doesn't get out of the car until you go around to his side, open the door. Then he creeps forth – all his movements cautious, wary. As if he thinks the ice on the tarmac underfoot is only an inch thick. As if the two of you are standing on a river, at risk of plunging through, like the skaters Marta mentioned, into the rushing, frigid waters. Tumbling into that furiously silent void.

You take his hand, feel the smallness of it in yours. Tell him it's okay.

The café is a portable building, of the kind that can be hauled anywhere on a trailer. Just four clapboard sides, a flat, sloping roof. A box. As you step in, a bell tinkles above the door. There is enough room for a counter, a kitchen, a till, and a handful of plastic tables. At the counter sit two men, dressed in jeans, boots, fur-lined down jackets. Truckers. Nobody is sitting at the tables. It's early evening – too early for any dinner crowd. If the place ever gets a dinner crowd.

You sit at a table, look at the laminated menu, peeling and sticky with grease. The items are all hand-written. No helpful photos depicting the dishes, like in the tourist restaurants in Prague. Without thinking you ask Gogol what he wants, and he looks at you blankly. You show him the menu and his expression doesn't change. Possibly – probably – he doesn't read.

You take the menu with you to the till. A woman about your age is standing at it, in a white blouse and apron, the front stained brown with grease and sauce and oil. She is hefty, muscular – her sleeves rolled up to show her forearms. You address her in English – you have no choice. You gesture at the menu, at the boy, and yourself. You say you want food. Fries or chips and burgers, and Coke. Assuming Coke should be universal. The woman listens to all this curiously. She looks to you, to the boy. Shrugs. Makes a rubbing motion with her thumb and forefinger. Money. Yes. Of course. Money. The spending money Mario gave you included some Ukrainian currency, some hryvni. For breaks like this.

You do the tourist thing – the hopeless gesture of travellers everywhere. You hold out a fan of notes, let her take her pick. She does so shrewdly, plucking two hundreds. She does not offer change. If the hryvnia is about as valuable as the koruna, she's taken just over five quid. Reasonable enough. She puts the money in the till, reties her apron, and waddles into the kitchen. You return to your table, feeling foolish, not as *smart* as you'd like to be. But you aren't perfect, and besides, there's no harm done. This time.

Gogol is waiting quietly. You sit across from him. Get a real look at him for the first time. He is almost unbelievably filthy – the dirt visible all over his face, in his hair. A layer of it, like make-up. More evident here, beneath the fluorescent lights. The dark hoody is soiled, stained, torn. His mouth is tight, always closed. One of his lips slightly twisted. His eyes hard, wary. He is not a beautiful or handsome child – not a classic diamond in the rough. Despite that, despite the obvious hardships of his upbringing, he has a lingering air of innocence about him. A mistreated, abused child. But still a child.

He has trouble meeting your gaze. He sits and stares at his hands, on the table in front of him. Still clutching his pieces of paper. You want to ask about that. You want to know. But the Cokes arrive, just then. In old-fashioned glass bottles. Placed down unceremoniously, but not rudely, by the server. Gogol's even has a straw in it.

He reaches for it, slurps at it zealously. Finishes it in less than a minute. Then sits there hiccupping – each one causing his whole body to shake.

When the food comes, Gogol doesn't attack it, as he did the Coke. He gazes at it in something like wonder, something like awe. A plate of chips and a beef burger. The grease congealing beneath the bun. He looks shyly at you, as if not quite daring to believe that this is for him. To eat it, he must let go of his papers. He tucks them in the pouch of his hoody, picks up the burger, and takes a bite. Tentatively. As if he fears it's a trick. As if you might be the witch in a fairy tale – the Baba Yaga figure – who is going to poison him, or put him to sleep, entrap him in a cage for fattening up. But when there are no ill-effects, he takes another bite, and another. He puts the food away without pleasure, without manners, without any sense of self-control. Just biting and gnawing and chewing. Like a starved wolf who's been thrown a scrap. His antics are such that the men at the bar look over, say something, laugh heartily. Not nastily. Simply awestruck at the sight of the boy's appetite, his lack of restraint.

Gogol is nearly done, and you've hardly started. You begin to eat. Still watching him. Oddly enough his clear and desperate need of it makes you appreciate the food all the more. The meat is gristly, overdone, with that old-liver taste. But it is something. You are eating, and breathing, and your heart is still beating. And this is all that matters, all there is.

As soon as he is done, he wipes his hands on his hoody – ignoring the napkins that are at the side of the table – and pulls out the papers again. Clenching them, as if he doesn't trust them to be safe in the pouch. You point to them. Ask him what they are. He looks at you shyly.

Then he spreads his hands, unfolds what lies inside. There are two pieces of paper. One looks like a report of some kind; the other is a newspaper article. Both are equally tatty, soiled, torn. He hands you the report. You spread it on the table in front of you. It is some kind of official form – all of it in

Ukrainian. You can't make any sense of it. One section, near the bottom, is highlighted in red ink.

You nod in approval, as if you understand. Offer it back. In exchange he slides you the other piece. It has been torn from a glossy magazine. You look at the article, the writing, in confusion. Then he makes a sound – no – and motions for you to turn it over. When you do, you see images of a rollercoaster and rides, a mock castle. A life-sized Mickey Mouse. A theme park. *The* theme park. The title and caption is entirely in Ukrainian, illegible to you, but the word on the sign above the entrance in the photo is in English: *Disneyland*.

When you look up, Gogol is beaming. You have not yet seen him smile. His teeth are rotten, yellow-brown, the canines crooked and sharp as fangs. He taps the image and nods eagerly. Says something that sounds like a question.

Yes, you assure him, sliding the advert back. Not brave enough to spoil his fantasy. You tell him you can take him there, to Disneyland. You *are* taking him there.

Understanding in that moment, this is the lie he's been told.

In the parking lot, before you even get in the car, he throws up everything he ate. The food too rich, or too much for his stomach to handle. It comes up in three full heaves – hitting the pavement in Coke-and-ketchup spatters. Reddish black, like blood that has been poisoned, tainted. You pat his back, both sympathetic and revolted. He wipes his mouth on his sleeve, looks up at you in suspicion.

As if you might be the witch in this fairy tale after all.

a stopping point

You drive by the inn on the first pass. It doesn't look like an inn or hotel or motel or any kind of establishment that you've seen. It's an old farmhouse, set back from the road. An estate. A relic of better times, of a completely different agricultural system. Even the satnav is confused, trying to find the place by the postcode. It tells you that you have arrived when you are in the middle of an open stretch of main road; the only building in sight, in the dark, is this old, decrepit farmhouse. The lights are on. You assume that must be it.

You spin a U-turn, crunching ice and gravel at the roadside, and head back to the gateway. There – you see it now. A painted wooden sign, with the now familiar and strange Ukrainian lettering. It's peeling, faded, the words barely discernible. But you can make out готе́ль and you know

– from your minimal guidance – that it means an inn, or lodgings.

Three cars are parked haphazardly in the driveway, near the front porch. On the veranda, a single light glows orange, and when you pull up and get out you can hear the bulb buzzing. You walk around to Gogol's side. Again, he doesn't emerge until you open his door. Again, he is cautious, watchful. You talk to him, even though you know now he doesn't understand. You explain that you're just staying here for one night. A warm bed and food. The act of talking helps keep you calm, clears your head – and seems to reassure him.

The front room of the farmhouse has been converted into a reception and drinking area: a long wooden bar, a motley selection of liquor. Sofas and chairs scattered around the place. The space is cold and practically empty, but at the same time quite raucous. At the bar sit two women and a man, talking animatedly. The man is, at least. Dressed in a pinstripe suit, with his hair slicked back, and wearing a pair of glasses with chunky black frames. He waves a short, puffy finger and declares something boisterously in Ukrainian, which makes the women laugh. They are dressed identically: mini-skirts, halter tops, heels, tights. Only the colours of each item are different. Both have bold, conspicuous hairstyles, sprayed and dyed pastel colours, like dancers in an eighties' music video. Off to the side, sitting together over a board game of some sort, are two men. One of them younger, in an ice hockey top, his face flecked with pimples. The other older, sitting hunched in a paint-spattered sweatshirt, with a wool hat pulled low over his brow. Builders, maybe? Contractors en route to a job? On the board between them are little discs or tiles, which they push around with their fingers. The pieces make a click-clack sound, like an erratic metronome. Something off. Not quite right.

You may speculate about these people, but that's all it is: speculation.

Behind the bar, a huge woman perches on a stool, so that her body mass spills over the sides of it. She has lanky, greasy hair that falls in ringlets to her shoulders. Meaty biceps, bare and tattooed. She appears stoic and firmly planted. Buddha-like. She looks at you (the others look too, momentarily quiet) but she makes no move to stand or greet you. So you go to her, say that you have booked a room, for you and the boy. You don't give her your name. You don't know if your name has been mentioned by Valerie. You just say that there is supposed to be a room. And there is. The woman nods again, causing her chin fat to quiver. She sighs wearily and shifts, easing her bulk off the stool. Emanating from her is the faint smell of body odour, yeasty as rotten beer. Her biceps, despite the cold, are slick with a sheen of sweat. The tattoo on the left one shows a skull, a snake woven in a figure eight through the eye sockets.

'Come,' she says to you, jangling a pair of keys.

She labours – that is the word for it – towards a hall. Behind you, the board game begins again – click-clack-click – and the suited man at the bar mumbles something that slowly crescendos to a punchline, explodes into more laughter, possibly at your expense.

Your room is up a flight of stairs, and seeing the innkeeper ascend them is something quite extraordinary: one step at a time, pausing to rest after each, like a climber atop Everest, sucking at thin air. You wonder why she couldn't just direct you. Maybe it's a matter of pride, or principle. Or maybe it's simply habit, what is always done. She reaches the first floor eventually, and makes a final rhino charge down the hall to reach a door. She throws it open with a gasp, motions you into the darkness beyond. You feel a pang of misgiving, of mistrust. But you shouldn't have anything to fear. You haven't fulfilled your main purpose yet. They hired you for the border. After the border is when you need to be careful.

Then you think: no, you need to be careful *now*, from here on in.

Or rather, you needed to be careful from the start.

As you step inside, you instinctively put a hand on Gogol's shoulder, guide him behind you so you are shielding him with your hip and thigh. Not that this would do anything. But it's revealing. You are already thinking of him as being under your protection. As being your ward.

A light comes on. No menacing figures, no men in balaclavas. Just the sight of a rumpled bed. The sound of the heavyset woman wheezing behind you. The smell of air freshener failing to mask the stench of stale smoke, of sweat, of sex. A sink in one corner. No bathroom. The toilet, apparently, is down the hall. You deduce this because the big woman points in that direction and gasps something, before throwing the keys on the bed, and lumbering back downstairs. As if she needs to descend without pausing too long, before her muscles cramp up, or her energy reserves run out. There has been no talk of payment. There will be no talk of payment. That has all been arranged by Valerie.

You put your bag on the bed. The only bed. Gogol can have the bed – you'll use the blankets, sleep on the floor.

You tell Gogol he needs a shower. He smells worse than the woman, worse than this room. Swaddled in a lifetime of grime. No towels have been provided. But there must be a shower. You motion for him to follow you, down the hall in the direction she pointed. Sure enough there is a toilet, and in the same room an old bathtub – the kind with brass clawed feet. It is greying, filthy. But there's a detachable shower head. You twist the taps, let the water run. It sputters. Pipes make

141

creaking and groaning sounds. The water is cold for a long time (you're checking it with your hand), but eventually it changes to a very mild temperature that can't be called warm, but is at least less cold.

Gogol is standing well back, watching defensively. His arms crossed in front of him. He looks far younger than he did in the car, smoking, or in the café, eating greedily. Such a little boy. His age seems to keep changing, fluctuating. As if he is some kind of changeling, playing at the role of child when it suits him. Like now. You pluck at his hoody, tell him to take it off. He does so with obvious reluctance. 'Come on,' you say. You mime exasperation. Point at the running water. 'Clean yourself up.' You tell him that you won't look, and turn away. But you hear nothing – no movement, no signs of obedience. When you glance over, he is just standing there, watching you timidly. You sigh, turn back to him. You tell him you're not going to hurt him but that he needs to have a wash. You help him out of his shirt and then motion for him to undo his jeans. The garments, when they hit the floor, look like puddles of grease or oil. So heavy with filth. When he's down to his tatty, threadbare underwear you pick him up under the armpits and put him in the bath, standing up.

He is unbelievably light. As if his body is hollow. A papier-mâché boy. You think he might melt away, dissolve in the water. But he doesn't. He is indifferent and listless and you begin to wonder if you're traumatising him, damaging him. Or if he has been damaged and that you're forcing him to relive it. You try not to touch him, but keep one hand held ready, in case he slips and needs your support. With the other hand you hold the shower head over him and let it run through his hair, which flattens and lies inkily down the sides of his head. His hair is unnaturally thin, and when wet his head looks like a sad little egg, the top painted black. His one leg – his left – is noticeably spindly and an inch or so shorter than the other, as if it has atrophied or not grown fully: the reason he limps.

The water pooling beneath his feet in the bath is dark, brackish, and you assume it's from the old pipes, poor plumbing, until you realise that this is the grunge running off of him, endlessly. Layer after layer. He makes half-hearted motions at scrubbing himself, though uncertainly, as if he has done this so few times he doesn't even know what to do.

As the grime clears and the paleness of his skin appears more clearly, you begin to see that his upper body is dotted with scars, as if he suffered from chicken pox or small pox or some kind of sickness. Except the scars are too uniform, too perfectly circular. They are small burn marks. Seeing this – knowing this to be true – is enough to make you look away, momentarily shield your eyes, pushing your finger and thumb into them, as if you can rub out the image. A startling reaction. You've been numb for so long, as if living under anaesthetic, that hardly anything has had the capacity to touch you. But this does. This boy's scars. You can't comprehend what he has suffered, what he has been put through. And yet you're altering his life. In a way that is hideously reckless, irresponsible.

These realisations prickle into you, like acupuncture needles.

All the same, eventually the water running off him clears, turns clean, and you take some small satisfaction in that. Satisfaction mingled with dread. Yes, you have been thinking about what he has been put through. But you haven't been thinking enough about what awaits him. About what Valerie and Pavel intend to do with him once you bring him back to Prague, hand him over to them.

Or perhaps you haven't wanted to think about it.

He is shivering now – the bathroom, like the rest of the house, is frigid. You twist off the taps, causing them to squeak. Since there are no towels, you remove your sweater and use it as a towel, wrapping it around his trembling shoulders and giving his torso a quick, vigorous rub-down. When you're done, you don't want to put him back in his clothes, in the soiled stink of his old life and all those associations, so you leave your sweater draped over him, and to keep it in place tie the arms about his neck, like a cloak. Or a noose.

chance encounters

This time when you enter the inn's lounge the effect isn't as apparent. The businessman and the two women scarcely glance at you – your novelty value has worn off. And the sounds of the men's board game only pause for a moment before the steady click-clack-click resumes, the gap so brief it's barely noticeable, like the beat that a heart skips. The big owner merely purses her lips at you from behind the bar, as if blowing a silent kiss. Whether this denotes approval or disapproval you can't tell.

Against the window is the scratching of wind-blown snow.

You have your mobile in hand. You cross the lounge, explain to the owner that you have no signal in your room, that you need to make a call. You say this in English, but make exaggerated miming gestures to demonstrate, holding the phone to your ear, shrugging your shoulders, holding your other palm out to imply the pointlessness of trying. You ask if she has a landline that you might be able to use. She shakes her head, no. Though whether this means she doesn't have one, or has one and doesn't want you to use it, you can't tell.

The man in the suit, who has overheard this, leans towards you and slaps the bartop with his palm. This to get your attention. He then hoists a shot glass, filled with a murky liquor, and tells you in English that he found some signal at the end of the lane – for his mobile network, anyway. You look at him uncertainly, wondering if this is a trick of some sort. Some fun at your expense. The two women appear unamused and uninterested in his titbit of helpful information. If it's a ruse, they're not in on the joke.

You look out the window, ask if he means back towards the road. Yes, yes, he nods, waving that way with one hand, knocking back his shot with the other. Only a bar or two, but enough to make a call. Then, leaning in confidentially, he tells you that he just called his wife, to let her know he's stuck in a snowstorm, and won't be home on time. Possibly till the morning.

He laughs uproariously again, and the women laugh along with him, as they're supposed to – even though it's unclear to you whether they've heard and understood. Either way, you thank him, tell him you'll give it a try.

Before going out, you return to your room to get your coat and hat. Gogol is lying on the bed, watching TV, still huddled in your sweater and his damp underpants. He didn't take them off and you didn't feel comfortable suggesting he do so. He's shivering a bit, but it won't kill him to sleep like that. He barely notices you: he's transfixed by the glow of the screen, his mouth ajar, his eyes unblinking. The show is a dubbed

American comedy of some sort, filled with slapstick spills as two men chase each other through a carnival crowd.

Having gotten dressed, you pick up his clothes from the floor. They are so soiled it's tempting to throw them out. But they're all he has. You take them with you, tell him you'll be back in a minute. He nods vacantly, too engrossed to care.

On the way out, you stop at the bar, again go through the act of miming for the woman – asking if she can wash the clothes. This time she seems to understand, or cares to. She nods, curtly. Taps her till to denote she requires payment – laundry wasn't included in your booking. You get out your hryvni, let her select some notes – about the same as you paid for food. In comparison it seems a bit steep to wash one set of boy's clothes, but you suppose she has to run the machine, the same as a full load. And it's not like you don't have the money. Just before handing the clothes over you remember Gogol's only possessions: the wrinkled and grimy pieces of paper. His dreams of Disneyland, and that form. You remove these from the pouch of his hoody, tuck them in your pocket. Thank her.

As you head for the door, you sense attention. An awareness. Not from the owner of the inn, or the three drinkers at the bar, but from the game players. As if they are watching you without watching you. When you step on the porch, you pause to light a cigarette. Use the excuse of shaking out the match to glance sideways, past the window. Catch the face of the older of the two men, angled towards you. Watching you. Definitely. Though whether it is pure curiosity, or something more, you don't know. You wonder if they are meant to keep tabs on you. Report back to Valerie. Let her know if you failed to show up, or if anything seems amiss. Possibly you're being paranoid, but it stays with you as you walk down the steps, past your car, down along the drive. Frosted gravel crunching beneath your heels.

You smoke as you walk – puffing and exhaling, puffing and exhaling – and hold your phone in the other hand, the screen illuminated, keeping it raised and following it like a water diviner sussing out a well. Halfway down the drive a single bar of signal begins to flicker on and off, and a little further along it solidifies, stays steady on the screen.

The phone is a simple clamshell model. You only have two numbers saved in the address book: Mario's, and the number you've been given to call. You highlight it, and the phone on the other end rings twice before somebody answers. They don't say anything. They simply answer. You can hear them breathing. You tell them that you have made the exchange, and are at the inn. The person doesn't give any sign that they're satisfied, but you assume they are. They begin speaking. They tell you that in the morning you will leave the inn at seven-thirty a.m. and drive straight to the border, to be there by precisely eight o'clock. The left-hand lane. It must be the left. The voice is male, flat, toneless. You suspect it's the man – Pavel – who was playing the harpsichord, but you can't be sure. Reception isn't good.

'What about the boy?' you ask.

The boy will be put in the boot, you're told. Make sure he can breathe. Tilt the back seats forward, an inch or two. They give access to the boot. The boy must live. Once you are over the border you are to call again – this same number – and they will tell you where to take him. At that point you will receive your payment in full and your job will be done.

'Do you understand?'

'Yes.'

'There will be no problems.'

'No.'

The call is ended. You stand for a time holding the phone, smoking, considering. Then you do something that you

148

haven't been told to do, but you haven't been told *not* to do, either. You call Mario. His phone rings several times before he answers. When he does, he sounds tense, anxious, asking immediately if everything is all right. You assure him it's fine. You have made the exchange.

'Ah, my snow queen,' he says. 'I knew I could count on you.'

But he is still waiting, expectant. You have called him, after all. To broach it, you explain that you're concerned: the people you gave the suitcase to did not seem happy. They threw things at you. Screamed at you in outrage. You're not sure why. And your passenger: it's this little boy. Only six or seven years old. What could they possibly need this boy for? You ask the question rhetorically, as if it's just occurred to you. As if you're thinking aloud, perhaps a bit rattled by the experience of picking him up.

There is a pause. Just enough to suggest this information is startling, even for Mario – that the job involves a boy. Then he tells you not to say any more, even though you're not talking. That he shouldn't even know this. That the boy is not his concern, and not yours either. Just do what they ask. No questions. It is better that way. Trust him. You will get paid, he will get paid, and they will all be happy. 'Of course,' you assure him, and casually explain that it just seemed strange, how the people were so upset. It's no big deal, though.

'A boy is no different to an adult,' he says, 'no different to any other package.'

'It's all the same to me.'

'You will still deliver him?'

'What else would I do?'

After you hang up, you tuck the phone in your pocket. Look up for the first time. The sky is a sprawling mass of black, against which the stars stand out starkly, in swirling clusters. You stare at the array, trying to make sense of them. Thinking of constellations, the star chart you had on your wall as a child. Chalk lines depicting creatures, heroes, goddesses. But those are just human fancies, images conceived to provide some meaning, and comfort. As simple as children's dot-to-dot drawings. Tonight, you can't make out a single constellation, not even the Plough. Up there, as down here, chaos is the rule. A void filled with futility. Chance encounters. Easy deaths.

You walk back slowly, thinking, placing one foot carefully in front of the other. You are moving more cautiously now, cat-footed, feeling your way in the dark. Aware of the danger that is looming, threatening, omnipresent as the stars.

Halfway to the house, you realise you are walking towards somebody, or somebody is walking towards you. A shadowy shape, coming closer – bold, and making no attempt to be discreet. You stop, stand ready. Feel the furious crescendo of your heart. But as the figure draws near you can see a face, lit up by the glow of a phone. The man in the suit. Looking down, composing a text as he walks. He nearly stumbles right into you.

He glances up, feigns fright: he was aware of you all along. He asks, gallantly, if you made your phone call, and you tell him you did. He jokes about texting his wife – to reassure her he is not doing precisely what he is doing. But the life of a salesman is lonely, and his wife uninterested. So what can he do? This with an innocent shrug. Then he pats at his pockets, in a way that reminds you of Mario – an affected gesture – and asks if you have a cigarette. You wonder if you timed his walk for this reason. You reach in your pocket for your pack of Smarts, and in doing so feel a rustling. Gogol's papers. After you slide out a cigarette, light it for the man, you withdraw the two papers as well.

On impulse, you ask the man if he reads Ukrainian. He jokes that he *is* Ukrainian, so he should hope so. You hold out the formal-looking document, ask him what it means. Squinting through smoke, he peers at it by the light of his phone screen. It is some kind of medical form, he tells you. A report or something, such as you'd get after a check-up.

You point to the circled portion, and he says it denotes blood type. Then, curious about your curiosity, he asks where you got it. Just something you found, you tell him, taking it back. You thought it might be important, but apparently not. He smiles, blows smoke – a long thin plume that billows up and out, like a steam whistle, screaming silently.

'Not unless you need a blood donor,' he says, and chuckles. 'Or an organ transplant.'

You fold it up, wish him luck with his wife. He laughs heartily, as if you've made an excellent joke, and continues weaving his way down the lane, while you carry on towards the farmhouse. As you mount the steps, you keep your head down, but have that same feeling of being observed, shrewdly, from the side. Just an instinctual awareness, on the periphery. But you don't look to check, try not to show any tells. Instead, you perform, play your part: rubbing your forearms vigorously to give the appearance of being concerned solely with being cold. Pretending you don't know they're watching. Pretending it's all going according to plan.

In your fist you are clenching the medical form, so tightly that your fingers ache.

the crossing

Three miles from the border, when the crossing and fences and guardhouses are still out of sight, you spot a disused side road, sheltered by a thicket of larch trees, and turn on to it. This morning, in the cold of the hotel room, after you'd dressed Gogol in his clothes that had been washed and dried by the innkeeper, you sat with him and tried to explain what was happening. Now, in the car, you go over it again, telling him in calm and patient tones that you have to put him in the boot. He sits with one leg – his bad leg – jittering anxiously, and looks at you, his expression baffled but trusting.

You open your door, motion for him stay in his seat. 'Just for a minute,' you say. Your shoes crunch on the frozen ground as you make your way round to the boot. You pop the latch and it swings up forcibly. You look inside. Clean and spacious, with room enough both for a duffel bag and a boy, it could have been just right. But it's not. Unfortunately, the Octavia doesn't have access to the boot via the backseats, like some vehicles. Like the Corsa – which they'd originally and deliberately instructed you to book. This presents a problem when it comes to air, and oxygen, for anybody hidden in the boot.

Your problem. You were the one who switched rental cars.

If you simply close the boot with him inside, he could suffocate. This so seemingly obvious, but it hadn't occurred to you till last night, lying on the bedroom floor, thinking through the steps ahead. And as you listened to Gogol breathing softly in the darkness, you had stomach-churning visions of him asphyxiating – a slow, quiet, stifling death. You've heard about something like it: a girl, playing in a car park, manages to lock herself in the boot of the family car. The parents, coming out, driving about frantically, desperately, searching everywhere, and not realising that their daughter is in the back. Until it is far, far too late. Like Tod's death, like so many everyday tragedies, this is both unimaginable, and all too easy to imagine.

It frustrated you that you didn't foresee this when you switched the vehicles, but you've adapted. Before leaving the inn you asked the owner if she had a nail, and though it took precious time to get around the language barrier, she provided one. You've brought it with you, couldn't risk anybody at the inn seeing what you're about to do. You get on your knees and use the nail, and a fist-sized rock, to punch small holes through the back panel, evenly spaced, above the number plate. It's surprisingly easy: like puncturing a tin can. This damage will no doubt be noticed by the car company, and will no doubt look suspicious. Still. It's all you could think to do. A necessity. Only now, you're wondering if it will be enough. How many holes will he need to breathe? How much oxygen to power a boy's small lungs?

You choose to make seven. Seven seems enough.

You quickly walk around to Gogol's door and open it for him, granting him exit, then lead him back to the boot. You point to your duffel bag, tell him that he must get in beside it. He doesn't understand, and instead reaches for your bag, assuming you have asked him to pick it up. You have to shake your head, no. Finally, you mime the act of clambering into the boot, awkward and clumsy, clown-like. You swing one leg in, then the other, and crouch golem-like inside. You point at Gogol, tap his chest, articulate the words for emphasis: You. Inside.

He nods vigorously, eagerly – not only understanding, but pleased to be playing this game. You get out and he climbs in beside your duffel bag.

When Gogol lies back, he looks fantastically small: he doesn't have to crouch, or curl up, or bend his knees to fit in the boot. He can simply rest there peaceably with his hands on his belly, like a contented sprite. A goblin-boy. He smiles up at you, and you put a finger to your lips, gently pat his head, tell him it won't take long.

And you shut the boot, sealing it like a coffin.

Then it's time to move, fast. You get behind the wheel, put the Škoda in gear, drive right at the speed limit the last three miles to the border. Eyes focused only on the clock, the dash, the road as it slides beneath the wheels and the border crossing rolls towards you. It's just before eight o'clock. You are right on time, right on schedule. The same border that you crossed over. But it looks different, from this side. Or perhaps you are different. No longer indifferent. The guardhouses look more threatening, menacing. The queues longer. They weren't this long on the crossing yesterday. You steer into the left lane, as you've been instructed to do. It's four or five cars deep, which doesn't seem a problem. But then you sit there, and sit there.

At the front of the queue is a large van of some sort, or small lorry. The guard talks to the driver for several minutes – too long for a typical exchange. Something is wrong. You feel it. If this guard is part of their scheme (as you suspect, due to your specific instructions), maybe he's trying to cover his tracks, create a defence in advance. Show that he's being extra meticulous this morning, not lackadaisical at all.

Or else, the plan has gone awry. He's the wrong guard. Not *their* guard.

Now he's walking around to the back of the lorry, calling over a comrade. Both of them dressed in the same blue uniforms, with rifles slung over their shoulders. At their request, the driver climbs down from his cab to join them, opens the big back doors. A brief, cursory check: boxes of vegetables, and tinned food. No people. No illicit cargo.

All this is taking time. And you are thinking of Gogol, locked back there. You worry that you have not punctured enough holes, or large enough holes. You worry that he will rustle around, kick your duffel bag, somehow block the makeshift air vents. You worry that the carbon monoxide leaking up while you sit stationary will poison him, kill him. You turn off the engine, to listen. You hear nothing. You are tempted to call out, but don't want to encourage him to make noise. You can do nothing. Except extend your will – willing him to be fine, willing him to be breathing: in, out, in, out. Those little precious breaths, like the fluttering of a moth's wings.

Time extends, elasticises. Until finally, you crack. Twist around, thump the backrest of the seats in the rear. Using your fist, hitting it twice. Thump-thump. Wait. Again. Like a paramedic using a defibrillator, seeking to jolt out a response, some sign of life. Faintly, you think you hear a reply. A muted echo from the boot. Subtle as a pulse, or a heartbeat. But enough to reassure you.

Then the queue is moving again, the lorry driver having passed. After that delay the next three cars are cleared in reasonably quick succession. Then it's your turn. It isn't the same guard as the day before, of course. This one is portly, black-haired, with a carefully groomed moustache. You hand over your passport, explain you were on a brief visit to the area, to explore your ancestral roots. Maintaining that plausible lie. He considers your photo carefully, then your car. At first you think he's looking at the dent on the hood – where the rock struck – but it's something else. He asks you where you rented the car. The question seems charged. Of course. The arrangements were for you to be in a particular vehicle.

Another thing you didn't foresee.

You tell him, casually, that you rented it at the airport in Prague. Mention that the company had to upgrade you, due to stock limitations. He looks at you, hard, but nods at this credible and straightforward explanation. He presses your passport to the scanner, and stamps it. The whole process only takes two or three minutes.

'Welcome back to the Slovak Republic,' he says.

And then you are driving, as fast as possible without drawing attention to yourself. Fleeing from the border, past those empty fields, dilapidated fences, barren trees. A lone wind-torn scarecrow who is guarding nothing, and has been for some time. As soon as you're out of view of the border you pull over at the road side, slam on your brakes. You're breathing heavily, feeling the heat – the burning heat – of dread, in your face, your throat. A tingling in your hands.

Out of the car, and around to the back. Fumbling for keys. Opening the boot.

And Gogol is revealed, lying still, his eyes closed, his arms folded. As if in a casket, for a viewing before burial. His hair sweaty, plastered to his scalp. A sheen of colour in his cheeks. Still and motionless. Clearly dead. Clearly gone.

A terrifying moment in which you're sure you have failed.

Until his eyes flutter open, squint up at you. To him, from his low vantage point, you must look like a shadow, an outline against the stark quartz sky. You don't wait for him to crawl out, but reach in, scoop him up – this act so easy, so natural. He puts his arms around your neck. His skin is incredibly hot, and you can feel the slickness of sweat on his forearms. You pull him out of the boot and he's like a duckling emerging from his egg, being born into the harshness of the world: into the wind and the cold and the noise and the light and the emptiness. And with only you for protection, against the elements. Against everything.

a change of plans

Time has changed again. Since yesterday time has only meant sticking to their schedule, getting to your waypoints and destinations. Staying on track. Time has been useful, but not valuable. Now it is. Now, time is vital, critical, not only valuable but invaluable. You don't just hear the clock ticking but *feel* each precious second, reverberating through your body, pounding in your head, pulsing in your limbs, your hands, your fingertips tapping the steering wheel. Time is life. Yours, and Gogol's. And if you waste it, squander it, you may run out of time completely. The moment in a board game when the sand-timer finishes: time's up.

It's hard to say precisely *when* you made the decision. In a way it wasn't a decision at all, but a realisation, a dawning awareness. You suspect why they want Gogol, what they intend to do with him. And that suspicion is enough. To alter course, to change the plans. To disobey them.

You have considered all the angles – at least, all the angles you can see. You could have chosen not to cross the border. You could have gone east, the other direction. But if you were being watched at the inn (as you felt you were) this might have been reported. Or it certainly would have been reported when you failed to appear at the border. You would have been pursued, probably. And caught. Likely. You have little knowledge of Ukraine. Your ignorance would have hurt you. They would have got Gogol anyway. No, you had to return to the EU. At the border you could have confessed to the guards, told them everything, tried to save Gogol that way. But clearly at least one of the guards is working for them. One has been bought, or blackmailed, or coerced. No. The border was not safe.

In Prague, you are convinced, you will find a way. A way home.

It won't be easy. Measures have to be taken, and risks. Risks that may or may not pay off. But you can hedge your bets. And the car journey will give you time to think, to adapt. For now, they still believe everything is going according to plan. You've made your pick-up, stayed at the inn, crossed back over. They'll be expecting you to call, soon. To find out where to meet them. That's the next step. And for as long as possible, it's important for them to think it's all going ahead. If they continue to expect your arrival, you'll have an advantage. Once they find out, that will change things.

Once they find out, they will be tracking you, hunting you, seeking to kill you.

For now, a strange time. The clock ticking even though the race is not on. Like watching the countdown before the starting signal, the green flag for *go*.

On the Slovak side, the roads are flatter and smoother, better tended. Humming beneath the wheels of the Octavia.

A gentle warm-up run. Surrounded by snow-crusted fields. Gogol in the seat beside you, his seatbelt on now, gazing at the scenery. You explain to him that you are in Slovakia, heading to the Czech Republic. You don't say you're a step closer to being safe, to safety. He wouldn't understand, and it wouldn't be true. You're going *towards* the danger, in order to escape it. In order to pretend all is in order.

Thinking this through, you become aware of a faint sound, inside the car. Almost indistinguishable from the noise of the engine, but definitely distinct. Perplexing. It has rhythm. A song? As if the radio is playing on low volume, only it isn't. It's Gogol. He's humming to himself. An upbeat rhythm. A pop song, possibly. Oddly catchy. He has a good ear, is perfectly in tune. You glance at him. He doesn't even seem aware that he's doing it. You imagine him in that tower block, hiding somewhere, sitting alone. Just humming. Something to cling to. Something to keep himself going.

He notices your attention, and stops, abruptly. As if he's been caught doing something wrong. As if humming is not allowed, and might trigger swift and harsh rebukes. Repercussions. Punishments. All those scars on his skin. He smiles tentatively, apologetically. His dark eyes worried. You nod, encouraging him, and pick up the tune to carry it. Humming with him. It has a repetitive refrain, like a march.

Forty-five minutes from the border, you pull over for a second time. You must call now. Waiting longer risks making them uneasy, even suspicious. But you've delayed long enough to maybe buy you a bit more time. If you're vague. If you say the right things.

You hold a finger to your lips, signalling Gogol to be quiet. Not that he is making any noise at all, having stopped humming when you stopped the car. You have three bars of signal, use the auto-dial to call back the number in your phone. They answer after one ring, ask immediately where you are. Not the man's voice, this time. A woman. Valerie.

'Just past the border,' you tell her. Your voice calm, steady. 'I'm calling to find out where you want me to bring the product.' It sounds comical – almost parodic – to refer to Gogol in this way. But you think she might appreciate it. Your cold formality. Clinical ruthlessness.

She asks when you crossed over, and you say, vaguely, about half an hour ago. There was a line, a delay. They were checking the back of a lorry.

'Yes,' she says testily, 'we know this. We know where you are, too. And that you are in a different car. Not the one that you booked.'

You can't help looking behind you. Bare and empty roads. A frozen expanse. A few alders. No other vehicles. You tell her what you told the guard, assuming he has relayed it to them: that there was a stock issue, that the agency gave you the upgrade. You didn't think it was a problem – and it hasn't been. You're through the border, on your way to Prague.

'Just tell me where to go,' you say, deliberately impatient. 'We're wasting time.'

She gives you an address. It's a warehouse on an industrial estate. On the outskirts of Prague, in Praha Thirteen – near Zličín. You tell her you'll drive straight there, though when she asks about your arrival time, you generalise. Say you'll have to punch it into your satnav, that it depends on traffic, and roadworks. Zličín is on the western side of Prague – you'll have to go around, or through the city centre. When she says they know all this, you assure her that based on the journey out, you shouldn't be later than seven. Seven o'clock. Giving yourself an extra hour or so.

Amid all the deception, you almost forget about the money (the money being so far from your mind), but you remember in time to ask, because Valerie no doubt expects you to.

'We will have your money,' she says. It sounds sly, the way she says it. You think of the rocks and soiled notes in the suitcase. Possibly they don't even plan to pay you. Possibly they plan to just take the boy, send you on your way with more threats. Or even kill you. Though to kill a foreign national seems risky, stupid.

Either way, if they aren't already planning to kill you, they will be soon.

'I'll be there,' you tell her.

She tells you not to delay. Seven, at the latest.

You hang up. Making a note of the address, which you never plan to reach. Sit for a moment. During the conversation your voice was steady, convincing. But you are trembling, all over. Like a reaction to cold when it's breaking, when you get the chills. The beginning of a thaw. The first trickles of a new emotion: not just fear, but real and genuine dread.

Gogol is looking at you closely, as if sensing your distress. 'It's okay,' you tell him. 'We're going to be fine. They're not going to get you.' He removes his scrap of paper. It's like a teddy bear to him. Or Dumbo's feather. Something he can't do without. His little picture of Disneyland. Yes, you assure him, we'll get you to Disneyland. After all this.

You put the car in gear, check the rear-view. There's a vehicle visible in the mirror now. Are they following you? Perhaps they had a car, waiting on this side of the border. It seems possible. Maybe as a precaution, or maybe Mario mentioned something to them. Maybe he told Valerie about your call, your questions. A mistake. You shouldn't have let on that you had any concerns about the trade. You already sensed it wasn't right, this plan – their sordid intentions. You would have figured it out, without Mario. What they intend to do to Gogol.

No more mistakes.

You wait the car out. It draws near without slowing, passes – a man and woman. Seemingly no threat to you at all. You pull on to the road, continue driving. They may not be following you, yet, but they know the make and model of your car, and the number plate, too. All that they will have got from their guard at the border, or accomplices at the inn.

You have to take measures, change your plans. You have to stay smart.

You can't assume you are one step ahead. You are possibly already one step behind. Playing catch-up. Endangering both the boy and yourself.

Next to you, Gogol begins to hum again, oblivious.

camouflage

Halfway across Slovakia, you pass a city – Poprad – with a mall and superstore on the outskirts. This is where it will begin. Your escape. You turn in, pull up, go around the car to let Gogol out. As you cross the car park, you talk to him. Low and clear. Convinced you have to – for his sake and yours – even if he can't understand. To keep you both calm. To convey the urgency of the situation. You tell him there are people who are after you, and him. This isn't true, yet, but it will be soon enough. You tell him you're going to take some precautions. For both of you. New clothes. A new look. A new you, and a new him.

The supermarket is big as an airplane hangar – all fluorescent lights, cool linoleum tiles. The same here as at home, as anywhere in the world. Shelves stacked high with cereal, rice and flour and dry goods, canned vegetables. In another section, beauty products, vitamins, healthcare, and – eventually – clothing. You walk briskly, but don't rush, trying to appear calm. In the boys' clothing section, you pick out jeans, two T-shirts, a hoody, socks, underwear, a winter coat and matching cap. All generic, low-cost, non-descript. You hold various items up to Gogol, guessing the sizes, not risking the time it might take him to try them on. He seems suited to the sizes for six and seven-year-olds. Even if he's older, he has a seven-year-old's body. He follows you around in wonder, stunned, not understanding that these new clothes are actually for him. Or perhaps understanding but not believing.

Your clothing doesn't need replacing like his, but your outfit will have been noted – either at the inn, or the border, or both. You stand out. You are recognisable. So, you buy jeans, a puffy down jacket, and a baseball cap with a sports team logo on the front. A Slovak hockey team. Then, from two aisles over, you add hair scissors and blonde hair dye. A children's toothbrush.

Closer to the front is a section of display fridges, with ready-made sandwiches, drinks and snacks. You gesture for Gogol to pick something, but he just stands there, overwhelmed – so you grab two ham sandwiches for you both, a few packets of crisps, two cans of pop.

When you have everything you need, you lead Gogol towards the front of the store. There are cashpoints there. You have plenty of money left – the amount they gave you was more than enough for the trip – but now you're planning beyond today, thinking long term. Of getting across Europe. You don't want to run out later, when it might be vital, and Slovakia is on the Euro. So you stop and, as you did on your first night in Prague, you withdraw the maximum cash your bank allows: around three hundred and fifty Euros. Gogol watches as the money spits out of the machine, crisp and clean. His eyes huge. You take the wad of notes and fit some in your wallet, stuff some in your pocket. Look around. Nobody has noticed. Nobody cares. Why would they?

You take the cash to the till and use it to pay for your purchases. The familiarity of Euros is reassuring after your fumblings with the Ukrainian hryvnia. Coming back already feels like the right decision. Later, if Valerie's people somehow check your bank records, they won't know what you bought: only that you stopped here, and withdrew some cash. They might deduce from it that you were planning all this in advance, which of course you are. But by then it will be too late for that knowledge to be of any use to them.

If they are already monitoring your banking, your transactions, then they are more powerful and mistrustful than you think.

The supermarket has toilets, including a separate disabled toilet. You go in there with Gogol, lock the door, tug on the light using the pull switch. It smells of bleach, of lemon-scented cleaner. You check your watch. You've spent perhaps only a quarter of an hour in the place so far. You crouch down, to Gogol's level. Explain to him that he needs to change – showing him by holding up his new clothes. He stares at you, gawp-mouthed, but complies as you tug off his old hoody, his T-shirt. Tear open the pack of new T-shirts with your teeth, remove one, shake it out, yank it over his head. A nice fit. Then get him to remove his shoes, his socks, his torn trousers, his threadbare underwear.

On the freshly cleaned tiles, his feet leave little prints of moisture, which fade after a moment. He steps into the boxers you hold out, then sits on the toilet to pull on the jeans – a laborious, lengthy process. Eventually you take charge, grab the waist band, and heft him right up so that he drops into them. Lastly, sitting him back to fit his shoes, lacing them up. And pulling him to his feet.

You step back, check him over. He doesn't look like an ordinary boy – there is still the thin hair, the paleness, the frailty, the rotten teeth – but he looks closer to ordinary. Less likely to be noticed, to stand out. You put his old clothes into the bag with a sense of release. Tie it off. Turn to stuff it in the bin. Then catch yourself, hold it up, ask him if it's okay. He looks at it, nods. No sentimentality there. He has already removed the only thing he cares about: his papers.

You push the bag, Gogol's past self, down to the bottom of the bin, then throw some toilet paper on top of it. Your turn next. The hair dye can wait. But your ponytail is distinct. A distinguishing characteristic. You reach behind your head for it, remove the hair elastic. Spread the hair out between your fingers, and hold it up like a top knot. With the hair scissors, you saw through it. Doing this carefully, to at least make a clean line.

When the last of the strands are cut, the hair comes free in your hand. You hold it in front of you, marvel at it. You've never held that much hair. It has substantial weight. Your head feels lighter. Gogol has observed all this mutely, but now he takes a step forward, extends a hand to the thick bunch of hair, and strokes it once, twice, three times. As you might touch a cat, or velvet, to see how soft it is. It makes you think of Valerie – her precious braid.

Then the hair goes into the hygiene bin, reserved for feminine products. You put on the baseball cap, tuck the remains of your hair up underneath it. Pull the brim down low. An IQ-slicer, Tod used to call them. A funny American term, the idea being that wearing a hat like this makes you dumber, slower, dim-witted. A redneck baseball fan. The impression of stupidity can't hurt – and it serves as a reminder that you need to be the opposite. *Be smart.* You pull the tags off the jacket. Ditch the old coat. Fit into the new one, zip it up. It's puffy and made of cheap nylon. You keep the jeans for later, turn to check your reflection. You do look different. More local. The high cheekbones. Prominent forehead. Maybe your past – your grandfather, your Czech blood – is significant after all.

Gogol comes to stand on your left, so that you are both looking at yourselves in the mirror, side-by-side. He seems to like what he sees. He smiles, showing his crooked canines. Reaches up for your hand. You imagine a camera taking a snapshot of you: click. The kind you might get from a booth in a mall or tourist destination. A little memento of the trip. A sentimental sequence of poses. A mother-and-son moment.

But, of course, for you there will be no time for anything like that. There's that old saying: time waits for no one. Certainly not you, or him. You are already running out of time. Can picture that little clockwork skeleton shaking his menacing hourglass. But also – until Pavel and Valerie find out your true intentions – you still have a few grains left, a little time on your side. You hope.

getting the bounces

You know the country, the culture, the language, but not well enough to make informed decisions. You must rely instead on memory, on guesswork, on luck, on hope. At least for now. Tod had a term for this. He called it 'getting the bounces'. Like many New Yorkers he was a hockey fan. He always insisted he take you to a game, when you were back there, visiting his family. The Rangers against one of their chief rivals – the Islanders, or the Flyers. Team names that were as meaningless to you as ancient societies. You didn't enjoy it, but you enjoyed how happy it made him, to be there, with you. Eating cheap popcorn and American hotdogs and drinking beer in plastic cups that tasted flat and sour. And Tod liked explaining the convoluted rules, the customs, the terminology: slap shots, hip checks, icing, high-sticking, getting 'rubbed out' into the boards, being 'caught with your head down'. Tod had played, as a kid, and often he would use these same terms in everyday conversation, apply them to his life. His favourite was 'getting the bounces'. Referring to the distinct movement of the puck, that disk of vulcanised rubber, skittering and hopping and caroming, off the boards, the glass, the ice. A stick or a skate or a goal post. If your team is getting the bounces, it means the puck is coming to you, working for you. In life, it means things are going your way. Luck is with you.

So far, this seems to be the case. But you haven't really strayed from your assigned path yet. Once you take that step, any faith in your compliance with their plan will be revealed as a sham.

You have considered all the options and, though you have no way of knowing this is the right choice, you believe it's the one least likely to be wrong. Or least likely to lead to your death, and Gogol's.

But you can't be sure. Not until it happens, or doesn't.

What you've decided to do is get rid of the car. They know the make, the model. Once you go off-course, they will be looking for this Octavia. You considered driving as far as you could go. Across the Czech Republic, across Europe. But if they have border guards on their payroll, they must have police and government contacts, too, and soon they'll all be notified to watch out for the car, the two of you. It wouldn't be hard for them to hone in on you.

Maybe you overestimate them. Maybe they are more small-time, more limited. Maybe it was just that one guard. But you doubt it. And better to overestimate than underestimate.

For the same reason, you've decided not to go to the police. Already. That simply isn't on your list of possible options. Even if you could find an official you were sure you could trust, Gogol would be sent back. Deported. He isn't an

EU citizen. He has a home, a mother. If you can call it that. If she could be identified. If she was even his mother at all.

And if not to her, then to some kind of orphanage. The social care system, in Western Ukraine. To give him up to that would be to give up on him. To never know his fate. A way to save yourself, and only yourself. And right now you are not thinking of yourself, except as an agent of his deliverance. Why else would this have all happened? Why else would you even be here, involved in this? A situation that is unthinkable, impossible. But it's happening and it's real and he is real: a boy sitting beside you, with his egg-pale face and thin hair and atrophied leg. A wounded duckling.

He's sleeping now, his mouth open, a thread of drool on his chin. Rows of chain-link fence blurring behind his head.

You will save him. And to do that you have to get rid of the car.

Like on the journey out, the Czech-Slovak border doesn't strike you as a real border. Marked only by a blue sign, and to one side a few toll booths for drivers entering or exiting the motorway. Wooden huts dusted with snow, like little gingerbread structures. Beyond, lining the roadside, tall birches rise grey and slender to the sky. Giant icicles. As before, it is no different from the Slovakian side, but this time it feels different. You've passed back through the looking glass and, like Alice, the journey has changed you. It feels reassuring to be in the Czech Republic again, to be that much closer to the known. From now on, that is what you will be seeking out: what you know, and home.

That will start in Brno, the second biggest city in the Czech Republic. It may not be the best choice but it's a place you know: you and Tod passed through during an excursion to the eastern side of the country, using your Eurolines bus passes. Brno was a forgettable stop, aside from the fact you were fighting, quarrelling over the petty things couples fixate on after spending too much time on the road together, too much time in each other's pockets, too much time in each other's lives, failing to understand that this time is limited – can be so easily cut short. When it seems perfectly reasonable to bicker about which hotel to stay at or where to eat or what to do in the evening.

Of Brno you don't remember much, but you remember the bus station. It was a hub – busy, bustling, dirty, chaotic. You hope it hasn't changed. If you are being followed – a legitimate possibility – then it may be your best chance to elude them. At least, for now.

It's late afternoon, and turning to dusk by the time you enter the city outskirts. From the motorway, you see a series of warehouses and storage units, and then sprawling outlet malls and superstores. You've programmed the satnav to take you to the bus station. So far, the route could still be one you might follow, if you were circumnavigating the city and carrying on to Prague. Not suspicious at all. But in two miles you will turn off towards the centre, and that will look like a mistake, or a deliberate attempt to do exactly what you are trying to do.

You check the rear-view. There are more cars now. Impossible to tell, but you think a brown saloon is one you've seen before. Maybe.

The turning comes up. You signal, slide around the off-ramp, get on to a wide avenue heading towards the bus station. Passing car dealerships, a large DIY store, then a neighbourhood of squat apartment blocks, underpasses lathered in graffiti. A billboard advertising *economický* software. You check the satnav. Just five kilometres from your destination, now.

You reach across, touch Gogol's shoulder. A touch is enough to wake him. He sits up with a start – in his eyes a raw fright that is heartrending. But when he understands he is in the car, with you, he relaxes immediately. His faith and trust in you now absolute.

You tell him that the two of you are going to leave the car and get on a bus next. That he must be ready to move quickly and follow you and do what you say. Then you repeat the crucial and core information: no car. We take the bus. The bus. He nods, repeats the word, confident in its articulation, if not its meaning.

Opposite the bus station is a multistorey mall, with retail stores, a hypermarket, McDonald's. The universal blue 'P' signs directing you towards parking. You almost follow those, then think of something else. Drive past, turn down a side street. The area here is seedy, sketchy, inner city. People standing in tatty parkas, with the hoods cinched tight over their faces. Smoking the air with their breath, huddled in circles, backs to the world. You park up alongside a group of young lads, yank up the handbrake. Go around to Gogol's door, let him out. Pop the boot. Grab your duffel bag. Slam the boot.

The men have stopped to watch this. Curious. Leering. You walk over to the one in the middle: a tall, big-nosed boy with a stud earring and a flame tattooed on his neck. You hold out the keys, and a thousand koruna. Tell him, in plain English, that he can have the car for as long as he wants, as long as he can. Until he gets caught.

He smiles, widely, looks at his mates. Says something in Czech and laughs. But he takes the keys and the money. Calls you crazy. Tells you in English they won't ever get caught. The car won't ever get found.

'Good,' you tell him. Handing him another five hundred. 'And we won't either.'

He calls you crazy. A crazy *holka*.

Taking Gogol's hand, you walk past them, back towards the mall. Near the entrance is a pedestrian footbridge, extending from the second floor over the street to the bus station. You cross this hurriedly, feeling you are potentially exposed to drivers and onlookers below. But the railings are high; the chances that you'll be picked out among other people, going both ways, minimal. One of those chances you have to take. Hoping you get a bounce.

You allow yourself a discreet smile, at the thought of the car. At the idea that it might not be found here near the station, which you were counting on. That it might simply vanish. Maybe get given a paint job, new plate numbers, or be broken down for parts. Too good to be true, too good to count on, but a seeming possibility.

It's getting near rush hour and the bus station is packed. People everywhere, queuing to buy tickets, standing in front of big digital displays, their heads tilted up to enable them to read the arrivals and departures, the numbers of the bus stands. You don't stop to look. You need tickets, go straight to one of the sales counters. You wait in line, holding Gogol's hand, the duffel bag slung over your shoulder. Every so often you glance around, casually. Checking left, right. Trying to keep a look out. But you don't know who you're looking for. They could be nowhere, or anywhere. No one, or anyone. You could be paranoid, or deluded, or both.

When the elderly woman in front of you finally figures out what bay she is leaving from, you step up. The clerk is an older man, grey-haired and unshaven, who seems in no hurry to serve you. You ask him when the next bus to Karlovy Vary is – one of the only destinations you're familiar with. The clerk answers without checking his system, tells you it just left. That the next isn't for another hour.

You rub a hand over your face. Wonder if a bit of slow driving cost you those precious minutes. You can't hang around here for an hour. Instead, you ask about buses to

174

Kutná Hora. This time he has to check. You can't get to Kutná Hora directly. It would be easier to take the train, via Kolin. Or a bus to the outskirts of Prague, and back out.

This gives you pause. Neither feels right.

'Is there any other way?'

He sighs, mutters something under his breath in Czech, but after some tinkering with his keys tells you that you could catch a bus to Jihlava, then grab a local shuttle from there to Kutná Hora. Says something about them running this month, for a local festival.

'That's fine,' you tell him. '*Dve vstupenky, prosím.*'

Two tickets to Jihlava: one adult, one child. It goes without saying you pay in cash, and the peculiar, unique itinerary seems serendipitous: more difficult for them to deduce your route.

He prints up the tickets, gives you them along with your change, and a receipt. Tells you it departs from stand nine. Gestures to direct you, but you're already moving, leading Gogol, having seen the sign for Jihlava and the queue of passengers loading their bags into the open luggage compartment. You reach the queue just as it's dwindling. Worry for a second the bus will be full, that you'll be left waiting, after all. But when you present yourselves and your tickets, the driver – a tall woman standing by the door – merely nods and points at the luggage compartment. You throw the duffel bag in, climb up the steps with Gogol. He is gazing about in satisfaction. He says 'Bus' and smiles, proud to demonstrate his knowledge of the English word, his ability to match the signifier with the signified.

You find two seats near the back – presumably left vacant since they're near the toilet. You take the window. You still have five minutes to wait before departure. While you do, you pull your baseball cap down low, keep an eye on the forecourt. You're feeling good, exhilarated, confident. You don't actually expect to see anybody you recognise, so it shocks you when you do. Or think you do. At a distance. Standing by the departures board. One of the men from the inn – the older game player, in the wool hat. Walking casually around the periphery. Studying people in the lines. His hands in the pockets of his jacket.

There are two layers of glass between you, one of them tinted, and fifty feet of space. But it's him. You're sure it's him. You think you're sure. Or are you simply imagining? The bus rumbles to life. Begins to beep, repeatedly, like a forklift, as it reverses out of its bay. You lose sight of the man behind a pillar. You turn your back to the window, angle your face away, lean over Gogol. Ask him to show you his magazine clipping, the ad for Disneyland. To keep him occupied, you point to each of the characters, pronounce their names. Mickey Mouse. Donald Duck. Snow White. He seems diligently fascinated by this.

Then the bus shifts gear, moves forward. The bay falls away. Other buses slide by. The man is gone, left back there. Whoever he was, he didn't see you. You squeeze Gogol's hand and think again of Tod, his hockey phrases. You're still getting the bounces.

killing time

Bones. Stacked up in four large piles, the ends of the fibulas and tibias aligned like matchsticks. Rows of skulls, most of them jawless, their upper teeth resting on the craniums of the row below, as if gnawing on each other, apart from the bottom row where the sets of incisors seem to bite the floor. And on the ceiling, skulls arranged in elaborate, cascading patterns. A bone chandelier hanging from one of the crossbeams, with femurs forming the centre piece, and vertebrae curving out and up towards the skulls that hold the candles. A nearby plaque explains that it contains at least one of every bone from the human body. Positioned around it, a set of matching bone candelabras loom at head height.

Bones. That's always what the town of Kutná Hora has meant to you, since the single visit you and Tod took. So many other parts of that trip have faded, gone – though some are coming back to you now, those delicate prickles of déjà vu – but the Sedlec Ossuary, the so-called 'bone church', has stayed vivid, and is exactly as you remember. The kind of place you don't forget, ever.

All these bones, arranged in artistic and architectural forms. The handiwork of a nineteenth-century woodcarver. A testament to human genius and sheer human audacity. It should be terrifying, menacing, foreboding. But you didn't feel that then and you don't feel it now.

You did worry about Gogol – how he might react. But, upon arriving in town and walking to the *penzión* you'd previously stayed in with Tod, you found its reception shut for a brief interval in the early evening. The chapel was right nearby, in the Sedlec suburbs. You remembered the location. The power of the macabre to embed a memory. You and Gogol got there a few minutes before closing, and just inside the entrance was a desk that looked like it should have been manned, only it wasn't. On top of the till an honesty box had been left for any latecomers. Perhaps somebody called in sick. A small boon for you: no curious clerk to ask questions. You paid the token fee for one child and one adult, and grandly descended the stone steps, oddly elated.

This late in the day, out of tourist season, the Ossuary is deserted. With nobody there to notice you, remember you, report you, you are free to kill time. Another odd saying: to kill time. As if you could slip the knife in Time's back, bash it on the head. Kill Time dead. And so, the two of you walk around the chapel together. Holding hands. Feeling the old, cold timelessness of the place. Gogol seems to share your understanding of it. Or else he simply takes his cue from you – it's okay because you give the impression it's okay. And for you it's not hellish or horrifying or repugnant (as you're sure some tourists must find it), but strangely

178

peaceful, calm and beautiful. The ultimate *memento mori*. It puts the Astronomical Clock in Prague, with its pathetic little skeleton, to shame. Here is death's *real* home – an entire chapel decorated with human remains. Or maybe not a home, but a domain, a dimension outside the ordinary, everyday world of flesh and blood.

As you move beneath the bones, between them, you can hear the joints creaking along with the timbers of the church. Keeping a natural rhythm, attuned not with human clocks but something larger and more eternal. The bones as numerous as sands in an hourglass. All that remains of countless people, dead for centuries, stripped of flesh, of face, of feature, of name, of identity, of everything except this: these cold, still, brittle, beautifully arranged bones.

Yet within your hand are the little fingers of Gogol. Warm, pulsing with blood.

An absolute contradiction. The absurdity of being human, of being alive.

Together you keep walking. The Ossuary, like so many chapels, is built in a cross. Down one of the branches hangs a huge coat of arms, the pièce de résistance, ingeniously constructed using a range of different bones. Scapulas fanned out like water-lilies; bundles of finger bones; delicate clavicles; slender ulnas aligned to form the shield, on which rest other bones that create the insignia and symbols of the aristocrat, or ruler, or whoever commissioned it.

In some places, the bones complement stone sculptures, painted figurines – little cupids, bizarrely and perversely kitsch – and colourful oil paintings. They do not fit at all. These relics of a typical church seem idiosyncratic, jarring. Gogol stands before a little painted cupid, with rouged cheeks and lips, gaping in that gawp-mouthed way of his. Then he tugs on your hand. Motions as if to speak. You crouch. He has said only a couple of words to you. Now he cups his hand to his mouth, and whispers a question, phrased as a single word: 'Disneyland?'

You smile. Yes. This could be Disneyland.

favours

The *penzión* has opened when you get back, but doesn't feel open. Upon entering, there's a small reception nook where the manager should be, but isn't. Off to the left, the dining room, just big enough for half a dozen tables, covered in vinyl-chequered table cloths. Above the fireplace, a boar's head, its mouth parted in anguish. It's half five but no guests are eating. The space is still and empty, so while you wait memories rise up like wraiths. You remember dining here, and even remember the table – that one, by the window – where you and Tod sat. You don't remember the food, but you remember the wine. It was red, and sour. Vinegary. You would have sent it back, but Tod always worried about complaining, about coming across as a brash American – typically loud and arrogant. To avoid it, he went too far the other way. Being in London and Europe had made him timid, mouse-like. At times you missed the boy you had fallen in love with. The one who'd thrown himself into Morecombe Bay, risked drowning to impress you. The one who'd kicked in a night club door because a bouncer had manhandled you.

Tod had become so diminished. Like a tree uprooted. Removed from its soil. The weakening, and loss of strength. It came back that night, when he thought you needed his protection, and he got himself killed.

The first time you visited this *penzión*, Tod had booked it as a romantic retreat, a luxury of sorts after a week of hostels, camping, backpacking. The two of you so young and eager, so *vital*. The only goals in your life to travel, to see, to eat, to get drunk at night and fuck, or fight, or both (in Kutná Hora it was both). Then wake up and do it all over again, in another town. The repetitive nature of it never tiring, never boring.

You know this to be true, but find it hard to imagine now. Hard to remember when that was all that mattered. It has gone. Dried up with age. Fallen away. Like leaves. Like Tod's thinning hair.

But what do we exchange it for? An office. Paperwork. A cramped apartment that we can't afford in a city that we don't hate, but certainly don't love. An economical car with a one-point-six-litre eco-fuel engine. Movie nights. Poker nights. Girls nights out. Getting drunk, but not *that* drunk. Having arguments, but without any enthusiasm – listless fights – lacking the crackling threat of recklessness, the possibility of real consequences.

And, ultimately, getting killed on a bus for no reason. No reason at all.

You and Tod would have stayed together, through anything. You know that. You'd already faced infidelity. You would have faced, and overcome, other challenges. Got by. Endured. Done more counselling. Signed up for evening classes. Taken yoga. Had kids – the big one. The big distraction, fulfilment, obligation. The best excuse to stay together. That parental stoicism you've seen in the eyes of people your age. That terrified pride. *Our kids!* Look at them, look at us. So well-adjusted. So content. Such a contribution to society.

So settled. So perfectly *functional*.

All that you have been spared. Maybe you should be grateful.

You notice Gogol yawning and pull out one of the dining chairs for him to sit on. There's no bell to ring, and so, after calling hello once or twice, you sit for some time too – a quarter of an hour – before the hotelier appears, coming down a dim hallway that, you see now, leads directly to her own apartment or living area. She rapid-blinks at you like a vole emerging from its tunnel. A very small woman, maybe six inches shorter than you, with hair that's gone wispy on top, revealing patches of spotted scalp. You can't remember what she looked like on your previous visit, or even if this is the same owner.

She isn't friendly but polite, professional. She doesn't seem curious about Gogol and, you suspect, has already assumed that he's your son, or at least your charge. And you suppose he is, now. She doesn't require ID and just asks that you fill in a form: name, nationality, phone number and address. You make these up on the spot: American, rather than British; resident of New York, not London. Using knowledge of Tod's family, trips to his home, to make it authentic – the pitiful truth being that Tod is useful to you now only as a ruse, a cover. You doubt the owner will be able to pinpoint your accent as British through the veil of translation. And, even if she did, you could simply be living abroad now.

She's pleased when you pay in cash. Accepts the notes, smooths them out. Tells you, in broken but clear English, that there are only a few other guests staying. That you can have the family room, for the same price. That you can have dinner or room service (you opt for the latter), and that breakfast is served from seven until ten in the morning.

All this is straightforward enough. Just what you hoped for. So you don't have to come downstairs again, you order dinner on the spot: beef goulash and dumplings and *smažený sýr*, the Czech fried cheese. She'll bring it up soon, at quarter to seven.

'*Dobrý*,' you say. 'That's fine.'

Your mind is moving ahead now. Thinking. The mention of seven o'clock has struck you, reminded you what's coming. Seven is when you're supposed to arrive in Prague, at the latest. Seven is when everything becomes very real and dangerous – more so than it already is.

Seven is when they will stop waiting for you, and start looking. If they haven't already.

Before then you have one thing to do. One favour. A risk. But a necessary one. You have decided. A debt owed. Somebody to repay.

You and Gogol go upstairs to your room. The bedroom has odd cedar wall panelling – chalet-style – that smells of resin, but not unpleasantly so. The bed is wood-framed as well. A glass-panelled door leads to a private veranda. The sun is setting and the light is fading, going, but beyond the veranda you can see a ravine dropping down to a stream. The dark sheen of the water rippling with movement. Not iced over. That sticks in your mind: a tiny detail. How the rivers have frozen, but not this little stream. Something to do with the flow rate?

There's no TV, which is a disappointment for Gogol. You can tell. But you assure him you'll have dinner, and play games. What games you don't say. You don't have any games.

But you can make up a game. Something. After you make a phone call. You tell him you will be just a minute, and go into the bathroom, shut the door.

The phone has been off. The idea being that, if they should phone, they will assume (or are meant to assume) that you are out of signal range, rather than simply letting it ring.

Now you switch it on.

You have signal. They have called – twice – but there are no messages. Both calls came from Valerie's number, not Mario's. But it's Mario you call now. He answers on the first ring. He must have heard from them. They are worried, so he is also worried.

They are, of course, right to be worried.

But Mario tries to put a brave face on it, in the first instance. Calls you his snow queen, tells you he hopes everything is going well. Says that he's heard you've crossed the border, that you'll be arriving in Prague soon. You tell him then. You tell him that you will not be delivering the boy to them. That you are reneging on the deal.

Your voice is level as you say this. You are looking at yourself in the mirror above the sink, as if talking to your own reflection, not him. He doesn't answer for a long time. When he does, it's not rage, but a whimper. A whine. 'You cannot do this,' he says. 'You have to hold up your end. They will kill you. They will kill me.'

You tell him that if you deliver the boy – you never use his name – they will kill *him*. They will cut him up for his organs.

This is just a guess, a test. You still don't know, until Mario tries to explain. Ineptly. Pathetically. That it is not all his organs they want. It is just his heart. His heart. To save another child, you see? A girl. A girl who is dying. This is not the kind of thing they do often, or ever before. It is a one-off deal. To save the child of a friend, or a family member. A life for a life.

You tell him you're sorry to hear that (though you're not sure it's true), but that it doesn't work that way. Life, death. Valerie and Pavel don't get to choose. You don't go on to say that death is simply out there, waiting, deciding at random, on a whim. You don't want to get into a philosophical discussion about it. Mario wheedles and cajoles, reminds you that you were the one who came to him, that you asked him for the job. He did you a favour.

'And I'm telling *you* this as a favour,' you say, 'to give you time to get away. They're expecting me soon. You've got maybe half an hour, an hour, before they guess what's happening. Go, now. Leave Prague. Run. We're already running. It's the only way.'

Mario says 'but' and then you hang up on him.

You put the phone aside. You look at yourself in the mirror above. A blotch of red on either cheek. The slow creep of colour returning. A bit of fury and fear. You twist the cold tap, use both hands to scoop handfuls of water to your face. It's ice cold – coming in from the pipes outside. You slurp it, too, feeling the chill on your teeth. You have to stay calm, cool, clinical. You have to be what Mario believed you to be.

As for him, you've given him a chance. That's all you could do. And maybe more than he deserves.

You twist off the tap, pat dry your face with a hand towel. Turn to the door. Gogol is waiting patiently for you, sitting on the bed, dangling his legs and kicking the side of the baseboard idly with his heels. You smile at him, leaving the phone and everything else back there in the bathroom. Food, you tell him. Time for food, and games.

games

The game you come up with for Gogol is very simple. You're
limited by the language barrier, and to games you can make
easily. There's a note pad next to the telephone, and you use
it to create a series of cards, twenty-four in total. On each
card you draw a shape: a diamond, a circle, a square, a star,
a triangle. Twelve shapes in total, and two of each type. The
simplest game of all: memory. The function that makes us
human. Or so they say. Or so you've heard, somewhere.
Memory being vital to our identity, our sense of self, our
capacity to consciously learn from experience, to develop
and adapt.

In preparation for playing, you and Gogol sit opposite
one another on the bed, which is covered in a floral-patterned
duvet, made from crisp nylon. You lay out the rudimentary
cards face down, in a five-by-four rectangle. Gogol intently

watches you place each one, as if he can perceive the images on the undersides, through telepathic force. To demonstrate the game, you turn over one card, and then another. A triangle and a square. You hold them up side-by-side, comparing, saying the name of each, and shake your head. Not the right match. You put them back, try again, until you find another triangle and hold the pair together. Triangle and triangle. Gogol nods vigorously, showing he understands.

Just before the game begins in earnest, there is a knock at the door. This startles you – sends a flare of fear through you – until you remember the food, the order you placed. Still. Best to be cautious. Before answering, you call to whoever it is – *just a minute* – and open the veranda door. You put Gogol's shoes on his feet, guide him outside. You tell him, calmly, that if anything bad happens (not defining what you mean by this) he is to run. You point to the woods, act out the motion of running.

You know this is hopeless: where would he go? How would he outrun them? But it seems safer than having him standing right there when you open the door. Which you do. Cautiously – just an inch, standing to one side of it, with your left knee under the doorknob. Ready to lean in with your full weight.

But it's the owner. Smiling tentatively. She has a tray in her hands, with two plates, covered in tarnished silver cloches. You imagine her putting the tray down, lifting a cloche, pulling out a gun. But, of course, she only places the tray on the large work desk that doubles as a table, and turns to you, nods. You can't tell if she's expecting a tip and when you hold out a one hundred koruna note she seems mildly amused.

But she takes it, then pauses, looks around. The bathroom door is open. Gogol is not in the room, not in the bathroom.

She looks at you, asks about your boy. You hold a finger to your lips, tell her you're playing games. Hide and seek. It is his turn to hide, yours to find him. She smiles tolerantly. Folds and pockets the note. Lets herself out.

When you step on to the veranda, Gogol is not there.

You feel a sick flutter in your chest, a double-beat of your heart. You scan the woods. Maybe he misinterpreted your explanation, thought you were telling him to run. But it's dark, and all you can see are the shadows of trees, shrubs.

'Gogol,' you call softly. 'Gogol?'

Rustling movement beneath you. And then, from under the veranda – from a space under the veranda that looks far too small for anything but an animal to fit in – appears a dirty face, followed by his shoulders, the rest of his body. Wriggling and squirming. Emerging worm-like into the night. When he's out, he rolls over, his hands rich with muck, his new clothes smeared. He grins at you, pleased by his deception. You are too. It may well have worked, if it had been them. Much better than your idea of running.

It occurs to you that he's more experienced at this than you. At evading, at avoiding those who mean him harm. At being smart. He was born into it. It's his whole life. To the extent it's instinctive. He's not just your charge, but your ally. Your helper. Your accomplice.

You hold out a hand, pull him to his feet. Crouch to lift him back up to the veranda.

Inside, you wash his hands – scrubbing the mud off them – before sitting him down to eat. He eyes his plate of goulash and dumplings suspiciously, perhaps recalling the food at the diner, the nauseating effect it had on him. You've had snacks on the go since then, but not another full meal. You explain to him that he must eat slowly. And eat less. You remove half his portion, shovel it on to one of the side dishes. You cup your hands around what remains without touching the food, as if measuring the size, and then hold your hands up to his belly. Demonstrating how the size is comparable. You give him the thumbs up, and he smiles.

You spoon a dumpling from your plate, take a bite, make a big deal about chewing it, slowly. Swallowing deliberately. Taking your time. Being calm. He does the same, with the first dumpling. But as he continues the pace soon accelerates, your advice forgotten – the dumplings disappearing down his gullet in ravenous gulps. Unable to help himself. But rationing his portion seems to have worked. He is not immediately sick, at least. Though once finished he does lay back and hold his belly, as if worried it might burst, or rebel again.

After dinner you leave the plates and tray outside the door, and return to your game. Now you're able to play it properly, without interruption. You take turns choosing pairs of cards, trying to remember, trying to find a match. Stars and triangles, circles and squares. Haphazardly scattered. Random patterns. Together, you slowly bring order to it. A very human endeavour. Sifting through, sorting, matching, arranging. Each pair being placed in a set together, and laid out in front of you. The simple act of categorising, of recognising similarities, is so natural, so fundamental to existence. Another way of making meaning.

Lately, you've been thinking more and more about this. About the meanings we make, about the conventions we've created to provide us with purpose. The rituals of prayer and worship and congregation that constitute our religions. The complex series of laws, set in stone – and then reset – that maintain order. The lines drawn on maps to establish political boundaries, national borders: utterly rigid, yet prone to change and flux. The customs specific to each culture and society, seemingly unique but also often similar, universal. The clocks and calendars we've devised to determine our concept of time. Sixty seconds in a minute and sixty minutes in an hour and twenty-four hours in a day and three hundred and sixty-five days in a year, except for those leap years that reveal the whole scheme as a ruse, a construct. But regardless we stick to it: a certain number of years spent in primary school, secondary school, college or university. Then into the workplace: minimum wage and eight-hour work days and five-day weeks and weekends and statutory holidays and monthly paydays and annual tax returns and P60s and P45s and pension plans and eventual retirement. All while adhering to other social norms: meals out and pub nights and first dates, and hen dos and marriage vows and baby showers, and Halloween fancy dress and Christmas parties and New Year's resolutions. All these established but wholly arbitrary traditions, accepted so blithely, regarded so gravely. All these routines and regulations and rules society has developed over time, to help us navigate our way through existence, and give it some meaning. Just like the rules in that old board game – *The Game of Life* – though at least in the game everything is simplified, and streamlined.

These thoughts are not new, nor particularly novel – just the meanderings of your mind while playing *this* game, gazing at shapes on white cards. And the thoughts have distracted you: it's your turn. Gogol is waiting.

You pick two cards. A star and a circle. No luck. In playing against a child, in categorising these basic cards, you expected to be merely pretending to play, while allowing Gogol to win by finding most of the pairs. But after Gogol picks out two triangles, two circles, and then two stars, in as many turns, you realise you must focus if you're to compete, let alone win. But you don't win – not in the first game, nor the second, nor third. Gogol doesn't make a single mistake, never forgets where a card is once he has seen it. In comparison, your mind is leaky, creaky. The old model. This pleases you – for his sake – but also worries you. Each time you get a card wrong. Each time you lose against a child.

What else have you forgotten?

What else have you overlooked?

consequences

You've forgotten about them. And the phone. Until they call. Why didn't you turn it off, throw it out? After hanging up on Mario, you simply put it aside, left it on the counter next to the sink. A black plastic shell. Innocuous as a cockroach. Lurking among the hand towels.

You don't even notice it as you cut Gogol's hair: standing in front of the sink, snipping the tufts. You can't do anything about the oddness of that, about a boy so malnourished his hair is thinning, patchy. But cutting it shorter hides that. Tod liked to wear his hair short for the same reason. He worried about losing it, going bald. It ran in the family. His hairline had started to recede. You found ads popping up, on your home laptop, for Regaine, for hair treatment clinics in London. The fear of aging, those small signs of mortality. You smile fondly at the memory. Tod. You are used to cutting hair, since he liked you to cut his. He was fussy and particular about it, never satisfied. But he preferred what you did to going to the barber. He was embarrassed, you think, for them to comment on it, talk about it.

So you are an old hand when it comes to giving Gogol a trim. Gogol watches himself in the mirror as you work this transformation. His black hair is silken, soft. Wisps and tendrils floating down into the sink, where they form complex patterns. You wonder if there are any traditions, any cultures, that used hair to tell fortunes. Like reading tea leaves, Tarot cards, or bone throwing. Hair seems a reasonable option, these delicate filament extensions of a person, carrying DNA, a genetic identity, removed and left to fall in prophetic patterns.

When it's done, the alteration is subtle but significant. As with the change in clothes, it makes him look more ordinary, regular, average. Hard to even notice how thin his hair is. Maybe it will grow back fuller, invigorated by a better diet, by protein and vitamins. His hair will grow and he will grow as well. You'll make him better. You'll make him a genuine, actual boy.

You catch yourself thinking these thoughts, then reject them. He doesn't have to be made into anything. He doesn't have to fit a mould, look like a standard 'type' or model of boy. This a hard lesson. This something you'll have to learn – to accept that he has suffered. And not everything can be made better, not all wounds heal completely. There will be scars. Far more than the burns on his body.

After his haircut it's your turn. Having hacked off your ponytail on the go, the results look less than elegant. In the mirror, with more time, you improve it. Evening out the back. Cutting away your fringe. Shortening everything, all around. The result isn't a professional job, but you're happy with it – short and spikey. Punked. You haven't had hair like this – so little of it – since high school. Your face looks narrower without the hair, your forehead higher. Not a new you, but definitely a different you.

Gogol sits on the toilet, watching. He seems content just to watch, to be. There's no restlessness in him, no manic little boy energy. He's not like other children in that way. You try not to dwell too much on what may have made him this still – his tense and instinctive wariness, watchfulness. Like the trick of a prey animal, avoiding the attention of predators. A stick insect. A butterfly, or moth. So much about him you don't know, may never know.

When the trim is done, your hair lies mingled with his in the sink, a tangled nest of strands. You scoop it up in a ball, deposit it in the bin. Next, fill the sink with water. Lean forward to dunk your head, wet your hair. Pour the blonde dye, rub it vigorously into your scalp, creating a shampoo-like lather. The directions say to wait for at least ten minutes.

Gogol reaches for the bottle, looks at you shyly. Points at his own hair. Him too? You can't think of a reason why not – and it might help disguise him. So you guide him to the sink, tilt his head forward, cup handfuls of the warm water over the back of his head, letting it run through until his hair is soaked, stuck flat to his scalp. You massage the dye in gently, fingers spider-walking his scalp, stroking his eyebrows to cover them too, being careful not to get any on his forehead, in his eyes. He beams up at you, his hair full of white foam, unaccountably happy just to be trying it – even if he's not sure what it does.

You twist your wrist, point to your watch. Hold up all your fingers, fanned out – hoping to signify ten minutes. He seems to understand that you have to wait, and so the two of you do – with him on the toilet, and you perched on the edge of the bath. It's so still and silent in the bathroom that you can hear the slow drip of water into the full sink, and even the faint tick of your watch, the second hand shaving seconds off the wait, the time, your life.

When the phone rings it's like an alarm. Abrasive, blaring.

You spot it then, lying among the towels. Where it's been all along. Waiting for you. There's no need to answer it. You shouldn't answer it. But you look at the display. You see that it's Mario's number, not Valerie's. Maybe that's why you answer it. Or maybe you answer because you need to know.

You press accept. You don't get the chance to say anything. The phone erupts with screaming. Screaming unlike any you've ever heard. The high-pitched, drawn-out shrieks of a human being in true pain. Closer to a pig or a lamb being slaughtered. A raw bleating.

Then it fades, as if the phone is being moved away. A voice asks you if they have your attention. It's Valerie, and you know then that Mario is dying, that he did the wrong thing. That he tried to go to them, explain to them. Cut a deal, make amends.

Valerie tells you that you just heard the sound of a man being operated on without anaesthetic. Of seeing his own organs being removed while still alive. The kidneys first, then liver, and then – before death – the still beating heart. She tells you that this is what they are going to do to you. Unless you bring them the boy. Now.

You don't answer immediately. You motion to Gogol to go out of the bathroom. Thinking of him, first and foremost. As you always will, from now on. Shutting the door behind him. Your own blood rushing, pulsing, throbbing. You tell Valerie that she can't have him. Not him or his heart. You're already halfway across Europe. You're going to escape and then report her and the authorities will find her.

She simply laughs at you. Says you are lying. Says the authorities will find *you* – on their behalf. 'We already know you got on a bus,' she says. 'There are only so many buses from that depot, at that time. We will find you soon enough. Then Pavel will do his work on you.'

As if to punctuate this threat, Mario's screaming crescendos again – either a renewed agony, or she is holding the phone closer, forcing you to listen. An unbearable sound, which evokes a physical reaction – you recoil, flinch, close your eyes. But that's worse. Against the dark of your own eyelids you can picture Pavel, his delicate hands. The precise way he played his harpsichord. The same precision he is using now, on Mario's body. The same as he will use on you.

'And then,' she says, 'he will see to the boy.'

The images are enough to trigger nausea, the taste of bile. Burning through your icy facade.

'No,' you say, resorting to denial. 'No.'

It's the only word you can manage, and you sound hoarse, unconvincing. The phone sticks hot to your ear. A leech, draining your faculties. Poisoning you with dread. Debilitating, after feeling so little, for so long. You want to hang up, know you should hang up. Shouldn't stay on the line too long. They might use it, trace you. Find you by the signal. But you can't leave it like this. With Valerie still gloating, in her position of power. Having found your weakness.

It's as if she's already won. As if it's over.

But it isn't. Not yet. You open your eyes. Look at yourself in the mirror, at the hard-faced woman. Her hair a spiky crown of foam. Glowing eerie white under the bathroom lights. A strange sight. A stranger. You hold her gaze. You are her. You are not you, any more. You don't just look different. You *are* different.

'No,' you repeat, clinging to that word, turning it into a renunciation. This time more forcefully. When Valerie tries to say something, taunt you further, you simply cut her off, speak over Mario's wails, somehow keeping your voice steady, level. 'You evil fucking witch,' you say, passing on the insult the Ukrainian man gave you. Then you tell her the bus was just a ruse – they can follow all the bus routes they want. They won't find you. They don't even know who you are. These words aren't just false bravado, but come to you like an epiphany, delivered clear and cold, ringing out with the force of prophecy.

Before Valerie can answer, you end the call. But even then, Mario's death cries still seem to echo – inside the bathroom, inside your head – so you shove the phone in the basin, fully immersing it, leave it there. As if you can break the spell through this trick. An irrational reaction, but it helps. You place a hand on either side of the basin, to steady yourself. Squeeze the porcelain, seeking comfort in its coolness. The tap is still dripping. You watch each drop hit the water, the effect calming and hypnotic. A steady rhythm your pulse seems to match as it slows, steadies. You want to believe what you said is true: you are not who you were. The woman you were – the wife, the widow – is not enough. You have to be more. You have to be better, stronger, smarter.

For him. For Gogol. The thought of him giving you strength.

Only once you've regained your composure do you open the door, smile at Gogol. He's waiting there wide-eyed, terrified – not of you but *for* you. He's heard you talking, of course. Even if he hasn't understood the words, he's felt the current of fear as if through a conduit. You draw him to you, tell him it's okay. You tell him that there are people out there, wanting to hurt you and him. But you won't let them. He is safe with you. You are learning a lesson of parenthood: you have to pretend it's okay, even when it's not.

He looks at you in a solemn, curious way – his hair still filled with white lather. The time's almost up, on your dye jobs. You lead him again to the sink. Turn him around, get him to tilt his head back, scoop handfuls of warm water over his hair, until the foam runs out, dissipates. Even wet, you can see it's worked.

Your turn next. Leaning over, dunking your head, rubbing out the dye. Then pulling the plug and letting the tap run, making sure you've got it all. Your hands are still trembling, from the call, the residual emotion. A charged, electric feeling. All through your body.

From the shelf, you take a towel, vigorously scrub your head first, and then Gogol's. You turn to consider yourselves in the mirror. Your hair looks identical: wet spikes, frosted with blonde. You are both so pale it looks quite normal, almost natural. And it makes you look more similar – his facial features not so different from yours, both of you thin, bony, and a bit emaciated. You've been subsisting on very little since arriving. You lacked the appetite, the will. But you have to change that. No time for romantic abstinence, for surviving on smokes and booze. You can't waste away. You both need to be healthy. Vigorous. Prepared. For whatever is coming next, now. For whoever is on their way.

Gogol beams, touches his hair tentatively. The change in hair colour is not the effect he expected. Seeing that, you smile too.

He could almost pass for your son. You could almost be family.

What do you do, when people threaten your family?

You put a hand on his shoulder. That sense of physical connection. That feeling of kinship, of protecting your own.

vigil

A still, clear, frozen night. From your perch on the veranda
– where there's a wicker table and two chairs – you can see
down into the ravine, and across to the hills. They're ancient
and rounded, worn by the elements, like the hills of Wales.
The moon is up and it casts a bone-white glow on the slopes.
The rounded domes look like skulls, the patches of shadow
forming the eye sockets, nostrils, gaping mouths, like a large-
scale version of the Ossuary.

To your right you can see the steeple of the Ossuary itself
and, beyond it, rooftops of buildings in town. Kutná Hora
is a quiet, sleepy place, a tourist stop, but only because of
the church, and not known for bars, nightlife. Most sounds
from the town tapered off around eleven. Other people are
asleep by now. Not you. You should try – you need the rest to
stay sharp – but you're too wired, too worried to sleep. The
exchange with Valerie still fresh in your mind. The sound of

Mario's screams. His piercing, shrieking terror. You wonder if he really made the mistake of going to them, or if they tracked him down, caught up with him. If they were monitoring his mobile, or yours. You don't think the idea's unfeasible. Various scenarios come to mind. Mario in his apartment, desperately loading a travel bag, when the door bursts open and they seize him. Or him down in Wenceslas Square, while trying to arrange his passage out, to elsewhere, anywhere. His last hustle. But too late – he's grabbed, forced into a car. Mario the magician disappeared like one of his acts.

However it happened, Mario is gone, and now they're coming after you.

You consider what Valerie said. They know you got on a bus. Could they really find out, through legwork, deduction, which specific bus? There'd be numerous buses leaving Brno, say, within a one-hour time frame. And all the various stops along each route. But they might work it out, eventually. If they have the resources. Or else Valerie might have been bluffing. You were bluffing her, so it's not unreasonable to assume she was doing the same. Trying to scare you. Hoping to get you to do something stupid, to reveal yourself. Flushing you out. Like pheasants from the underbrush.

But you can't assume that. Can't be certain that they won't show up here, during the night. Which is why you're sitting up, vigilant. Frightened of going to sleep, and waking to discover you've let your guard down, failed. The punishment for this not death but torment, a grotesque fate like something out of Bosch, those mediaeval paintings of hell. A scalpel across your abdomen. Your glistening organs being handled like jewels.

You sit up, physically shake yourself, seeking to banish those thoughts, dispel Valerie's nefarious influence. She'd want you to dwell on it, grow sick and stupid with fear. Make a foolish mistake.

Focus, instead. On the here and now.

From your perch, you have a view of the main road in and out of town from the east. A small bridge crosses the ravine down to the right, and vehicles travelling from Brno would likely use it – the direction you came from, the direction you assume they would be coming from. Every so often a vehicle appears, its headlights strafing across the stones and brickwork. You can't see the car park of the *penzión*, but you can see the driveway. So long as you're awake, and alert, you'll be able to tell if anybody arrives.

You get out your cigarettes – you're down to your last few Smarts – and light one more. In the cold, the smoke feels soothing in your lungs. The rest of your body is numb. Even huddled in a coat and cap, various layers of clothing, if you're not moving, not doing anything, the cold creeps in. You feel as if you're seizing up, crystallising, going solid. Turning into an ice sculpture, not a snow queen.

The thought of that nickname saddens you. Poor Mario.

You can't sink into stillness, sentimentality.

Regardless of whether or not Valerie was lying, bluffing, or partly telling the truth, you need to move. And when you move it has to be fast, purposeful.

Flying would be ideal, but it's not an option. Gogol can't fly without a passport, and he doesn't have one. Clearly. He doesn't have any ID whatsoever. Aside from his sad little medical report – his ticket to what he thought was Disneyland, but was actually death. So it has to be overland. Trains might work, but are a risk. To be in plain view, easily spotted. Your new haircut and dye job revealed as a paltry and feeble disguise.

No, driving would be safest. Driving would be best. You can drive straight west. The borders in the EU are no longer real borders. There are no checkpoints. There would be nothing to stop you. The main problem is finding a new car. One that they can't track, can't recognise. Not a rental – not anything that requires your name, a record. No, a private sale would be best. There must be something for sale in this town. An old beater. That's all you'd need. So long as it runs. Unless there's another option. Something you haven't thought of yet.

You stand and stretch. Shrugging off that numbness, the lethargy of cold. You lean against the railing, gazing out. Thinking it all through has calmed you some. But the anxiety is still there – like a ball of hooks, tangled in your guts. You think it might be there for good. Even if you get away – today, tomorrow, this time – will you and Gogol ever be safe? Ever be able to relax? A week from now? A month? A year?

Those timescales are meaningless. What matters is now. Tonight, tomorrow.

You open the sliding door, ease yourself inside. Gogol is a dark lump on the bed. A little cocoon of a boy, enshrouded in sheets, the duvet. You pull a chair over to the window. If you're going to stay up, you may as well be inside, near him, where it's warm. You position the chair so that you have a view of the driveway leading up to the *penzión*. You'll be able to see any vehicle as it arrives.

A stirring from the bed. Gogol. He's sitting up. He asks you something, in his own language. Talking to phantoms. Haunted by his old life. The words are lost to you, but the meaning, the fear, is clear enough. 'Everything is okay,' you tell him. 'Go back to sleep.'

He does, and you settle down to wait out the night, like a sentry on duty.

running

Morning. A line of pink light on the horizon. You're not any safer, but the light makes you feel safer. There were no cars in the night, no ominous knocks at the door, no violent intrusions. Valerie was bluffing, after all. Or they've come up against the limitations of their resources, the vastness of the bus network. After all, how would they track you down, even knowing you got on a bus?

Feeling triumphant, you stand for a minute at the veranda door, smoking, and watch Gogol sleeping in the soft light of dawn. His hair is dry now and the dye-job more striking, the strands all silken and pale, like the fuzz on the head of a duckling, newly hatched. He's on his belly, one arm folded awkwardly beneath him, the sheets a tangle around his legs and torso. He does not sleep well, or easily. His dreams troubled, his soul unsettled. He woke half a dozen times in the night, always looking to you for confirmation and affirmation: 'It's okay,' you would repeat at such moments, 'I'm here. You're safe.'

You shower and change and when you come out of the bathroom, he's sitting up, looking bashful, embarrassed. He's clutching the sheets, eyes downcast. You go to him, suspecting, and see that they're damp. The smell of urine emanating from them. You take the bundle, chilly and wet, from him, speak in a cheerful, friendly voice, tell him not to worry about it. You'll explain to the owner.

To take his mind off it, you lead him into the bathroom, help him brush his teeth. They're so brown and ruined you thought he might not even know how, but he seems confident enough, scrubbing up and down with the toothbrush, grinning at you through the foam. When he spits, it's pink with blood.

Downstairs, the owner has set two tables – one for you, and presumably one for her only other guests, who apparently aren't awake yet. When she comes out to take your order, she glances curiously at the hats you're both wearing indoors (to hide your change in hair colour), but makes no comment. She thinks you're American tourists, after all, and Americans wear caps all the time. Instead, she takes your order – bacon and eggs and toast, for both of you – and ducks down her little hole-in-the-wall corridor, towards the kitchen.

You sit and sip coffee, bleary-eyed, dazed by lack of sleep, feeling almost peaceful. Gogol has a glass of orange juice, which he drinks very dutifully, with the utmost concentration. Sip after sip. When the food comes, he eats, if not slowly, then at least less ravenously, having begun to understand that there will be more meals like this, that he can enjoy the experience, that he can taste the food. You eat as well, and are surprised by your own appetite. The eggs go down easy, the yolks rich and warm as blood. The bacon is thick-cut, crisped to perfection. The kind Tod would have liked. You have to remind yourself that a man died last night, a man you knew. Tortured to death. But it doesn't ruin your appetite.

Your revived empathy has its limits. Ironically, you're still Mario's snow queen, even if he's no longer around to call you that. You'll hold on to the name, the title. Draw strength from it. It gives you an edge. An edge you'll need.

When the owner comes back to clear your plates, she mentions that your friend called earlier. Asking after you. You look at her dully for a moment, full of food and contentment and overconfidence. Unable to process her cheerful, passing comment. You have to repeat it yourself, aloud, as a question: my friend called?

'She was not sure what hotel you'd booked into.'

Still you are blank-faced. The owner pauses, with the plates held expertly in one hand, the other on her hip. 'It must be you,' she says, getting impatient. 'A woman, and a little boy. Here on holiday. That's what she said.'

You reach for your cup of coffee, lift it. Replace it without taking a sip. The cup rattling against the saucer. 'How long ago was this?' you ask her.

She tells you it was this morning, just before you came down.

You knock back the coffee, push away your plate, and when the woman asks if you'd like more coffee you tell her to be quiet and listen – *listen*. 'The woman who called is not my friend. They will come here, looking for us, if they aren't here already. Whatever you do, don't tell them we are going east. Tell them we are going west, to Germany. Do you understand?'

The woman's expression reminds you of Gogol: wide-eyed, open-mouthed, awe-struck. You have to repeat the question – *do you understand?* – before she confirms that she does, she does understand. You're already getting up, motioning to Gogol. Heading for the stairs. Not knowing how they found you, but knowing that they have.

You spend less than five minutes in the room. Simply throwing everything into your duffel bag, pulling on your jacket and shoes, instructing Gogol to do the same. He is quicker to act now. Able to read your moods, take his cue from you. And maybe able to understand more than you realise. Sensing the urgency, certainly. And the aura of fear, of being hunted, of having to run, to hide. This he knows all too well.

Then, out the glass door on to the veranda. Into the cold clear morning. Taking Gogol by the hand. A three-foot drop, landing next to his hiding spot from last night. The ground is hard, frozen, but there's no snow. Just a covering of frosted leaves, mottled brown and red. Crunching underfoot like shards of glass. With the duffel bag slung over one shoulder, and your other hand holding Gogol's, you make your way down the slope of the ravine, until you're out of sight of the *penzión* and below the road into town.

Not sprinting but hurrying, moving efficiently, walking with an odd lurching gait due to the angle of the descent. Your breath puffing out in front of you. It's hard for Gogol, because of his leg. His weak leg on the downslope. Thin and seemingly as fragile as the twigs that snap underfoot. But he doesn't complain. Simply tries to keep up, keep pace.

You think of all the time wasted through the night, when you were so smug and content. So certain you'd eluded them, that you were still *being smart, getting the bounces*. Really you were being overconfident. If it costs you, and they catch you, they will make good on their promises. Pain and death.

You cling to the hand of the boy following you, trusting you, relying on you.

Along the side of the ravine, you head towards the bridge. It's a modern structure, a simple concrete arch, with two abutments supporting it. You reach the abutment on your side and scuttle beneath it. When vehicles pass overhead the whole structure seems to hum and vibrate like a giant tuning fork. On the other side there are hills and woodlands, offering concealment from the road.

That's where you go.

Once up the opposite slope of the ravine, you cut back towards town. You can only see the road intermittently – occasional glimpses of grey pavement between trunks, branches, pine needles. As you walk, you explain to Gogol your goal, more for your benefit than his. Talking it through. Telling him that you're heading for the train station, in the centre of town. There's a minor station, Sedlec, that's closer, but it's only for a local line – you'd have to transfer at the main station anyway. Safer just to go straight there. You've got your innate sense of direction, which Tod always envied and admired, and you know Kutná Hora station is on this side of town. You're confident you can reach it by working your way through these woods overlooking the road.

All this you explain while pulling Gogol along, and not once does he falter, tug on your hand, lag behind. You have the feeling that, loyal as a dog, he would keep going until his legs gave out, until he collapsed from cold, from exhaustion, from dehydration. He may be hindered by his leg, but he isn't weak. He is, on the contrary, stubborn and resilient and tenacious. As much bulldog as duckling.

The hike goes on longer than you expect and you wonder if you've misjudged, if in your fear and panic and the rush you've got turned around, somehow. If the town centre is back in the other direction, and you're heading away from the station, out of the suburbs and into the wilderness. Yet another mistake, on your part. Yet more wasted time. The time they need to find you.

But the fears are unfounded. Through the trees you glimpse buildings now. Houses. A hotel. And behind you the steeple of the Ossuary. It helps guide you, provides a means to get your bearings. That monument of death that seems to preside over the whole town. Possibly the whole country, the whole world. These crazed thoughts flutter up, frantic and frenetic. Using the Ossuary you can work out how close you are to the town centre, the train station, and turn downslope in that direction. You emerge on a one lane track that winds through the woods, then connects with a side road that skirts a residential area. End up a few hundred metres from the station. Just a brief walk past a junction and some shops.

It's very early. Hardly anybody is about, aside from a man opening his café, scattering salt on the cobbles out front, huffing in the cold, and a woman in a high-vis bib, plucking a can from the gutter with a litter-picking stick. You walk cheerfully with Gogol, swinging his arm, acting as if you don't have a care in the world. A tourist mother with her son. Brisk and ambitious Brits, setting off for a day of sightseeing. Heading to the station, to catch an early train. Ta-ta. Cheerio.

When you get there, you mount the steps, risk a backwards glance. Nothing. Nobody watching. Nobody that you can see, at least. You wonder if you will spot them, before they find you. Or if it will simply happen, if they'll blindside you, kidnap you. A black hood over your head. A Kleenex full of chloroform. A discreet blow with a sap. Or however it is they do it; the same way they might have got Mario.

Inside the station, a few old-fashioned monitors display train departure and arrival times. It takes you a moment to differentiate, decipher the Czech. When you do, as far as you can tell, it looks as if all the destinations are local: somewhere in the Czech Republic. Which isn't what you want. You go to the ticket booth (there are no other passengers) and ask the clerk – a young man, dopy, bleary-eyed, smelling faintly of last night's beer – if any international trains run through Kutná Hora.

He shakes his head, yawns. Explains you have to go to Brno, or Prague. All the high-speed, inter-city European trains run from one or the other. They don't stop here.

Brno, or Prague. Both places where *they* will be looking for you. Closing in.

You ask the man when the train for Prague departs, and he tells you they run every half hour, the next being in fifteen minutes, at quarter past eight.

You buy two tickets. Stand with Gogol at the far end of the platform: him wearing his winter hat, you wearing your baseball cap. There's no shelter, no waiting room. Out there, in full view, your little disguises don't feel so effective. Your haircuts and dye jobs seem comically inadequate, rather than clever and deceptive.

Above your head, a digital display shows the platform number, the destination of the next train due – Praha – and the current time. You have never felt time move like this, so slowly. Each minute seeming to extend, stretch on and on forever. You stand clutching Gogol's hand, shivering, knowing you made a mistake, an error in judgement, and so deserve this – consigned to a hellish limbo where eight-fifteen seemingly will never come, and trains to Prague never depart.

backwards

When the train does arrive, it's small – just three carriages – and also backwards. The control cab at the rear, pushing it, rather than pulling it as you would expect. This is not unheard of. This is not all that irregular. Still, in your heightened state of fear and alertness it's disarming and strange. A backwards train. Movement in reverse. The front (or rear?) still glazed with frost, as if it's only recently come from the trainyard, just awakened from a long hibernation. It trundles to a stop in front of you, sighs, shudders, and falls silent.

When it's motionless, the oddness of the carriage arrangement is no longer evident – it just looks like a train and you must get on it. There's a six-inch gap and foot-high step between the platform and the doors. You put down your duffel bag and lift Gogol up first, placing him directly in front of you.

You stoop to pick up the bag and, when you straighten, he's gone. Like that. You feel that panic-surge and leap on to the train, looking first one way – towards the vestibule between carriages, the toilets – and then the other, into the aisle. And Gogol is there. Of course. He simply stepped to the side to make room for you, and the bag. They haven't taken him, can't have taken him. How would they have known to get on the train before you? It's the shock of the shift, from complacency to flight, and your own paranoid brain. Playing tricks on you.

You reach for his hand, seeking and giving reassurance, and guide him further into the carriage, which is nearly empty. Find seats on the side away from the platform, where you are less noticeable. Watch the station and platform carefully, with Gogol right next to you, the duffel bag cradled on your lap. Willing the train to move, which it does, eventually. Sluggishly. As if it has forgotten its own purpose.

No pursuers step on to the platform, or peer out of the station and ticket office. They either haven't arrived in town yet, or they've gone straight to the *penzión*, where they will find only the landlady. Frightened and confused.

She will tell them everything, that much is a given. They will make sure she does. But she will tell them first that you went to Germany, and then – when forced, threatened – that you're actually going east. Of course, neither is true. A simple ploy on your part, to feed her that double-lie. But you hope it's an effective one. Even if it buys you only a little extra time.

The train is picking up speed now, the platform falling away. Another set of tracks glides along beside you, every so often wiggling left, or right. Shifting. You try to recall which direction the train came into the station, and if it continued on in the same way. You think it did, which means you are now moving backwards with it. It wasn't merely a case of backing into or out of the depot, as you've seen before. Shrewsbury station operates like that. To get to Aberystwyth, on trains from Birmingham. Not in Kutná Hora. Backwards is simply the direction this particular train is running today, it seems.

You can't help but feel that time is moving backwards with it. Drawing you back to Prague, the last place you expected to go. You remember a sequence of film clips you saw, during a lesson on time in A-level physics. The specifics are gone, lost, but you recall the shots of a train running backwards, automobiles racing along in reverse. And more: demolished buildings reassembling themselves, the flowering flares of bombs shrinking to brilliant seeds, fallen bridges rising, levitating into place. Then stars, rushing first outwards from each other like fireworks, and slowing as if on elastics, and eventually reversing, moving back towards each other. The opposite of the Big Bang. All the elements of the universe rushing towards each other, ultimately neutralising and eliminating one another.

The Big Crunch. That was what they called it. Maybe that's what this is.

Whimsical thoughts. Thoughts you're better off without. Better to think backward in practical terms. How did this happen? How did you end up like this, on the defensive, fleeing in fear, when you had all the advantages?

But that's delusion. You never had the advantages. You just believed you did.

The man at the bus station. It could be incredibly simple: he *did* see you. Even though you didn't think he had. Caught a glimpse of you, noted the number of your bus. Or, if not, how hard would it be to ask around a bit, perhaps check some of the security camera footage. Him and his accomplice posing as police officers. Maybe they *are* police officers.

You imagine it being played out, and reversed, like those clips from your class: black and white footage of you and Gogol, getting on the bus, getting off, getting on, getting off. Freezing it just as your faces are turned in the right direction. The man demanding a close-up of that. *That's her, all right.* Both of you looking nervous and uncertain. Furtive. Easy prey.

From there, how hard would it have been to track down the driver, ask her if she recalled you. Probably she did. The British woman, in the hockey cap? A little boy with her? Seems to walk with a limp. Oh, yes. She would remember you. Could provide the needed information: the two of them got off in Jihlava, transferred to the festival shuttle bus. In the early evening.

Or maybe the driver didn't remember. Maybe it was a matter of graft, guesswork. Looking at all the stops on that route. Checking various inns and hotels and *penzións*. A long series of innocent-seeming phone calls, until they finally struck pay dirt, found the one you were at. You can imagine how Valerie would have sounded on the phone. You're convinced it was her, personally. It had to be her. Her voice friendly and charming and relaxed. Completely convincing. The owner shouldn't have told her. If a man had phoned, asking after you, without even calling you by name, would the owner have been so forthcoming? Not that it matters now. It's on her: she'll have Pavel to deal with.

You reach for your Smarts, pinch out the last one. Hold it and tap the filter repeatedly against the cardboard box, making a soft tocking sound. The scenario you've come up with – the means by which you were found – seems plausible enough. If not that, a variation on it. And yet you've only been able to piece it together in retrospect. Like being able to assemble a puzzle once you've seen the finished image.

Not good enough. You have to be better. You have to think ahead, see ahead. And never assume they aren't right there, following. Waiting to take him from you and kill him, butcher him, sell his organs like cutlets. Though your mind skitters from such thoughts you force yourself to think them: these are the stakes. And after torturing you in vengeance they'd likely find a similar use for your organs. Valerie strikes you as very pragmatic. Not one to waste an opportunity for profit. Your kidneys going to one buyer, your liver and spleen to another. And, of course, your heart – the real prize. Placed in a case, still beating, on a bed of ice. Like a giant ruby resting amid diamonds. Priceless.

You squeeze Gogol's hand. You have not let it go since you sat down.

You only let go when the conductor makes his way through the carriage. He heads straight for you, having seen you get on in Kutná Hora. He is tall, thin, grey-haired. Smiling pleasantly. Happy to be doing his job, to be so perceptive about noting his customers, finding them, checking their tickets. It occurs to you that all conductors, out of necessity, are good at this – spotting new faces, recalling which passengers they've checked, so as not to ask again and potentially offend. You offer your tickets up with a polite smile. Try to keep your head slightly averted, your features shielded with your hat brim.

An ineffective ploy, really. He will remember you. You must assume that. They will learn from the owner of the *penzión* that you rushed off. They will be checking bus schedules, train schedules. They will guess, or figure out, that you lied about where you were headed. They will be after you again, or waiting for you at the other end.

Gogol reaches into his pocket, and pulls out the little stack of memory cards that you created together for your game, the night before. He remembered them, even in your rush to get out, to get away. He lays them down now on the small side table in front of his seat, just below the window. Looks at you hopefully.

You almost shake your head, no. Your insides wound up too tightly even to humour him. But then you check yourself, nod. Put the duffel bag on the overhead rack and take a different seat, opposite him.

As the game begins, you focus on the cards, on the symbols. Rub your temples with your forefingers. Hoping for some lucidity, some clairvoyance. As if studying a tarot spread. Trying to determine a way out of this that you haven't foreseen. Haven't considered.

If you haven't yet, maybe they haven't either.

key

Gogol will provide the key. Unintentionally. A chance occurrence, his natural fascination, his childish curiosity, which inspires the lateral leap you need to solve this locked-room mystery, escape this Schrödinger's box.

Not knowing this, you have already committed to a plan of action. Logical, obvious, uninspired. Flying is not an option, and your idea of finding a car – buying one, or borrowing one, renting one under an alias – has faded with the knowledge that they've found you, could be right behind you, may have figured out already that you're on this train, going back to Prague. Since you can't turn yourselves in, put your faith in authority, you've reached the simple conclusion that in Prague you'll have to transfer from this regional train to another train, an intercity train – heading out of the Czech Republic, to Germany, most likely. Dresden or Berlin, or all the way to Hamburg.

And, from there, you'll keep going. Either to the Netherlands, the ferries there. Or south into France, up to the port at Calais. And home. There must be a way through. People smugglers do it all the time, and you would have the advantage of a British passport, no criminal record. Rent a car and drive through the Channel Tunnel with Gogol hidden in the back, or perhaps try the ferries. You and Tod did that with cases of wine – so why not a boy?

All these scenarios flitting through your mind, as you chug past frozen fields, copses of birch and alder. Hurtling towards your fate. You want to believe it can work, this plan of yours – but it still feels too predictable. And even if you make it, will you be safe back in the UK? How far will they follow? How desirous are they, for this boy's heart? Is it simply for the money, the crass cash sale, or is it a one-off like Mario said? For the daughter of a friend, or family member? Maybe you've consigned this other child to death. Maybe Valerie is her aunt, her godmother. Maybe she and Pavel will seek you out, forever and indefinitely, simply for the sake of revenge.

Those fears can wait. Right now, you just have to get out, and trains seem the only way. A quick change at Praha hlavní nádraží, the central station where this train terminates. Find the first, and fastest, intercity train leaving after you arrive. And simply buy your tickets and hop on. Go. Moving quickly, hoping your disguises are sufficient, hoping they don't have people watching the platforms, that they have less resources than you fear.

It's not much of a plan. Part of you worries this is another misstep, another mistake. Still. It's all you have. It's what you've decided to do.

Until you reach the outskirts of Prague. See the spires and domes, shrouded in smog. The inversion layer – with its sensation of stasis – has not dissipated in the few days you've been away. It's still here, waiting. Unchanged. You have the feeling you've been drawn back, on this backwards train, into a vortex. Funnelling you right to where they expect you to go, and where they will be waiting for you. One of the men from the inn. Or your old friend Denis. Awaiting a chance to grab you and Gogol. In the chaos of the station, a foreign city. Amid the stamp of passing feet – all those passengers going in various directions, nobody to hear your confusion, fear, strangled cry, or notice a boy and woman being accosted, secreted away. Taken to your fates. The feeling is so strong it's almost like a premonition: a vision of your future. It's improbable that Valerie would be there in person, but she would be presiding over it all, the guiding presence. The one you have to ultimately outsmart, outwit.

And not by doing this. Not by staying on these tracks, doing what's logical, what she expects. There must be some other way to save Gogol from his grim, macabre, fairy-tale fate. A heart. *Bring me his heart.* Like the stepmother in Snow White. Wasn't there something about a heart, in that one? The hunter used a pig's heart as a decoy. That's what you need: some ingenious, sideways solution. A curveball.

But you're tired, weary, your mind clouded, foggy. Like a dull sow in a cattle car, you are being carried towards your final end reluctantly, resistantly, but without any real hope of escape.

Not Gogol. He's sitting up, child-giddy, awed by the sight of this city. What was it that woman on the flight had called it, the one who'd had the fit? The mother of cities. The golden city. The city of a hundred spires. For Gogol it must appear magical. Mythical. He looks back at you, shy and sly, and even before he asks you know what is on his mind. This, surely, must be Disneyland. The *real* Disneyland, as opposed to the bone church. It even has a castle, visible in the distance, rising above the other buildings, like the photo in his cherished newspaper advert.

No, you tell him. Prague isn't Disneyland. But you'll get him to Disneyland, eventually. He presses his face to the glass, peers out, fascinated all the same. You can see the fog made by his breath, creeping up the pane. Shortly after, you cross a bridge with a stretch of river shimmering beneath you, and he stands up on his seat, craning to peer at the water. People are rowing down there. Some kind of longboat race. Half a dozen oarsmen in each, clad in shell jackets and Lycra, pulling in unison. Gogol points, confused, and asks you: *Where?* Just that word. Picked up in the last few days, or before. His developing English. *Where?*

You tell him, vacantly, that they're having a race of some sort. Against each other, or against the clock. You begin to explain that they aren't actually going anywhere – just rowing up and down the river. Until you remember the river *does* go somewhere. Very far away in fact. *Where?* One simple word. A child's curiosity.

You lean over the table, kiss Gogol gently on the forehead, blessing the epiphany. Consecrating his new plan. You're three stops away from Praha hlavní nádraží, where you intended to change trains, but you stand to take down your duffel bag from the overhead rack. Tell Gogol you're getting off at the next stop. He has provided the key, and like the tumblers in the safe, all the other elements begin to fall into place, allowing you to open up this door, this escape route. A Houdini trick. Just what you need, and it's been right in front of you – or right behind you, in your past – all along.

By the time you reach the next stop, you know exactly what you have to do. You step down on to the platform, lift Gogol after you. Set him down guardedly. Aware that you are here, now, in their territory. On their turf. The air is dingy, cold, heavy – city air still laden with smog. People are waiting to get on – a woman with a striped handbag, a man holding a rolled-up newspaper like a baton – but nobody seems to be waiting for you, or watching. Their eyes drift over you, past you, registering you only as an obstacle to navigate around.

You've already spotted a payphone across the street, and after stepping away from the platform you thumb through your wallet, searching for a crumpled napkin, that number, which you never expected to call. Until now. Until you saw a chance, a last gambit. Until it seemed the most logical thing in the world.

And that's when you called me.

old friends

How strange, that phone call. To have it come out of the blue. After assuming, of course, that you would never contact me, had no real interest in or use for me. And how odd that your call, and what followed, is why this account exists. Why I have a story to tell. Your story. Of all the minute observations I made in that language class, all the pages of character sketches, dialogue snippets, scene breakdowns, in the end I found nothing that truly interested me, nothing that haunted me. That came from the Welsh woman, who dropped out of the class, who seemed shrouded in mystery.

What I knew at the time was minimal: a call from an unknown number, and when I answered, background noise – the murmur of voices, passing traffic, the sense of an outdoor space. And a voice I didn't recognise, at first, until you reminded me – explaining that you were from my class, did

I remember you? Of course I remembered. You said you had a bit of a problem, and needed help – somewhere to stay. You used those words. Not 'hide out' or 'refuge'. I said yes, you could come to my apartment. I was thrilled, flattered, which seems mortifying to me now. I was still intrigued by our short meeting – a few beers, a shared pack of cigarettes, your impervious persona. I gave you my address – the apartment in Praha Three where I was staying.

You must have been nearby, or at least not too far away. You said you would be there soon and hung up. You didn't say exactly how long, but after about half an hour my doorbell sounded – a short old-fashioned buzzer that grated on the eardrums – and I let you in the building, opened my door.

Initially, I thought I'd been tricked, or somebody had made a mistake. I was expecting you, but then coming up the stairs was this boy, followed by a woman, wearing a cap pulled down low, partially shielding her face.

But when you glanced up, I recognised you. The angular features, the fierce eyes. Looking a little strung out, hyper-alert. At the time, I wouldn't have used the term hunted, but of course that's what you were. You and him. The surprise must have shown on my face, since you said, matter-of-factly, 'This is Gogol.' And then – as if that was a key, or password – I stepped aside. Not inviting you in, but simply allowing you in. Granting you access.

Nothing noteworthy about my flat – just a one-bedroom apartment, the kind you would find anywhere in Prague. A cheap rental, with a kitchenette, for tourists, travellers, students. Or would-be writers. I had a desk in one corner. A plywood bookshelf, lined with books so portentous and weighty they may as well have been slabs of concrete.

When you removed your cap, the change was disconcerting – the haircut, the dye job. The way it matched the boy's.

Before I could ask about that, you asked me if I had anything to eat. Gogol needed lunch. He was watching me, cagily. I could tell that there was something wrong with his leg – he favoured it, and moved with a slight limp. I thought perhaps he had sprained it, hurt it. I smiled at Gogol and dug through my cupboards and said, flustered, that I didn't have any macaroni but that I had Pot Noodles. As if, in my head, a little boy would only eat one or the other. Nothing else.

You said Pot Noodle would be fine, that you could explain things after. Food first.

So, I played host, to you both. I made tea for you and me, hot chocolate for him. I put the Pot Noodles on. I chatted frivolously as I went about these tasks, as if you were an aunt or cousin come to visit. Or an old acquaintance. How have things been going? What have you been up to? You never answered these questions directly. Didn't provide specific information. You weren't ready. I sensed that, but kept up my frivolous chatter all the same. I didn't know how else to behave.

When the noodles were done, I dumped in the sachet of salt and flavouring and ladled it into two bowls. Put them down at the table. I remember the boy's appetite. The way he devoted himself entirely to the act of eating. I noticed his teeth, too. They stood out. You don't often see children with teeth so stained and crooked, these days.

You ate differently. Mechanical and distracted, your mind elsewhere. Knowing you had to eat something, I imagine, but uninterested. Your body a machine. Just refuelling it.

After you'd both finished, I showed Gogol around. He had brown, wary, watchful eyes. He didn't trust me – I could see that – but he trusted you enough to listen to me (it took me some time to deduce he couldn't understand English). I apologised for not having a TV, any games, things for kids

224

to do. I'd cut myself off from all that, to focus on my writing. No distractions. Though, of course, I'd written nothing worthwhile. He didn't look too bothered about the lack of entertainment, but was clearly fascinated by all my books. He began to take them off the shelves, look at the covers, flip them open. It seemed fine to leave him to it.

You and I went out on the balcony to smoke. You needed to bum one, since you'd run out. I had my own carton of cheap cigarettes, though not the Smart brand you seemed to like. We smoked in the cold. There were patches of ice on the concrete underfoot. My balcony overlooked an inner courtyard. Not much down there – just gravel, a dead tree, some rusted bikes, bits of litter. Nobody to overhear. It was safe to talk, so we talked. You told me, as far as I know, pretty much everything – starting with the job you'd mentioned before, explaining about crossing the border, picking up Gogol, and the slow realisation that they were going to kill him, to sell his organs. Or, at least, his heart. This according to the man you called Mario, who was, from what you said, now dead. I stood and listened to that and sucked rapidly on my cigarette and responded in inane, ridiculous ways, saying the kinds of things you would say when somebody tells such an incredible story. Why you told me everything, I can't be certain. I suspect you needed to confide. To pass it on. As much as you could. In case you didn't get out.

This way, at least one other person would know the truth.

Regardless, for whatever reason, you had chosen to trust me, perhaps sensing in me my eagerness to please, and my fascination with you. Maybe even sensing some similarities to Tod, or a young version of him. With my books and literary interests. Immature but well-meaning.

I asked you what your next step was. I was taking my cue from you, trying to act as cool as you. For me, of course,

225

it could only be that: an act. Whereas your detachment, your taciturn indifference, was seemingly deep-rooted, authentic.

That was when you told me you needed me – another reason you had to confide at least some of the backstory. And you laid out your new plan, that I was to go see your landlady. Marta. Valerie knew your name, would have tracked down your address in Prague, by that point. They would be watching Marta's building. But I could go there, without drawing suspicions. I was to tell Marta you were in serious trouble and needed to travel on her boat, down the Vltava. To Dresden, if possible, or if not there then as far as she could take you. I'd arrange the time with her. Then come back, fill you in. That was all.

You said all this with an impersonal urgency. I could be of use to you, and that was why you had come – no other reason. In that way, you displayed the same cool detachment as the woman I'd met before, but your facade showed signs of thawing. Not a superficial softening, more of a subliminal smouldering. A slow-burn within. A kind of kindling. You had begun to *care*, something you'd lost when your husband died. You reminded me of those religious zealots who hand out pamphlets, go door-to-door. You had found a clear, spiritual, single-minded fixation. A devotion. Everything so simple. Dedicated to one purpose, one end – not God, but one of God's creatures. A flawed angel. An ugly duckling. Your Gogol. You would do anything to ensure his salvation, to deliver him from evil. And I was to help.

walk-on part

Could I do it, this favour you needed? Of course. But, before going ahead, I asked (and I really wasn't trying to get out of it) why not simply phone her?

You said that you couldn't trust the phones. They could be monitoring the phones. I looked at you sideways then. Wondering how far you'd fallen into paranoia. Wondering if that was even possible – surveillance and tracing. Wiretaps and hidden mics.

But you also could have been right, and either way I wanted to help. It wasn't far to Marta's building, over in Vinohrady. You gave me the address, and showed me on the map of Prague I'd picked up at the tourist information centre a few months back. To make the ploy convincing, I called ahead, told Marta I was a Canadian living in Prague – wondering as I spoke if they really were listening, and if my acting sounded authentic enough – and that I wasn't happy at my current let. I was interested in renting a flat from her. She said she'd show me one she had available and could I come later that afternoon, perhaps four o'clock?

When I arrived at the house Marta was waiting. A stocky woman wearing jeans and a flannel shirt and work boots, smoking in the porch alcove. She looked like she'd just got back from fishing, and maybe she had. She shook my hand and turned to unlock the front door for us. Only once we were in her foyer did I explain, in low tones, that I wasn't really interested in renting a room; this was about something else entirely. This was about you. I didn't give too much detail – only that you were in trouble, that you had a boy with you, that you needed to get out of the city, and that you needed Marta to help.

She held a finger to her lips, led me up to her apartment, shut the door behind us. She did not ask the obvious question: what kind of trouble? Instead, revealingly, she asked me if you had done anything wrong. It might have been the language barrier, but the word choice struck me – not if you'd done anything illegal, but *wrong*. The emphasis on morality, rather than lawfulness. I told her no – that you were in this situation because you had done something *right*, not wrong, that you were taking a great risk to save a boy's life.

That was enough. Marta didn't have to think about it. She nodded, approvingly, and said, '*Ano.*' She would take you in the morning. Her voice heavily accented, gruff, but I detected real emotion. She'd known you were going away for a few days – you'd fed her that phony story – but she had been worried about you, all the same. Travelling alone. Grieving. So my covert appearance with news about you was not solely unsettling, it was also something of a relief.

228

She did not offer me coffee or tea. There was no pretence of hospitability, now that the charade of my looking to rent from her had been dropped. Still. We stood for a time, as accomplices, in her living room. It had vinyl flooring, functional wooden furniture, a few modest photos of her and a man – her dead husband, presumably – and smelled faintly of homemade bread. I remember thinking she made a great ally – level-headed, resourceful, practical. I didn't linger, just thanked her and left, returning home via a random, circuitous route – taking in a few sights and stopping off at the market hall in Vinohrady, riding the metro across town, then back. Pretending it was just another afternoon for me, while hoping I might lose anybody following.

Feeling thrilled and foolish to be playing the part you had given me.

When I got back to my place, you and Gogol were sitting on the floor, looking at a strange book I'd found at a second-hand store, on human anatomy. Other books were piled around him, having been checked and discarded. The ones filled with English words probably weren't of interest to him. The anatomy book had pictures, drawings – garish and gory, archaic diagrams of the lungs, of veins and arteries, of nerve endings and blood cells. I'd bought it on a whim, thinking it might be fodder for a horror story, some day. An ancient text, with an authentic gothic creepiness.

You two were looking at the page on the heart. Whether you had chosen it, or he had, I don't know. But he was fascinated. The diagram depicted a close-up sketch of the human heart's four chambers, the valves and ventricles, the direction of blood flow. All the mysteries of life and death and love and time contained in one compact, powerful, invaluable organ.

You looked up from that, bleary-eyed and hopeful for news. I was happy to be able to pass on that my modest quest had been a success. Marta had agreed. You let your eyes close once, as if in prayer. A subtle, telling sign of relief.

Gogol held up the picture, pointed to the heart – showing me, and you. And he said that word, one of the words in his growing English vocabulary: *where?*

You tapped his chest, explained that it was inside him. He looked down at his own body, marvelling at the secrets it contained, at the hidden strength and magic he had in him.

I was hoping you might put him to sleep and stay up, so we could hang out, smoke and drink like we had last time, in the cellar bar. But the truth of the matter is, you were beyond exhaustion, ready to collapse. You asked me one more favour: to let the two of you lie down, for a time. You needed sleep. It was hindering your capacity to think, to stay alert. You felt stupid from fatigue. I was to act as look out, with the front door locked. Not to answer if I heard a knock.

In this, too, I was eager to help. I said I'd sleep on the sofa, showed you both my room. I did a quick clean, removed a few dirty clothes, changed the sheets. You thanked me, vacantly, perhaps already thinking ahead to morning. Before bed, I remember you brushing his teeth, washing his face, him seemingly so comfortable in your care. Then, saying good night. A few minutes later, when I went to knock to ask if you needed food for the morning's journey, I got no answer. Worried, I tried opening the door an inch, but it was blocked. You had barricaded yourselves in there, perhaps with a chair wedged beneath the handle. You didn't feel safe enough with me to overlook that. But you felt safe enough to sleep, apparently. I suppose I should take that as a compliment, along with the idea that you would think to ask me for refuge, when you needed it, when your life depended on it.

According to you.

I had doubts, of course. About your sanity, about the veracity of your incredible account. I wondered if *you* were the kidnapper, a great fantasist. A confabulist. That you had found a life's purpose, after your husband's death, through your own invention. Or wanted a son so badly you simply bought one, took one. Telling yourself it was an act of generosity, to remove him from that mother, that world. Or whether only some of what you said was true, and other details merely the result of delusion, paranoia. The product of your sleepless nights, and grief, or a potential psychosis. I wondered, for example, about these people who you claimed had hired you – a syndicate or mafia or whatever they might be – and whether they could really be as powerful and influential and malevolent as you believed.

And I might have kept wondering, had I not received a visit, soon after you and Gogol left. Nothing noteworthy about your departure – you simply woke up and had some tea and toast and went. My paltry parting gift a few packs of cigarettes and some snacks – cheese and crackers for Gogol. I stood at my window, watching you walk down the street, until you were gone. I thought that would be it. But the very next day, two men came to my door, and invited themselves in – or, at least, I felt obliged to let them in. To sit with me. One flashed a badge, though it was impossible to tell what kind of badge, and if it was authentic. I wouldn't know that back home, let alone in Prague.

The one with the badge – big, ruddy-faced, overweight (he at least *looked* like a cop) – did all the talking. He said that they were looking for a woman and a boy. They asked if she might have come here. They were checking with all the people in her language class. I knew then that you had told me the truth, at least for the most part. That in a way I held

231

your lives in my hands – or my head. Any inkling that I knew something and they would get it out of me.

I also wondered, were they really asking all the people in class, or had they already connected you to me, and me to Marta? Had I blown the whole thing, been followed home, after all?

Fortunately, I had a lot going for me. Firstly, that I was a foreigner, Canadian. That I am friendly and always give off a feeling of wanting to help, in any way I can. That I have a bumbling, clownish persona often drawn on when in trouble with authority figures of every sort. It's second nature, instinctual with me. I said I did remember you, the British woman. That you came to class for a couple of weeks, that I even ran into you the day you were leaving the school. I acted eager to help, pretended to be concerned. I said I had a brief chat with you then, and it sounded as if you were involved in something, that you seemed distracted, troubled. I told him I hoped it wasn't anything serious. Is she all right? I asked, repeatedly.

He assured me you were okay. He looked disappointed. In me, in the information I could not provide. If he'd been alone, I might even have been convinced he was a real policeman.

But the other man, the one who did not speak, was wearing wire-rimmed glasses with yellow tinted lenses. He had a thin mouth, and very long, slim fingers. He spent the entire time watching me. You had told me enough for me to suspect this was him – the musician and surgeon. The one Valerie called Pavel.

I worried that he could see through me. Was looking at my organs. Considering how they could be accessed, and surgically removed. Weighed and dissected and studied for signs of my honesty, or my duplicity. The book of anatomy was sitting on the table, where Gogol had left it, and seemed painfully incriminating.

I would like to think I fooled them. I want to believe I did, that I gave nothing away. If I had, I have to admit, I would find it hard to live with myself, and the knowledge of how I'd let you down.

part three

waterways

Marta is waiting on the boat, standing with her arms crossed, at the stern, looking towards the bridge. The engine already running, billows of smoke rumbling up into the cold dark. Not long before dawn – seven in the morning – but it may as well be night; there's no light on the horizon. Flakes of snow falling gently, and sticking to the ground, where a thin layer has built up, maybe half an inch thick. The steps to Marta's jetty have been cleared and salted, but all the same you are mindful of Gogol. You descend ahead of him and reach back to hold his hand, help him balance. The steps look as old as Charles Bridge, the centre of each one bowed, carved out by the passing of time, by hundreds of thousands of feet. All those years, all those generations, all those people long dead, in whose footsteps you follow.

You can remember being the woman who idly fantasised about being dead, leaping from this bridge, into this river. But you can't fathom it now. It seems foolish, juvenile. It has the same unreal feel as looking back on a childhood memory, or some of your times with Tod. Third-person images. As if it happened to somebody else. A you that's no longer you.

From Marta, you don't know what to expect – curiosity, chastisement, uncertainty? But she simply greets you and treats this as she might any other morning excursion; she has even put up her chalkboard sign, with rates and times. That seems smart. Proceed as if it's simply another day. Business as usual. From the jetty, you hand her your duffel bag, which she hefts on to one of the rear seats. You then grip Gogol under his armpits and hoist him – so light in your arms, your hollow-boned boy. Pass him across the gap to the gunnel, where Marta is waiting to receive him. Once he's aboard, she instructs you to untie the lines, which you do, recalling the routine from last time, and tossing them aboard without being directed.

As you do, you hear her make a clicking sound at Gogol, to get his attention, and she asks him something in Czech. Then, seeing that he doesn't understand, she tries again, using different words, a different language.

This time he smiles, answers back. The confident sound of his voice a surprise.

'I know some Ukrainian and Russian,' she tells you. 'For the tourists.'

It occurs to you that Marta knowing those languages might make her one of them, that she – as a landlady, a property owner – could be knit up with them somehow. An irrational fear. You don't even know if they're Russian. Valerie said they were from here, there, everywhere. As if they are too diabolical to belong to any one country.

Besides, you've already put your trust in Marta. Gogol is already aboard. She extends her hand. You take it, hold it, each of you grasping the other's wrist. You leap across the water to join them, pat her shoulder by way of thanks. The deck is stable, cleared of snow, with a pebbled grey paint that provides grip. The boat, untethered and caught in the current, begins to drift away from the jetty.

Marta asks you to stow the lines as she goes to take the wheel. When she eases forward the throttle and begins to turn the boat around, the noise of the engine sounds perilously conspicuous in the morning quiet. The banks of the Vltava are lined with neoclassical buildings, most of them hotels or apartments. All those windows. All those drawn curtains. All those potential eyes, peering down on you.

You take Gogol into the wheelhouse. Just in case.

You huddle beneath the fibreglass canopy, which provides shelter for Marta's clients in the event of rain or snow. Still exposed to the air, but warmed by the heat of the engine. The bench seats can accommodate several passengers, but of course you and Gogol have one entirely to yourselves. You sit together and peer out at the buildings of Prague sliding past, screened by a veil of soft-falling snow. The fluttering flakes land on the water surface and linger for a few seconds, hovering like water bugs, before melting, dissipating. The river doesn't smell – it lacks the thick mud-stink of summer, or the mulch-stench of autumn. The cold has frozen any scents right out of the air.

The boat glides over the glassy surface like a sled on ice. You pass beneath another bridge, and past Letna Park. In the middle of the park, visible for miles, even in this dim morning light, is a giant sculpture: a red metronome, fully-functioning, seventy-five feet high. You've seen it before, but have never learned its meaning or purpose – and this morning it seems ominous, slow-ticking the time as you drift by. Beyond, more bridges and the sweeping oxbow bend that encloses Praha Seven. You are heading north out of the city. Downriver.

The opposite direction from which you travelled with Marta previously. The river is about five hundred metres across and as the buildings of the city give way to fields and stands of poplars, you feel safer than at any time since picking up Gogol. All that water, between you and shore. Between you and them. Like a moat. Impossible to cross. The boat your little castle. This was the right decision, the best way out. The only way out, maybe. You are impervious, for a time. At least until you dock again.

Over the noise of the engine, you thank Marta for doing this. She looks back at you as if she doesn't understand. Then you realise she understands the words, but not the need for thanking her. She just waves a hand. It's nothing. 'But,' she adds, 'you will tell me.'

She means what's really going on, and what you've gotten her involved in. She isn't asking you to tell her now. The noise of the engine, the presence of Gogol, prevents further discussion of the matter. You have time to think, to consider how much she needs to know, how much she *should* know.

Gogol taps your knee, leans over to whisper something to you. His main English word: *where?* Not where are we, you presume, but where are we going? You explain that you – the two of you – are going to a place called Germany. That it will be safer there.

Marta, overhearing, reaches up to a shelf above her windscreen and brings down a book. It's a map book of the waterways in the Czech Republic. Locking the wheel, she lets the boat steer its own course momentarily while she flips through the pages, soon finding the one she wants, before handing it to you. It's the two-page spread depicting the area around Prague.

You hold it open on your lap, point out to Gogol your approximate location. The map is deliberately simplified, with limited detail of the topography, not intending to show any differentiation between buildings, or streets. Prague is a pink blob, around which snake the various streams and tributaries of the Vltava. It is startling, the complexity and number of waterways, so many usually left out of regular motorway or tourist maps. The whole image reminds you of the book Gogol was studying the night before – a heart in close-up, with the accompanying tangle of blood vessels, some wide and vital, arterial; others thin as capillaries. Our circulatory systems, at least in that respect, seem to mimic the natural water systems.

You trace your finger along the large vein of the Vltava – for Gogol's benefit as much as your own. Pause at the junction, north of Prague, where it meets the Elbe, then continue further west along the Elbe, past Litomerice, and Ústí nad Labem, and Děčín, and beyond to Germany. To see what lies in that direction you have to turn the page. Dresden is quite near the border – another pinkish heart, entangled with the veins of waterways, roadways. You tap it, showing Gogol. There. We are going there. You don't explain it's only a waypoint, the place you'll have to disembark, find other transport – it seems too complicated. Besides, you harbour the hope – the *belief* – that if you reach Dresden, get out of the Czech Republic without them deducing your plan, then you will be safe. You will make it out.

You half expect him to ask about Disneyland, but he doesn't. Just bites his lip and stares at the destination. Maybe he's come to understand that Disneyland doesn't factor into this. He's too perceptive, too attuned, to have not guessed much more is at stake than that.

You lean forward, ask Marta how long the journey will take, having to raise your voice over the engine. She tells you tourist cruise boats do it in seven days – when puttering at a leisurely pace of ten or fifteen miles a day, stopping in all the cities. You should be able to comfortably do it in two days, with one overnight stop. You nod, relieved. The scale of the map made it look much further.

You ask her if you and Gogol can stand by the bow. She nods, gestures to encourage you. You take his hand and lead him out the back of the wheelhouse, around the side – where the deck is narrow, only about two feet across – and up to the foredeck. You stand together and look down at the water parting silkily around the prow. The reflection no longer shows any buildings. Only trees, hills, openness.

Two days. Just two days to safety. And from there: Britain, Wales, Ceredigion. Home. A new life. You put your hand on Gogol's shoulder. Staring far ahead along the smoothly flowing river, you can almost see it, like a mirage reflected in the water surface.

terezín

At lunch you stop near Litomerice. Marta adjusts the throttle and rotates the wheel, deftly turning the boat a hundred and eighty degrees, so the prow is pointed upriver before she drops anchor. Currents push the boat back until the anchor chain goes taut, holding you in place as the river flows by. It's snowing harder now and the cloud layer has thickened. There's no definition to the sky. No sense of freedom, like when you last left Prague. This time it feels as if the inversion layer has expanded, followed you. You're making progress, you're moving, but you can't escape the sense of claustrophobia and confinement.

Marta has brought lunch: ham and coleslaw sandwiches, crisps, a can of Coke for Gogol, beer for you and her. You go below deck, where there's a small cabin, typical of what you'd find in an old trawler. The galley is just big enough for two adults and a child, with a square table on a single post, and bench-seats. A two-burner camp stove. Directly opposite, a hatch opens into a V-shaped sleeping berth nestled at the prow of the boat.

The meal begins in silence, the only sound that of chewing and slurping echoing the lap and slop of currents against the hull. Gogol eats far more slowly than you have come to expect. At first you think this is due to the fact that he is simply no longer starving. But he is also distracted, gazing vacantly around the cabin. Another new experience. He's never been on a boat before, and to him the existence of this small living space tucked within it must be amazing – a magic trick.

Marta asks him something in Ukrainian and he shakes his head. She asks another question, and he swallows, nods vigorously. You look at her, curious and a little envious. She can communicate with him in these simple ways that have eluded you. She explains to you that she asked him if he has ever fished, and if he would like to.

Then it's Gogol's turn to ask her something, his voice a quiet but firm warble, looking from you to her. You pick out a word that sounds like 'Maty'. Hearing it, Marta's face creases into a smile. A soft chuckle. She shakes her head, no. She says Gogol wanted to know if she was your mother. Unabashed, he asks something else. That same word. *Maty*.

This time she doesn't answer right away, but looks to you. Explains that he asked if you are going to be *his* mother. Her tone, in passing this on, is cautious, neutral.

'Yes,' you say, unquestioning. 'I will be.' It sounds like a vow. Then, you ask her how to say it in Ukrainian, so you can convey it in his language, his words: *Ya tvoya maty*.

He smiles widely, showing his tarnished teeth, and it feels fierce and bright and warm as sunlight.

'*Dobrý*,' Marta says, and drains the rest of her beer in toast. 'Now, we fish.'

With a delicate burp she stands, and pulls herself up the step-ladder that leads to the wheelhouse, going out on deck. You put your own beer aside, not willing to risk losing an edge, sinking into complacency. While you and Gogol finish eating, you hear her up there, opening and closing compartments, traipsing back and forth. Getting the fishing gear ready – the same as when you went on your day jaunt, the widow's expedition.

As these preparations take place Gogol keeps sneaking shy glances at you. Painfully pleased at the prospect of staying with you, being in your care – not just for the present, but indefinitely.

When everything is ready, Marta returns and motions for Gogol to follow, which he does – leaving the remains of his sandwich. You take it up after him, along with his can of Coke, the act feeling somewhat motherly already. Marta has readied two rods at the stern. She demonstrates to Gogol how to bait the hooks: slicing chunks of sausage with her fisherman's knife, sliding the meat over the barbed hook, and then tossing the float, weight, and bait overboard into the water. The reel makes a ratchet-sound as she spools out lengths of line, sending the little red float bobbing downstream – the strand of filament thin and delicate as spider web.

With the other rod, she repeats the process but gets Gogol to help. He is avid and eager, a swift learner. Once both lines are out, she shows him how to hold his rod – with one hand above the reel and the other below, so it won't be pulled from his grasp. Then she fits her own rod into one of the holders on the stern. Tells him to call her if he gets any bites. He nods, eyes still on the lines, accepting his duty with solemnity.

With that done, Marta turns to you – gestures to the bow. The two of you go up there and stand leaning against the gunnel, from where you can still see Gogol. Marta produces a pack of cigarettes, offers one to you, and lights them both. Your first exhales hang in heavy clouds around you. There's no wind at all, and the river surface appears stagnant. Marta cuts a hand through the smoke decisively, and says, 'Now, you must tell me what is happening.'

You have been thinking about this, waiting for this. There's no reason not to tell her the truth, unless you don't trust her. And if that was the case you wouldn't be on this boat. So you explain, in as concise a way as you can, about meeting Mario and accepting the job and crossing the border and picking up Gogol and realising that they intend to kill him and your decision to not let that happen. You are getting well-versed in the tale, and though it should be shocking, the way you relate it is straightforward, factual. This is simply what has occurred, and where you are at.

You expect Marta to ask about going to the police, but she doesn't and you wonder if, over here, corruption is more commonplace – and your decision *not* to seek help from the authorities therefore an obvious and sensible one.

Marta folds her arms, gnaws angrily on the butt of her still smouldering cigarette. 'We will get you to Dresden,' she says. Then adds something to herself, in Czech, before translating: but will that be far enough? You ask if she thinks they will follow you there, and she snorts – loud and pig-like. She says that, regardless of where Valerie claims they are from, they are most likely Belarusians, or Chechens. It's clear they're powerful and established and can't allow you to cross them without repercussions. And if they'll kill a child, then they'll do anything. Whatever it takes. Such people always make you pay, eventually. She states these things with a certainty and bitterness that implies she speaks from experience. She'd told you her husband died of heart failure, that their business was going under. But now you wonder: what made his heart fail? Maybe he took on a bad loan, which he was unable to pay back. Maybe he was in debt to people like Valerie and Pavel. People who found other ways to make him pay.

If so, she doesn't confide in you, and you don't pry; it's not the past that matters now. In looking ahead, and thinking it through, it occurs to you that Marta could rent you a car in Dresden. Your money, her name. You suggest this and Marta has no problem with it. She is going to help, any way she can; she is committed. But she also seems to understand what you are up against. Having discussed it in such plain terms, the severity of the situation is clear as the frozen air, to both of you.

You glance to the stern, where Gogol is dutifully manning the lines, looking too small for the adult deck chair. You admit to Marta that you can't understand it. Can't *fathom* it. How this could be something they want to do, and presumably have done – the murder and mutilation of people, of children, for body parts. Marta gazes at you for a long time, either considering your words or how best to respond. She points with her cigarette, off the starboard side, towards shore. Beyond the sedge grasses and nearby wheat fields, some buildings are visible in that direction. That is Terezín, she tells you. You have heard of this place?

You have, but can't recall why, or when. So she explains. That during the Second World War it was converted into a ghetto for Jews deported from other areas of Czechoslovakia, Austria and Germany, and beyond. It was presented as a fully functioning town, with schools, shops, places of work, a doctor, a dentist. The International Red Cross was invited to inspect it, to attend theatre shows, performances by the Jewish orchestra, to observe the community spirit, the well-adjusted citizens, to see all the children doing their schoolwork, playing sports and games. Terezín demonstrated that what was taking place under the Third Reich, there and elsewhere, was truly a 'relocation' – not anything worse, as some were saying, as the rumours implied. The inspectors went away happy, wrote up reports full of praise.

You listen to all this grimly, your fingers prickling.

Marta proceeds to explain that Terezín was merely a show town, of course – a charade. With limited capacity. Most of the children, the musicians, the teachers, the townsfolk were sent on to Auschwitz, to Bełżec, to Treblinka. To make room for the next citizens, and the next.

Now Terezín is preserved, a museum: tourists can visit and see the buildings, the theatre, the orphanage, the drawings done by the children. Read about where they ended up, how each one died – at one of those places, sometimes just weeks after completing a picture of grassy fields, a shining sun, smiling stick figures.

Marta taps her cigarette. Ash falls from it, lands unceremoniously at your feet.

'These are the things humans do,' she says.

And it's true. Stark, brutal, undeniable. There are no explanations, no words. No point in discussing it further. The two of you walk solemnly back to the stern. Gogol is still sitting very still, diligently overseeing the lines. Marta calls to him, questioning, and he shakes his head, no. So far, no bites, no nibbles. She tells you that it's time to go; it's best to keep moving. She's going to start the engine, raise the anchor, but Gogol is welcome to sit back here, watch the lines, trawl for a while. She has to proceed slowly, anyway – speed on the river is limited, and it would be foolish to draw attention by breaking the law.

From below deck the steady rumble-thrum of the engine begins, followed by the slow grinding of the anchor chain, link over link. A backwash of water from the stern as the propeller churns, and the boat is moving once again. You sit out on deck with Gogol. Watch the lines trailing after the boat, dropping to the surface about twenty metres back, between the endlessly parting wake. The two floats mark the point of contact, bobbing and dipping on the foam. They strike you as discretely menacing. So bright and red and friendly and obvious. Yet underneath, hidden from view, hangs the weight, the bait, the fatal hook. The real danger is always hidden from view, always kept out of sight.

evil

You puzzle over the nature of evil, as you chug down the slow-flowing river between snow-covered fields and frosted trees that lean out from shore, seeking the light of a sun that isn't visible. While Gogol regards his fishing rods, you smoke a short way off, peering into the depths. All is dark, murky, opaque. There are evil deeds, but are there evil people? What Marta told you of Terezín seems evidence enough. A fake town, a halfway house on the way to the concentration camps. Everybody being made to perform, play their parts, before being sent on.

All those children.

You look over at the child beside you, staring so intently at his lines. Hoping for a catch, as if it's all that matters in the world. And maybe it is. Food is a matter of survival, after all. You would like to think he is blissfully oblivious to evil, to the things that men do, but of course he is not. He knows it better than you. Has lived through much more than you.

You take a long drag on your cigarette, your fingers numb except for where they touch the filter, feel the heat of the smoke passing through. You'd like to believe otherwise, but you know that the abuse and cruelties he has suffered are part of human nature – just as much as the nurturing, caring instincts. Both sides are in us. And under certain conditions brutality and callousness and sadism can spread, take over, metastasize.

How else to explain Terezín, the camps, the Nazis?

You don't know enough about that, the psychology that enables it. But you know – we all know – that even amid those horrors there were those helping, trying to counteract it. Hiding families in attics, in cellars. Or working to secure safe passage. For friends, for relatives, for strangers. Or else simply refusing to inform, to comply, to give up others.

People trying to do what they could, to save those they could.

Gogol looks over, perhaps sensing your scrutiny, and you smile through a cloud of smoke. He extends a hand, asking for the cigarette, and you hesitate. You've told him you're going to be his mother: when will you start acting like it, fretting about his penchant for smoking – as well as so many other concerns, aside from pure survival?

You compromise. Hand him the cigarette, but hold up a finger. One drag. He nods, seeming to understand. Draws deeply, making the most of it, before checking his line, huddled in his coat and hat. A miniature version of a fisherman. A boy playing dress-up. An image you'll remember, you know. The boy as man: everything he could be, could become. After his one drag, he obediently hands the cigarette back to you.

This gives you an idea. While you watch the lines, on the smooth floating stillness of the river, you teach him numbers

251

in English, demonstrating with your fingers: one, two, three, four. Ticking them off on your hands, and then doing the same to his. The lightness of that touch, fingertip to fingertip. His cuticles still ringed with a grime that doesn't seem to wash off.

He is an apt pupil. Gets it quickly – recites them back to you. Then, shyly, he holds up a single finger and says, '*Odyn.*' His word. One. You nod. He's right. This has to be a two-way exchange. You hold up your fingers, reverse the game, let him count them for you, inducting you into his language: *odyn, dva, try, chotyry.* The words difficult and awkward in your mouth. Not easy. And it won't be. None of it will be.

In the middle of your lesson, Gogol's fishing line goes taught and the rod leaps off his knees, skittering to the deck. No time to wonder, just react. He's quicker than you. Diving on it suddenly, not grasping the handle but just grabbing the entire rod as if wrestling a snake, the line whizzing out now, and you joining him, taking hold of the handle, trying to slow the reel, both of you side by side on the damp cold deck, laughing and shouting, panicked and breathless and exuberant. You call Marta's name, and she leans to peer out of the wheelhouse – then grins at your agitation and mimes a reeling motion, shouting, 'You are fishing, I am steering!'

So it's just the two of you, facing this on your own. And it takes the two of you to slow the whirring reel, halt the progress of the fish. Then, cranking the handle around and around, reeling in line, one inch at a time. An arduous grind. The weight of the fish heavy, steady, but every so often jerking into life, the tip of the rod jittering this way and that. Your fingers, locked over Gogol's on the handle, ache from the strain, sting from the cold. Until finally there's a feeling of release, a sudden bouyancy – the fish has cleared the surface. You both stand, peer over the gunnel. The thing looks so small, after such effort. Not at all like those photos of proud fisherman, cupping a pike as big as their arm, their leg, the length of their whole body. No, this is just a river perch. A foot long. Speckled greyish-green. Pink-finned. Flicking its tail and whipping about, desperate to free itself. You and Gogol swing it over the gunnel, lower it to the deck, where it goes still, stunned, its eyes terrified, its mouth pursing at the hook.

You call to Marta, announcing your success. She takes time to peer from the wheelhouse, nods approvingly, gestures to the tackle box. Where she keeps her hooks and bait, her fish-bat and knife, which she showed you last time. You fetch the bat, squat next to Gogol over the prostrate fish. He is gazing down at it in rapture. You don't know how he'll respond to what happens next, so you talk him through it, mime the act of hitting the thing. Check that he's okay with it, that he doesn't want to throw the fish back.

He doesn't. He just nods, accepting, understanding more than you think, as usual.

Pretending you know what you're doing, you clumsily put a palm on the fish – gripping it when it starts to flap – and tap it with the bat. It jerks, twitches, and you hit it again, harder. Something crunches. Its skull, perhaps. And the fish goes still. A seam of blood appears at its gills. The job done. Gogol pats it, tenderly, as if to say: sorry, little fish. But he doesn't appear sad, or distraught. He gazes up at you, his eyes gleaming, and says another English word, which he has picked up on his own: 'Dinner?'

Yes, you tell him. We'll have it for dinner.

You marvel at his toughness, his resilience. You are trembling, from the excitement of landing the fish, and the thrill of killing it. You have only ever killed flies and bugs and spiders before. This is a new sensation. It lingers as you and Gogol use Marta's knife to extricate the hook from the fish's mouth, then rebait it and let the line out behind the boat again. The perch goes in Marta's cooler, resting curled on a bed of ice, looking strangely peaceful and snug.

You watch the lines with newfound optimism, as the boat carries the two of you towards a snow-coated valley, the hillsides spiked with pines, like the gates of a giant portcullis. You ruminate on swinging the bat, the killing blow. Just a fish. But still. It felt illicit and powerful. To know you have it in you, too, that capacity for life-taking, for death-making.

A soft pressure on your hand. Gogol is holding it, the fingers you counted together, as if sensing your queasy exhilaration. You can feel your pulse through his palm. You can feel, too, the certainty that you will do anything to protect him, will do anything to those who seek to harm him. The knowledge is powerful, all-encompassing, electrifying – as if you've just plugged into a vital current, are charged with life.

All your previous musings regarding good and evil now seem abstract, esoteric. Evil deeds or evil people: it's pure semantics. *They* are evil. Valerie is evil. An evil witch. Just as the man at Gogol's building said. A proclamation you've passed on to her, like a curse. Seeking to commit this small-scale atrocity, to kill a boy – to kill *your* boy. That won't happen. You know it. But you know something else, too. Feel it through the lifeline, the ley-lines, you are plugged into for that brief moment. It jolts you with the power of prophecy. A frozen void. Blood in the snow. A desperate struggle. There will be killing, before all this is through.

The boat floats on, over the placid water. Off the stern a crow arcs like a boomerang through the air, nearly catching itself on the fishing lines before slinging away. Your feeling of clairvoyance fades, dissipating in the cold, but you are left with that ominous sense of an ending. You squeeze Gogol's hand, as if seeking reassurance that you can protect him, be the guardian you need to be, when the times comes.

dinner

The churn and spit of spray. The flecks of foam and whitewash flashing in the dark like tiny teeth. Gnashing the water where the river grows shallow, near the bank.

You've moored overnight behind a riverside inn, with a simple dock running parallel to the bank. About a dozen moorage berths. Empty except for two boats, both battened down, covered in blue tarps. This being the off-season, there aren't many holidaymakers or sightseers around. And not many vessels on the river taking long journeys, aside from the cruise boats running from Prague to Dresden, and vice versa. The lack of river traffic worries you, as does the lack of guests staying here, at the inn. It makes you stand out. It makes you feel exposed.

But Marta said dropping anchor, as you'd done for your lunch stop, wasn't an option overnight. It was illegal, a hazard. Going against that could potentially draw more attention. And trying to navigate the river at night, in this old boat – no satnav, no digital maps, no depth sounder – was not just foolish, but risky and unfeasible.

So a riverside marina or an inn like this was the only option. Marta has gone to sort the moorage fee with the owners, while you and Gogol prepare dinner – the perch he caught. There is satisfaction in the routine: a struck match, the hiss of gas, the little camp stove burner igniting with a whoosh of flame, lacing a circle around the hob. You tell Gogol that he can be your helper, your assistant chef. He imitates these words – *helper, assistant chef* – articulating the syllables slowly. Trying them out. Sounding more confident with his English.

You drizzle oil in a pan, set it on one burner. A pot of water on the other. While both heat up, you get Gogol to peel potatoes, using a rusted peeler from Marta's drawer. Showing him how to do this, without cutting himself, working outwards, away from the other hand. He sets to it with his typical zest. While he does, you get out an onion, slice it on an old white chopping board, cross-hatched with years of marks. Like slashes in a sheet of ice.

When that's done, you brush the pieces into a pan, set them sizzling, and move on to a carrot. You are so fixated on watching Gogol, ensuring he is careful and doesn't cut himself with the peeler, that you forget to pay attention to yourself. Make a basic, beginner's mistake by cutting into the tip of your left thumb.

Not a deep cut, but definitely a cut. The blood comes immediately – appearing along the slice, forming droplets. You swear, turn on the tap, run it under the cold water. The red turns pink, washes off. Spirals around the tin basin, whirlpooling down the drain.

Gogol has stopped peeling to watch, his eyes wide, worried.

'It's okay,' you tell him. 'Just a nick.' Even if it's a little worse than that. Severe enough that you have to wrap it up in a paper towel to continue clumsily prepping the dinner.

When Marta returns, she eyes your bandage – bloody now – but doesn't comment. Just takes over the cooking duties. You are demoted to a second assistant, like Gogol. With her long-bladed fishing knife, she begins gutting the perch. Clean-slicing a line from its gills to tail, prying open the flesh, letting the innards spill out in a glistening bundle. All those tiny organs. This, of course, makes you think of Pavel. The knife not so different to a scalpel. That surgical precision. You shiver. Marta, unaware, tips the guts into the bin, scrapes the rest of the fish clean, then lays the perch in the pan, covers it with a lid. As it fries, the smoke and stink fill the small galley.

When it's done, Marta drizzles the fried fish oil over the potatoes, and dinner is served. The perch meat is firm and white, with a mild, almost sweet flavour. Gogol chews the first few bites thoughtfully, considering – another new taste for him. Partway through the meal, you notice a drop of blood on your plate and get up to the change the bandage.

Marta finishes first, having devoured her food lustily. Sitting back, she belches and dabs her mouth with a napkin, takes a swig of beer. 'I told the owners,' she says, 'that we have two passengers, two women. The boy, I did not mention. In case these people looking for you have figured out our plans, with the river. You see?'

You do see. You thank her, get up to wash the dishes, but she intervenes, explains it is not good to wash dishes with that thumb. Tells you she'll do the cleaning up, that you can look after the boy.

257

Beneath the galley bench, Marta has some games. Given the choice, Gogol picks chess – an old set with a wooden board and carved stone pieces. Marble and onyx. You show him how to set it up: pawns in front, rooks, knights, bishops and royalty in the back. The rules are difficult to explain without the language, so you attempt to demonstrate – pushing the pieces around, showing him the ways they are meant to move. He watches, follows, imitates. When he's grasped the basics you reset the pieces – black for you, white for him – and play an informal game together. The rules are only loosely applied, but Gogol intently pursues your king, regardless. Then, mid-game, he mischievously plucks his queen from the board and moves her to Marta's map of the waterways, open next to you on the table. Places the piece there, going off-piste. The queen has escaped the boundaries of her board.

You smile, slide her towards your position, nearing Dresden. The endgame. Leaving her there, you play a few more moves before conceding the win to Gogol. It's time for bed.

The two of you are to spend the night in the forward berth – the one shaped in a V. Marta gives you sleeping bags, and lumpy pillows that smell of mildew. After doing Gogol's teeth, you help him into his sleeping bag, lie with him for a time – your feet pointing at the door of the galley, your heads close together in the bow.

Despite having decent sleep the last few days, Gogol still looks pale, fatigued. A lifetime of mistreatment, malnourishment, sleep deprivation – these things won't be remedied in a few days. He lies on his side, very still, gazing at you in the dark. His face a pale moon. His eyes dark hollows. Giving him a grub-like appearance. Something not yet fully formed. He burrows closer in the dark. His hand finds yours and he touches the makeshift bandage on your thumb. 'Okay?' he asks, emphasising the two syllables separately, like two words: O-K.

'Yes,' you tell him. 'I'm okay.'

Heartrending, how easily that reassures him: you say it, and he believes it. And after being comforted he falls asleep immediately. Like narcolepsy – just dropping off.

You extricate your hand from his, slip out the hatch, ease it shut behind you. Marta is doing the dishes, drinking another beer, humming to herself as she washes up, the tiny tin sink brimming with soap suds.

Seeing you, she grunts, reaches for a tea towel. Tells you she ought to take a look at that thumb. You sit across the table from her, feeling foolish as a child yourself, and hold the wounded hand out. She puts on her spectacles, peers downwards at the cut, and frowns. 'It should have a stitch,' she says, but explains she doesn't have a needle in her First Aid kit. What she does have is iodine – the ochre disinfectant you recall from childhood, now largely obsolete but still effective. She splashes it on, and you wince at the sting, accepting your punishment. She dabs it dry – the residue has stained your skin – and puts on a butterfly bandage to compress the wound.

'You need to be careful,' she says, and it sounds both motherly and foreboding.

It occurs to you that you haven't thought of your own mother for some time. It's as if you have severed yourself from that aspect of your life – your past in Britain, in Wales and London. You don't have space in your psyche for it, for the person you used to be.

All you have is this, now. Him, escape, and safety.

With your wound tended to, you and Marta go to have a smoke on deck. You sit huddled in your jackets, the river

259

looking black and still, but movement evident in its sounds – the steady churn, like a cauldron on the boil.

As you sit contemplating your chances, Marta gets out her fishing knife. It has a leather sheath with a strap to hold it in place. She unbuttons the strap, slides the blade free of its sheath. Offers it to you by the handle. Tells you it would be good for you to keep on you.

'For protection,' she says.

You take it. Hold it. Cold as an icicle in your palm but not nearly so heavy. You are surprised by its lightness, its seeming delicacy. You comment on this. Marta grunts – a noise you recognise now as habitual. 'Not heavy, but strong,' she says. 'It will do what needs doing.'

You run your finger along the cutting edge. Marta keeps it sharp – the blade wickedly curved, with a serrated back edge for gutting, scraping. You grip the handle, remembering a similar handle, protruding from Tod's chest. Imagine the stabbing motion that put it there. Just one thrust was all it took. The reaper's rattle. Easy death. Right here, in your hand.

The wound on your thumb throbs. You are gripping the handle too tightly.

'Is Czech,' Marta says, with a hint of pride. 'Finnish steel. Very good.'

Marta takes the weapon back, gently. Brings out a sharpening stone, about the size of a bar of soap. Demonstrates how to hone the blade, running it along first one side, and then the other. The soft rasp of steel on stone. As she does this, she tells you about her husband. That he in fact didn't die of a heart attack – a truth you'd suspected. His heart did stop, she jokes bitterly, when he fell in the Vltava. He had those debts. Their boat business, their apartment lets. It was not going well. He borrowed money, and couldn't pay it back. It was ruled to be an accident, which meant she got the insurance. And maybe it was. Or maybe it was accidental suicide, or accidental murder. Either way, they killed him – this she knows.

The tale both similar and different to what you'd imagined, though you don't mention this, and don't question Marta about the people her husband owed. It's clear it wasn't Valerie and Pavel, just as it's clear that it must have been the same kind of people.

Marta re-sheaths the knife, hands it to you along with the sharpening stone, which is to be yours, as well. 'It is important they don't get their way,' she says. 'It is important that we all do what we have to do.'

You accept this gift, and this wisdom. You think of your cut thumb, of all the little lapses in attention you've had along the way. You can't only focus on Gogol; self-sacrifice won't be enough. If you don't survive, he won't either. Your fates are entwined, now, like strands in a rope.

closer to the end

Hoar frost has settled on the tie lines, stiffened the knots. With numb fingers you pry at the hitches, having to work each loop before it will loosen. The sky grey and flat and featureless, dark as flint rock. Paling slightly towards the east. No sign of the sun, and there won't be: the arrival of dawn must be deduced, inferred. The smokestack of the boat sticks up in stark silhouette, spewing a black column that widens as it rises. The engine rumbling, ready.

You awoke in the dark, the cold. A small shape curled towards you, seeking warmth. Your feet gone numb. Marta warned you of this – the boat's heating system runs off the engine, so overnight the cold creeps in, stealthily. It was like waking up in a freezer. You felt Gogol shivering, wrapped him in an extra layer of duvet. And you came out here, on deck, at Marta's request. Time to go. Time to cast off. Time to head for Dresden.

The final knot loosens, slackens, allows you to undo it. Gathering the line, you toss it on deck, where it lands heavily, like a coiled snake. You palm the gunnel, vault it – more confident in doing this now – and Marta begins reversing the boat out of its berth.

While departing, you watch the docks, the gangplank, the premises. Staying vigilant. The marina is directly behind the rear of the inn. You can imagine this as a lively stopping spot, during tourist season. But now there's hardly anybody around. Except, up on the back porch, near the bar area, you notice a man standing by the rail. Smoking a cigarette. Looking down. At the morning view of the river, or at you? Impossible to tell in the half-light. His face is obscured by shadow, marked by the cherry-red tip of his cigarette. Like a single eye.

You raise your hand in acknowledgement. Testing. There is no response. Either he is not looking at you, or is pretending not to. Either way, the inn will have a record of your stay. And it might be possible to track you using the name of Marta's boat, painted so obviously on the hull. She had to use it to check in, along with her own name, as the registered owner. A few phone calls, or somebody acting as lookout, and they'll know where you've been, and be able to guess where you're going.

As Marta navigates the boat downriver, you join her in the wheelhouse. You start asking her about these concerns but she shakes her head. Tells you, tersely, that the river here is still narrow, and steering by sight in the half-light requires all her attention. You go to make coffee, and while the kettle heats up you check on Gogol – still sleeping – and study Marta's map of waterways. Gogol's chess piece from last night, the white queen, still marks the spot where you were moored at the inn. You adjust it, slide it downriver.

Soon you'll cross the German border and, shortly after, you'll arrive in Dresden. You haven't thought about that enough, about what happens next.

One step at a time is not enough. You need to think two, three steps ahead. Like a good chess player. You pick up the queen, jump it to Dresden, to Bruges, to Calais, to London. Still such a long way to go. And if you think too far ahead, you may miss what's happening now, right in front of you. How to do both?

You hold the queen in your palm a moment, feeling the weight of the marble.

The kettle is boiling, screaming for attention. You twist the camp stove burner off, fill two mugs with instant coffee, and take one up to Marta, who accepts it wordlessly. You cradle yours, feeling the warmth of the liquid seeping through the ceramic, passing into your fingers. When you put it on the dash, the steam creates a cloud on the windscreen.

Dawn turns to early morning. In time, the river widens, becomes more languorous in its flow, and the landscape changes. The banks rise steeply, lined with spruce and alder, and plateau in frozen fields – possibly for cattle or sheep, though no livestock are in sight. You sense a change in Marta too – the dissolution of tension. A more casual driving stance. You wait for her to speak. When she does, it seems she too has been thinking ahead.

'In Dresden,' she says, 'we must get you both to the car rental agency. Quickly. No time to waste.' You ask her if she thinks they've figured out your plan, and may be following, and she says that whether they have or haven't doesn't matter, you need to act as if they have. Then, as an afterthought, she adds that it will be best to stay in public places, and public spaces. They are less likely to try anything drastic with witnesses around.

'We will get you a car,' she says confidently, 'and you will go.'

'What will you do?'

She says she is due a vacation. She will likely keep going. Up the Elbe. Maybe all the way to Hamburg. She has always wanted to see Hamburg. You don't ask her when she'll go back. You fear that she may not be able to. Giving up her apartment lets, her home. Her whole way of life. All to help you.

You thank her, again, as earnestly as before, and her response is just as nonchalant.

'How is the boy?' she asks.

'Cold.'

'He should eat, drink. Keep his energy up.'

You gather the mugs, feeling chastised – being absent in your mothering. And take them down, drop them in the sink. You enter the cabin with the intention of waking Gogol up. But once you shake him, and he fails to stir, you find yourself lying down next to him. He is completely huddled in his sleeping bag, downy dyed-blonde hair poking out the top. Like the furry head of a caterpillar.

You lay with an arm around him and stare at the hatch overhead that allows in a small square of daylight. The glass glazed with frost. Slowly thawing as the cabin heats up. It occurs to you that something is different from last night: you can feel the engine, rumbling not just through the mattress but all around you – in the hull, the walls, the deck. The engine has its own thrumming rhythm that seems to rise and fall. You feel safe and secure in here. A single vessel floating down this artery of Europe. You check your watch, tell yourself you can afford five minutes. No thoughts of Dresden, no thoughts of being caught, or escaping. Just this womb-like comfort, rocking on the water, in the belly of a boat, the slow pulse of the engine reverberating right through your flesh and bones. Gogol, sensing your nearness, wriggles closer without peeking out of his bag – just finding you intuitively.

In time, you become aware of something jutting into your hip, hard and uncomfortable. You shift position, pat the mattress. Feel in your pocket. The chess piece. You tucked it in there when the kettle boiled. You remove it now. Study it. The solemn marble queen. A crown on top of her head. A face white and nearly featureless, emotionless. Hollows for eye sockets. Despite being in your pocket, she feels cool to the touch. A snow queen. A reminder of who you must be, to get through this. You stand up, gripping her tightly, like a talisman.

dresden

The city appears in miniature on the horizon, emerging from the snow and haze. A vague jumble of shapes. Not as striking as Prague, from afar. Far fewer towers, spires, and turrets. Far more blocks, squares, and rectangles. Not a postcard city – not like *the city of a hundred spires* – but a city that's more practical, functional. Or so it seems.

Gogol comes to join you at the bow, stands beside you in silence. Perhaps sensing your apprehension, picking up on your anxiety, in that way children can. Or in the way he can.

For you, Dresden is an unknown. Dresden is merely a collection of images, imprints. Not a real city yet – since you've never visited it – but a reported and recorded city. The impression of a city created through books, and media. All you've heard of Dresden is what most people have heard: the Allied attack, the firebombing. Firebombing that turned into a devastating inferno, ravaging the city. Indiscriminate annihilation. Not military targets or resources, but houses, hospitals, schools. Men, women, children. Civilians. Innocents.

You eye the dull sky uneasily, picture bombs scattered like seeds, dropping towards the earth. Flowering into towers of flame. Blossoming billows of smoke. You put an arm around Gogol's frail shoulders, instinctively, as if that would be enough to shield him from such an onslaught, or any unforeseen attack, calamity, disaster.

This the mistaken belief of parents throughout history, that they are all-powerful, that they can somehow protect their own child from harm. Like the figures of Pompeii – the child turned towards its mother, the mother embracing it, seeking to shield it from a volcanic explosion, the obliterating waves of ash and hot gas. An apocalypse.

The poignant impossibility of that.

The parents of Dresden must have done the same. Still seeking to save their children. Right up to the hopeless end. And yet, the city is here, again. After the war came the rebuilding. Reconstruction. A chance to start anew, all over again. You hope that's what Dresden represents.

That idea – of rebuilding, reconstruction – reminds you of that physics class, of time unwinding. Something your teacher said about an author who wrote about Dresden, describing the firebombing in reverse, just like the film clips. The flames on the ground diminishing, extinguishing. Damage miraculously repairing. Buildings rising, reassembling. Bombs leaping up like fleas, to be drawn straight into the bays of the planes with magnetic, magical force. The squadrons returning to their bases, landing. Time flowing further and further back, like a river reversing its course.

You gaze down into the river beneath you, at the reflection of Dresden there. Shimmering and rippling. Hard to tell which way the water is actually flowing. The Elbe could be running south towards the Vltava, pulling Marta's boat with it. All the way back past Terezín to Prague. Disembarking. Bidding goodbye to Marta. Driving back across Slovakia to Ukraine. Dropping off Gogol, leaving him to his fate. Mario reanimating – the magician reappears. And for you a return to indifference, a return journey to Prague, then all the way to London. And further, further back. To before the funeral, up to that night. The knife in Tod's chest. Removing it. Getting off that bus. The cinema. Walking backwards with him, walking back to your house, your life, still waiting.

And yet. You wouldn't go back even if you could.

This, the stark truth. This, not a betrayal of Tod but an acceptance. An understanding. What's real, what matters, is this moment here, looking towards Dresden. Your arm around Gogol's shoulders. Believing it's the beginning of your journey with him, not the end.

When Gogol points to the city, you explain that you will be getting off the boat there, renting a car. You mime the act of steering a wheel, to make it clear. Try to imitate the sound of an engine. We drive. We drive home.

He considers this. Then, falteringly, asks, 'Where is home?'

It is the most complex sentence you've heard him say in English. Articulated slowly, deliberately, it has a profound aura about it. Like a proverb or Buddhist mantra. You begin to say that home is Britain, Wales. Not London, but the hills of Ceredigion. The sight of the sea. But then you stop, knowing none of that means anything to him. So, you simply place your palm on his chest, and then on yours. That is home. Your home. His home. Together. Like another old proverb: where the heart is.

He smiles, accepting this explanation. Knowing it to be true.

A faint tapping behind you. Marta is knocking on the windscreen from within. She motions for you, beckoning you inside. You go join her, bringing Gogol with you. She says the boy should stay below deck as you enter the city. No sense taking chances.

You lead him down there, get out the chess board for him. Help him arrange the pieces. The two of you found time for a rematch after breakfast. As with your homemade memory game, Gogol has picked up the rules quickly. Needs no further coaching on the moves. You tell him you can't play with him this time, but he seems content to try on his own, shifting and sliding the pieces around, playing both sides. The dark king and queen against the light. Trapped on the board in their small-scale, endless struggle. You leave him to it.

Up in the wheelhouse, Marta explains that she knows of two places to dock in Dresden: the marina in the city centre, and another further out, south-east of the city – the direction of your approach. Though the central marina is closer to public transit links, and car rental agencies, she thinks it would be prudent to dock on the outskirts, make your way from there. If you've been noticed on the river, or if they've figured out that Dresden is your potential destination, they will most likely be watching the main marina. They may not even know of the other, which is smaller, not used by tourists and cruise ships. A spot for local vessels, with a members' club and long-term moorings, but also a few overnight and casual berths.

All this makes sense to you; you have no reason to doubt Marta's judgement, and are encouraged by the impression that she may know something they don't, may even know a bit more about Dresden, which isn't their home turf. Later, perhaps, you will think back, and wonder if there were mistakes made along the way. Or perhaps know that mistakes were made, but be uncertain what they were. Such is the benefit, or curse, of hindsight. But, for now, you must trust, and hope, and believe this is the right course of action, the *only* course of action. This is the path that leads to safety.

mooring up

The marina sits within a wide, oxbow bend that has been extended and expanded. Divided from the rest of the river by a pair of breakwaters – imposing jumbles of stone and concrete block, mottled with algae, rising from the water like the pincers of a giant rock crab. Boats must pass between to reach the docks and wharf. The marina isn't meant for larger vessels; the entrance deliberately narrow to limit access to crafts like yours.

As Marta steers towards the gap, she instructs you to stand on the foredeck, to ensure she doesn't grind the hull or gunnels against the breakwaters – there is only about a foot leeway on either side. You stand ready to act as fender, pushing off against the edges if needed, but Marta negotiates the passage expertly, without incident.

Once you're through, you begin to flip the buoys over the side, letting them dangle and bounce against the hull as

Marta chugs towards the short-term berths. The marina is the largest you've passed on the Elbe, perhaps fifty or sixty vessels, arranged in a maze-like grid of floating docks. Many of the boats are not in use, the windscreens covered in blue tarpaulin, the hatches battened down, the sails stripped to the rigging. But a few boats have people on them, and others are being cleaned, or repaired – either by the owners or tradesmen.

The short-term berths are on the far side, near the members' club and office. On the approach, Marta drops the throttle into reverse, expertly slowing to stillness. Points to the bow, barks an order at you. Taking the rope, you clamber awkwardly over the forward gunnel – there is a four-foot drop to the deck – and manage to lash the line to a cleat, though in your rush and nervousness you forget the knots Marta has taught you, instead simply looping the line in a series of figure eights. It seems to hold.

By then, Marta is already out of the wheelhouse, tossing the other lines down to the dock for you to tie off. When that's all done you climb back aboard. Your hands are numb and you're breathing hard, your throat filled with the copper-penny taste of cold.

Marta tells you she will go pay the moorage fee, and while she does you head below deck to get Gogol ready. He's still engrossed with his one-man chess game, having eliminated the majority of the pieces from both sides, except for the kings, queens, and a pair of pawns. The empty board is a field stripped of its variables and options. Pared back to a final confrontation, leading to the only – and maybe inevitable – outcome.

You tell him it's time to go. Go – another word he now understands. He doesn't complain at all, but is happy to leave the board set up like that, frozen in stasis, the two sides still at a deadlock. You pull on his hat, work his arms into his jacket. Fit his shoes and cinch the laces – the distressing thought floating to you: *he may need to run*. You both may need to run, before this is through, so it's best if his shoes are tightly laced.

Your duffel bag is packed, ready. Near your bed. You go fetch it, but before bringing it above deck you unzip it, take out the knife. It's no use in there, out of reach. You check its sheath, try fitting it in the back pocket of your jeans, or the pouch of your hoody. Neither suits. The best place is the inner pocket of your jacket. For easy access. Snug against your chest, near your heart. It fits like an extra rib. Nice and discrete and light. But weighted, too.

You hear footsteps up top, on deck, and Marta calls down into the galley, 'We go now, yes?' The urgency evident in her tone. You sling the duffel bag over your shoulder, step back into the galley, smile encouragingly at Gogol. Motion for him to precede you up the steps. You're half-expecting some terrible twist – to walk out on deck and see Pavel, or one of Valerie's other men holding Marta with a knife at her throat. Having walked right into their trap.

But no, Marta is standing alone, waiting anxiously at the port side, sucking avidly on a cigarette. Hearing you, she turns to take a look, and nods approvingly. 'Good,' she says, then repeats in Ukrainian for Gogol. She flicks her cigarette over the side, and you hear the fizzle-hiss as it hits the water.

You walk down the narrow docks in single file, winding your way through a maze of vessels and masts that tip back and forth, clinking and clacking, like giant metronomes all in a row, all in unison. A man sitting on the deck of a pleasure cruiser, braiding a rope, looks up as you pass and raises his hand. Nothing menacing in it at all, just the friendly gesture of one boater to another. Marta waves back politely.

Then up a gangplank and along the wharf – wider, built on sturdy pilings and paved with concrete – towards the members' club, a chain-link fence, a parking lot full of new saloons and hatchbacks. Glossy and polished as beetles. An upmarket marina, the members seemingly affluent. Though you know it could well be misleading, this puts you at ease – the presence of money, of wealth, of people who are valued by society. The seeming safety and security of the place.

Here, surely, you won't be accosted or attacked without somebody noticing.

As you walk, you hold Gogol's hand tightly, your fingers interlaced with his. Marta explains that she asked about transport when registering for the berth, and there's a bus station nearby. The three of you can catch a bus to a car rental agency in Blasewitz – an eastern borough, quite close. It seems a good plan. A way of avoiding the city centre entirely. She is talking as she walks, and you are listening so closely – caught up in the seeming ease of it, the allure of it all working out – that you don't notice anybody behind you until an arm loops around your shoulders, as if in congenial greeting – *just an old friend!* – and something sharp and cold and hard is stinging your lower back. It feels physically wrong, the pain so intense.

'Keep walking towards the car.'

These words, murmured warmly in your ear. Then something about a scalpel, and your kidneys. You know the voice. That soft falsetto. Pavel. Her musician and surgeon. You can smell his sweat and cologne, his breath and nearness. When you try to look over – at Marta, and Gogol – Pavel's arm tightens, squeezing pressure on your neck, keeping you looking ahead and moving ahead. Gogol's hand still clenched in yours; they haven't tried to separate you. Perhaps knowing they don't need to. They have you now. They have you both.

This, the nightmare. This, everything you feared. Waiting for you all along, here in Dresden. But how strange – now that it's happening it feels not just probable but inevitable, something that *had* to happen. And yet, you're not defeated by it. Your heart flutter-pulsing, yes. Your brain dizzy with fear, with surging blood and oxygen, yes. But the knife still weighing in your pocket, hidden, undetected. The hope of that, the possibilities it implies. A desperate, fervent belief that this is not finished, that you can still get out of this. Somehow.

Not yet – you can't reach for the knife. Even if you could, you wouldn't be able to use it in time. You are disposable. Only Gogol is valuable. They would not think twice about simply doing away with you, and Marta too. A glimpse of her then, in your peripheral vision. Still with you. Her face tight with fear. Somebody else guiding her, forcibly.

This occurs to you: the only reason you and Marta are being kept alive – and may be kept alive for some time – is so you can be punished, tortured. Like Mario.

Their car is just ahead now – you're approaching it. Moving on automatic legs. All of it feeling slow and dazed, a hallucination. Impressions of a beige, non-descript vehicle. A standard SUV. Wheel wells spattered with slush. Expensive, but not flashy – not attention-grabbing. Deliberately unobtrusive. Tinted windows. No sense of what or who is inside. The back door opening, the interior dark as a cavern, into which you are forced to enter.

a long drive

Pine-scented air freshener; leather polish; cigarette smoke; sweat; nerves; the possibility of violence; blood and death; hopelessness; fear. These are the things the vehicle smells like. It is spacious inside, wider than a normal car. Wide enough to accommodate three seats in the front. With an extended rear hatch. Hearse-like. You and Gogol have been put in the back. Gogol against the door, and you in the middle. The man called Pavel easing himself in beside you. Transferring the blade he has against your back to your side. Doing it quite casually, quite naturally. In profile his features are sharp, bony. A ridge of nose. A pointed chin. Those thin lips. He's so close you can see the hairs in his nostrils, the way they quiver when he breathes.

Marta is being put into the front by another man, with a shaved head. The stubble fine as wires. Big, bulging eyes.

Mario's old accomplice, Denis. Denis the Menace. He has a gun in his hand – a small pistol. He waves it towards the front seat and, when Marta hesitates, he merely forces her in next to the driver. Manoeuvring her in a practiced, impersonal way.

Beside you, Gogol does not cry or whimper. Instead, he has gone quiet, tense. Sensing the threat, the potential for violence in this situation. Relying on his instinctive stillness and suppressing any signs of fear. His way of playing possum. He knows drawing attention only makes it worse.

The doors lock; the engine starts.

Caught so easily, led so willingly. You wonder if you should have shouted, screamed, kicked and struggled. Would Pavel have stabbed you, silenced you, killed you, in a parking lot at a marina, in plain view, during the middle of the day?

Directly in front of you is the driver's seat. The driver a small woman, hunched forward. Wearing a flat-cap and leather gloves. Perhaps this is even her main role, in their organisation – a dedicated driver. She turns to look behind her, backing up, and you see she has a gaunt face, her cheeks pockmarked with acne scars. While she reverses, she gazes past you, beyond you. As if she hasn't even registered your presence. As if you aren't really there. Or are invisible, to her.

Not so Denis. He catches your eye, and smiles – showing his small yellowed teeth. Says it is a happy day for him. Apparently not having forgotten how you embarrassed him that night, when he slipped on the ice. You ask him, quite calmly, if he knows what they did to his friend. He leers, shakes his head.

'Not my friend,' is what he says.

Then the car is moving forward, turning out of the parking lot. Accelerating. The ride eerily smooth. Cushioned by big four-wheel drive tires, faultless shocks and suspension. As if floating. A magic carpet ride.

You're breathing heavily, without even knowing it. The situation both unbearably fraught and somehow banal, boring. An everyday drive. You turn your head, just enough to look over at Gogol. His eyes are on you, only you. Hoping. Hoping this is okay, or will be okay. Hoping you have a solution, a way out. But you have neither.

You have a knife, but that's it.

And you also have a knife in your ribs. Or a scalpel, if Pavel is to be believed.

Where his blade jabbed your back, you can feel a wetness. A leeching, burning sting. The slow bleed of a flesh wound. You ask if you can put Gogol's seat belt on, and you ask this of Pavel – assuming that he is in charge. He doesn't bother to reply. Your idea is that if you can reach across Gogol, you might be able to grab the door handle, tug it open, jump out with Gogol. Maybe when the car slows down to turn a corner, or at a light. Then run. Scream for help.

Madness. You don't even know if the door opens from the inside. It would be stupid, on their part, if it did. You try again anyway, telling him that Gogol is valuable. 'Valerie won't be happy if he gets hurt,' you say.

Pavel removes his glasses and massages his temples with his slim fingers, as if he has a headache. As if your words are like the buzzing of a mosquito: irritating and inconsequential. 'Please stop talking,' he says, so softly it is difficult to hear. 'Please stop talking to me. The boy does not need a seatbelt. We are not going to crash, are we, Lenka?'

'We are not going to crash,' the driver says. Lenka.

Unwilling to leave it – to resign yourself to silence – you ask where you're going.

Pavel says, 'You are going where you are going.'

Denis snorts at this. 'You are going to the lake,' he says loudly. 'To have a vacation. To swim. To fish. To swim with the

279

fish.' At this cleverness he laughs. A loud and loutish sound.

Pavel politely tells him to please shut his mouth, and Denis does. Pavel replaces his glasses, pushes them up the bridge of his nose with a forefinger, ending the interlude.

Outside, a wide, snowy boulevard. Shrubs and bushes dusted with white. Rows of residential houses, all modern pastels. A few errant, fluttering flakes of snow. The whole scene pleasant and wintry. And through it you move, locked in a hearse, rolling steadily towards your fate.

Unless you can think of something. Do something.

Try. You have to try. You tell Gogol it is going to be okay – speaking clearly and earnestly – and let go of his hand, for the first time, so you can reach over to pat his knee – the one closest to the door. Afterwards, you slide your hand a few inches further, fumbling for the handle. Your fingertips have just touched cool chrome when you feel a sharp sting, wasp-like, against your ribs. Pavel murmurs that you are not to try anything idiotic like that, or he will simply stab you, deeper. Your fingers linger on the handle, longingly.

'It doesn't matter if you bleed,' he says. 'As long as you are alive.'

You let go. 'So you can torture me,' you say. Your voice flat, emotionless.

He makes a sound in his throat, acknowledging the truth of this. He studies you to see how you will react and, when you don't, he nods, as if in grudging approval. Maybe he's accustomed to victims begging, pleading, beseeching, and appreciates your impassiveness, since he surprises you by mumbling an ominous apology. Explaining he would rather not. It is simply a result of what has happened. The trouble you've caused. Valerie cannot allow such a thing to occur.

You ask him how much further you have to drive, but the simpatico moment between you has passed. He shakes his head, so slight it seems like a twitch. No more questions.

Time passes. The car rolls on. The scenery changes. Buildings giving way to empty lots. A proposed development, the fencing draped in large posters, renderings of what the area will look like, one day soon. Two-bedroom terraces and three-bedroom detached houses. Smiling children and laughing parents. A communal park. None of the houses completed yet, none of the foundations laid. All of it a frozen dream right now.

Pavel reaches into his jacket pocket for a mobile, thumbs through the numbers to speed dial. Somebody answers, and he mumbles something in their language. Letting Valerie know they have caught you, you suspect. He repeats a word that sounds affirmative – *dah, dah* – and then hangs up.

Denis reaches forward and turns on the stereo, as if he has been waiting for this moment. A heavy throbbing bass fills the car, and an explosion of vocals. European techno-pop, wild and frenzied, the words lost on you except for the nonsensical chorus in English – *Love you love me love us love them love everyone love forever*. The dull beat thudding, thudding, thudding. Loud enough to make the windows vibrate.

You pass the city limits, and Lenka turns smoothly on to a long stretch of road. You discretely study the road signs, trying to keep track of where you are, where you are going. You couldn't tell which direction you travelled from Dresden, but there are frequent signs denoting the distance to the Czech border. It's getting closer, now only thirty miles or so. You're being driven east, maybe back to Prague.

A sound, beside you. Gogol. You look over. His eyes are wide now, anxious. You think the situation has finally become real to him, overwhelmed him. Until you notice that he is sitting with his hands between his legs, squeezing them together. He casts his eyes down, signalling.

He has to go pee, you tell them. Then repeat it, louder, over the music. Pavel says something, and Denis turns down the stereo. Pavel leans forward in his seat, looks across you at Gogol. Murmurs something to him, softly. In Ukrainian, or Russian. Checking the veracity of your claim. When Gogol nods, Pavel sighs.

He and Lenka exchange words, seeming to debate it. Perhaps deciding if Gogol should be forced to pee in his pants. Ultimately, though, Pavel says something to Lenka, who slows down, pulls on to the side of the road. You think this is it, your opportunity. Feel an electric tingle in your scalp, the prickle of anxiety in the build up to movement, action, violence. Maybe what Tod felt, just before the fight on the bus.

Lenka leaves the engine running, gets out. Opens Gogol's door – dutiful as a true chauffeur – and cold air rushes in. The scent of snow. Altitude. Gogol slides down from his seat, is led by Lenka to a fence post a few feet from the road. She holds one hand on Gogol's shoulder as he stands in the cold, and a small stream of urine patters the snow, turning it yellow. You shift your arm, ready to reach for your knife, and Pavel takes a firm hold of your elbow, leans on his blade in your ribs, making you gasp, go rigid. Each time it must be cutting you, going deeper. You just don't know how deep. It's clear there will be no great escape here. Not with Pavel so close, right next to you.

Marta tries anyway. She begins to make a move, attempting to clumsily scramble out Lenka's open door. Seeing this, Denis merely reaches across and catches her by the neck, shaking her like a misbehaving cat. Cracks her head once on the dash. When he releases her she slumps brokenly in her seat. Stunned. Her lesson learnt. Resigned now to confinement.

Gogol is still peeing, has not seen anything. When he finishes, he wades back to the vehicle, sinking up to his knees in the snow. He retakes his seat, shivering. Lenka shuts his door and walks around to her side.

'And you?' Pavel asks you. 'Do you need to go, too?'

You glance at him, to see if it's a taunt. But his eyes, behind those tinted lenses, are unblinking, serious. You try to imagine it. Stepping out, pretending to go, while intending to run. Is this the place, the time? But Gogol will be in the car, with them. You need him with you. You need a better opportunity, better odds. You have to wait, and hope.

You shake your head. No.

Lenka sits back in her driver's seat, releases the handbrake, shifts the gearstick. The car keeps going, that smooth ghosting motion. The sky in front of you is dull and lifeless, glazed with grey. Beneath your coat you can feel the warmth of your own blood on your ribs, and back. The three nicks pulsing persistently, repeatedly. A reminder of the mistakes you've made, and a portent of your pain to come.

the cabin

Rumbling over a gritted track through trees all cowed and snow-bent, like figures twisted in agony. Trapped in purgatory. At the roadside large mounds of snow, stained brown and flecked with grit and dirt. The track descends and becomes rougher, the SUV bucking and rocking, the tyres occasionally spinning before the four-wheel drive kicks in. Where the treeline ends, the terrain levels out and you see that you have indeed been brought to a lake. Maybe a mile across, oval shaped. Possibly man-made. The surface completely grey and frozen except for a dark patch of water in the very centre, like a target.

The lake is encircled by pine and fir, closely bunched, creating a natural barrier. One other vehicle – a black truck – is parked at the end of the track, and on the far shore of the lake sits a cabin. An old A-frame. The roof shingled. A porch out front. Smoke leaking from the stove-pipe chimney. The cabin is innocuous enough, even cosy-looking, but the sight fills you with horror and dread. Simply because this is where they have brought you. This is where it happens. This is their place. Their slaughterhouse.

The truck has its engine running, smoke spewing from the exhaust, spreading into a haze that clusters around the wheels and bumpers. Like a miasma oozing out of the ground.

Lenka pulls alongside it. Leaving about a metre of space between the two vehicles. There is somebody sitting in the driver's seat, but from your angle you can only see the shadow of their shoulders through tinted glass.

Pavel is talking to you. 'Now we are going to get out, slowly,' he says. 'All of us.'

He gets out first, extending his hand to help you after him, like a coachman. A lackey to your doom. You grip the doorframe – noting how cold it is on your bare fingers – and pull yourself out. The sky is dull, featureless. The mountain air unbelievably fresh and clean.

Behind you Gogol emerges, blinking and wary, sensing the threat and menace of the situation, seeking your hand again immediately. Any short spell of separation is upsetting to him, and you too. From the front, Lenka appears, followed by Denis – pulling Marta out after him. A lump and patch of dried blood on Marta's forehead, already flaking. Her eyes darting left, right. A hunted, haunted look. But when you catch her eye, you think you perceive something else there: a discreet signal. A mutual understanding. She knows you have the knife. Knows there is a small chance.

She says something, not to you but to them – an uncertain question in Czech that is simply ignored, in that way of theirs. Denis stays close by her. Not bothering to hold her or restrain her, simply within reaching distance should it be needed. His gun hanging casually at his side.

Once you're all out, and assembled, the driver's door of the black truck opens.

Valerie descends from the driver's seat, grandly, like a queen. Stepping first on to the footboard and then into the snow. Even here, in the remote wilderness, she has her own distinct look. Black snow boots, functional and fashionable, that come up to her knees. Dark fur gloves, svelte and glossy. And a heavy woollen shawl, worn like a poncho, patterned with muted browns and greens – as if chosen to match the surrounding forest. Her hair is in that thick braid, and she's left it hanging outside her shawl, deliberately on display. So long it reaches her waist. Tied off with a black silk ribbon, the same sheen as her boots.

There is nobody else in the vehicle. Just her, waiting. Her smile both beatific and murderous. A killing smile. She barely glances at Marta. Focuses – fixates – on you, before padding, predatorially, through the snow to Gogol. She bends at the waist, lowering her face to his. Pets his head, murmurs something in Russian. Something reassuring.

The attitude of the others is deferential, reverent.

'I don't often come up here,' she admits. 'I leave these things to Pavel.'

She goes on to explain that for you, she made a special trip. She wanted to see you, to see some of his work. She inhales the cold air deeply, savouring this moment. Then, as if it has just occurred to her, she asks you if you would like to scream. Even urges you to. As a test. She explains that you are miles from anyone, anything. You can scream all you like. And, of course, you *will* scream, she assures you. Later.

You say nothing. She has defeated you and she knows it, and there is nothing to say. You could not speak if you

286

wanted to. Your throat is tight, your veins humming with fear.

Lenka asks her something, in their language. A short exchange follows. Valerie ends it by nodding, agreeing, and only switches back to English to summarise, and drive the point home: 'You can go. We just need the truck for the drive back – only three of us will be returning.'

She smiles at you, deliberately.

Lenka jingles her keys and holds up a hand in farewell, heads for the SUV as if grateful to be spared witnessing what's to come. From the boot she removes your duffel bag, tosses it casually into the snow. She still hasn't looked at you or Gogol, or truly acknowledged you. For her, you suspect, you don't really exist. You are dead already. She has been driving ghosts.

The rest of you watch, the act oddly ritualistic, as the beige SUV reverses and leaves via the track you arrived on. As it trundles through the trees, Valerie reaches into the cab of her truck, twists the keys to turn off the engine, but leaves them in the ignition, presses a button to keep the heater running. Clearly there's no need to lock it out here, and this way the truck will stay nice and warm for her, presumably until she is finished with you.

Still. It's a detail you note: there are keys in the truck.

'Come,' Valerie says. 'Bring them.'

You are made to walk. To the cabin. A path has been cleared across the lake – it's easier to walk over the ice than through the snow. They lead you close to shore, where the ice is thickest. All of you shuffling in that cautious, flat-footed manner one adopts on ice, to avoid slipping and falling.

You glance down at Gogol, just to meet his gaze. Hoping you can convey love and reassurance through a look. Hoping you don't simply appear terrified, petrified. Failing to be the mother he needs.

Valerie, who has taken the lead, slows down and falls into step beside you. Pavel has to move aside, to give her room. It's the first time he hasn't been right there, holding you or pressing the knife to you. You see now that he does indeed have a surgical implement of some sort – a long, curved scalpel, slim and silver as a crescent moon, except for the very tip, which glints red with your blood.

Valerie links her arm in yours. As if you are two friends, out for a walk. She talks philosophically about the foolish decisions you have made and how none of this was at all necessary. She and Pavel always hold up their end of these bargains and their business dealings are usually smooth and trouble-free. They rarely have to resort to ridiculous measures such as you've forced them to use: scouring the countryside, calling in favours, sending people to look for you, drawing unwanted attention, taking great risks in order to track you down.

And so, they have to kill you, of course. As an example. But, also, to punish you. You need to suffer before you die. Not the boy. It will be quick, painless for him. Just going to sleep.

She looks over at Gogol. 'Isn't that right, little one? Just a nap.'

He stares at her warily, like you might a viper. Sensing her wickedness and power.

The long walk and her menacing chitchat have a strange effect on you. You can feel the cold settling in, leeching the warmth from you. But with the warmth goes the panic, the fear, the dread. You are able to think more clearly, more clinically. You feel that once they have you in the cabin you are lost. You will be dead. So whatever is to happen must happen before you get there, in the remaining – and ever-diminishing – distance.

Valerie says something to Pavel, and he murmurs an answer, points across the ice.

'*Da*,' she says, and smiles sweetly at you. 'Come, this way.' She changes direction, adjusts course. You're still heading towards the cabin but at an oblique angle, away from shore. You see now that there's a machine or mechanism of some sort, out on the ice. A large bore or drill. You think at first that this is a terrible instrument of torture, huge and impractical. A nightmare contraption.

But no, as you get closer you see holes in the ice, of varying sizes. The machine is a large auger – the kind used for ice-fishing. To drill a hole, access the water below.

Valerie is not looking at the holes, or the drill. She releases your elbow, walks in a circle, studying the ice, an intent expression on her face. Finally, she snaps her fingers and says, 'Ah-ha' and takes two steps to the right. 'Look,' she says, pointing down.

You don't want to look, don't want Gogol to look. When Pavel touches your shoulder, urging you forward, you let go of Gogol's hand, allow yourself to be guided over to Valerie, to see what Valerie wants you to see. Beneath the ice there is a face. Pale skin, cloudy eyes. A gaping mouth. Features twisted by pain, rigid with death, but recognisable as Mario nonetheless. Just below, hazy through the ice, you can see his torso, stripped bare. Striated with incisions. A twisted map that leads to a gaping hole in the centre of his chest.

Pavel nods, solemnly, as if acknowledging responsibility for his work.

'This is where you go after,' Valerie explains. 'Frozen all winter, and fish food come spring. There are big carp in these lakes. They scavenge the bottom, strip clean the bones. Nobody else ever comes up here, you see.'

Pavel adds, 'It is our place.'

They are standing side-by-side, looking down, in awe and appreciation of themselves and their capabilities. Their poses and profiles so similar it's eerie. In that moment, it occurs to you that they may be brother and sister, or related in some way. And, in that same moment, you know that this is the time: now. With the two of them beside you, but no scalpel at your back. With Pavel still gazing at Mario, fascinated by his own handiwork. With Gogol close to hand. With Denis a dozen steps off, guarding Marta but looking slightly away, maybe even unnerved by the sight of his onetime friend.

With all the pieces arranged, just so, on this chessboard of ice.

You make a soft gagging sound – as if overwhelmed by what you are seeing – and double over, clutching your guts, pretending to retch, while discretely sliding your hand up to your jacket pocket, reaching for the handle of the knife, so perfect and powerful in your grip. Valerie makes a sympathetic joke, about how unfortunate this is, this whole nasty business, and while she chuckles about that you slip the knife free of its sheath and straighten up and turn towards Pavel, using the force of your pivot to shove the blade into his chest, right where his heart should be.

It slides in so cleanly, like a key in a lock. Fitting where it's meant to go.

The gasp of his breath. Not inwards but out. A sound you know. The sound you remember from the bus. The sound of life escaping. Soft and deafening. A small-scale cataclysm. An ending for one. Only this time you are the one holding the handle.

In the aftermath: a shocked stillness. Everybody standing silent as Pavel slow-topples backwards, his legs folding, his head hitting the ice first with a dull, fatal clunk. The handle of the knife sticking straight up from his chest, firmly planted, stuck in its final resting place. A moment in which you all remain in a frieze, not believing, before realisation sets in.

Then the stillness snaps and Valerie shrieks and Marta falls upon Denis, punching and kicking, grabbing at his gun. Screaming obscenities. Surprise on her side, and the ferocity of desperation. Her last-gasp effort adds to the chaos, heightens your chances of escape. Denis can't shoot, and as he grapples with her the gun gets dropped, skitters across the ice like a little black bug. Marta is screaming at you to go, run – *save the boy* – and you grab Gogol's hand and together you begin to run, as best you can, across the slippery and treacherous ice.

Not even sure which direction to go, at first. Simply moving away from them, then having to adjust. Heading back towards the truck. Thinking of those keys. This time, rather than circling around the shore, you cut directly across the lake. The distance that much shorter. You glance back once and see Denis kneeling on Marta, his hands at her throat, choking and strangling, and glimpse Valerie crouched over Pavel. Checking him, or trying to save him. This you know to be useless. You felt the certainty and satisfaction of it: his death.

Then running for another thirty metres – the truck, just get to the truck – before you check again. Denis is in pursuit now. Having left Marta behind. A lump on the ice. Sprawled and motionless. Marta.

Valerie pointing after you, repeatedly shrieking. *Stop – stop this!* As if casting a spell, as if she is so delusional regarding the extent of her powers that she believes she can actually stop you that way.

Gogol labouring beside you. Not crying, but focused entirely on the act of running, which is a struggle. His bad leg. The truck still so far off. No way you can outrun Denis. Stopping, turning. He's there. Coming for you. He isn't shooting yet. Not wanting to risk wasting bullets, or not wanting to risk hitting Gogol.

You stand resolute, holding Gogol's hand, as Denis closes the distance.

Seeing that, Denis slows down, stands maybe ten metres off, panting and puffing breaths of frost. But grinning – showing his yellowed teeth. He knows he has you. The truck is still a few hundred metres further. And he has his gun. When he raises it, you try to guide Gogol behind you – a last act of protection – but instead Gogol steps in front of you. His face furious and fierce and defiant. Not a child's expression at all. Your changeling.

'Maty,' he says. 'Mother.'

Denis pauses. From that distance he can't shoot; he can't be sure he won't hit Gogol. And so there is a moment of deadlock. Denis laughs – at the seeming absurdity of this temporary dilemma – but stops laughing abruptly. Goes still. Looks down.

You heard it too. The ice. Creaking. Cracking.

You've sprinted straight across the centre of the lake, close to the patch of water, where the surface hasn't frozen over. Now you can see that the layer beneath you is precariously thin, laced with cracks. The result is a strange impasse, as Denis tries to decide what to do, and you do too. Run, and hope the ice holds? Or will the first person to move, to break the stand-off, be the one who plunges through into the water?

You shoulder-check. There's still a long stretch of thin ice between you and the truck. But Gogol could make it. So much lighter than you. He could scoot across it like a duckling. You whisper to him, 'Go to the truck. The truck.'

Perhaps Denis hears, or decides he must act. With a reckless shout he charges at you, but, rather than flee like he expects, you push Gogol towards the truck, urging him on his way, and turn to face Denis, standing your ground, and as the two of you come together Denis slips – his legs shooting out from beneath him. A slapstick repeat of his clumsy attempt at mugging you, on that first night. And in falling this time he grabs you and pulls you down with him and you both land heavily and there is a sound like a tree branch splitting and then a dropping sensation and a brutal shock of cold and you know you have broken clean through the ice into the freezing waters of the lake.

the void

So this is how you'll die. In a vacuum. An emptiness. Cold as space. The shock so great that it sucks all the air from your lungs, seems to seize your body and squeeze. Your eyes clench automatically. You're still entangled with Denis, slow-sinking together, struggling – him gripping your arm just above the elbow. You feel him thrashing wildly, violently, panicking. You force your eyes open. See a strange sapphire darkness. Light filtering down through the layer of ice above you. Denis's blurred face, his contorted features, right there in front of yours.

You shove at him. Using the heel of your palm. Short, jabbing motions. Recalling something from swimming lessons – what to do if a drowning person clings to you. Aim for the nose. Beat them back, or they'll drag you down with them. It seems to work. There is a kaleidoscope of bubbles as he cries out soundlessly. Blood clouding the water.

But he has let you go. It gives you a chance.

You kick free, kick away. Peer through the murk. Denis just a shape off to the left now, pawing at the water, having dropped his gun. It spirals down, turning lazily as it falls, straight down into darkness that is endless, that swallows it. Gone. You're still sinking too. In these moments, when you're in the open palm of death, you don't think of Tod or your mother or your childhood or any important memories. Your life doesn't flash before your eyes. You don't have visions of a bright light, or sense any benevolent or malevolent forces at work.

You don't experience any of those things.

You know then that death isn't a spiritual or mystical process. It's only – or purely – a biological one. The act of a living organism shutting down. Of body heat draining, of cold leeching into skin and flesh. Of muscles cramping, seizing. Of air no longer reaching the lungs, of oxygen no longer reaching the bloodstream, circulating to the organs. Of electrical impulses slowing. Of the heart fluttering, sputtering, followed by stillness, by silence, by nothing.

Death is just a stopping.

And yet. Working against all that, the fierce, vicious, ferocious, furious, desperate, raging, all-consuming desire to survive. Burning in your nerves, your limbs, the centre of your chest – your heart a hot coal – fuelled by thoughts of Gogol, of that little boy. Still up there, above you, in the world of the living. Crying out. You can hear him. Calling to you. *Maty*.

Look up. The surface is a vast white sheet, a glow of diffusion. Already so far away. How did you sink this deep? You're flailing, kicking. It doesn't feel like swimming. Draped as you are in clothes, weighed down as you are by shoes. It feels like climbing, like dragging yourself through slush.

You wriggle out of your jacket, then jack-knife in the water to yank off your shoes. Keep trying, keep going. Your lungs aching, straining, threatening to burst in your chest.

Maybe that will be how it feels. A last bubble-pop of life.

Except, a star-shaped patch above. You're floundering towards the hole in the ice by instinct. Your old sense of direction. The primal part of your brain. Guiding you as it would an animal, a fish or amphibian. All those years of evolution in you, on your side, triggered by the urgent sense you are dying – and dying to live.

You're getting closer to the surface. But the opening seems to be moving away. Staying just out of reach. Until it isn't. Until your fist claws up into open air, shoving aside thick chunks of broken ice. Followed by your head, breaching, and your mouth.

Now breathe. Breathe. That first gasp like being jolted back to life by a defibrillator. A violent seizure. Air filling your lungs. And again. Breathe. Ragged, burning inhalations. And each time the cold shoves the air right back out of you. You flounder and splash amid the puzzle pieces of broken ice. Struggling to find the edge, something solid. Something to grip. But the sides of the hole keep breaking, again and again, cracking off in chunks. No way to make progress. And all the while the water pulls at you, dragging you down. The cold seeping into you, leeching your strength. Until, finally, the ice doesn't break. Your fingers find solidity, but, even then, you can't gain purchase – clawing repeatedly at the rough, slippery surface of the lake. Your nails scraping, cracking, going bloody.

Not going to work. Something else. Try something else. Extending both arms flat out in front of you. Leaning your weight on your elbows. Kicking furiously, to raise your torso, seal-like, your upper body now pressed on the ice. You understand: this is your chance. Your one chance. You don't have the strength to do this again. Find your focus. And pivot sideways, lift a leg, raise the sodden weight clear of the clinging water, up on to the frozen surface. Use the leverage to work the rest of your torso out, your other leg. And then roll. Away from the hole. Towards the shore, the thicker ice, safety.

Then a terrible cramping sets in. Unlike any cold, or effects of cold you've ever experienced. Your whole body contorting, contracting inwards. Spasms and shudders. Wracking your bones, rattling your teeth and skull. As powerful as a seizure.

Somewhere, far off, you can hear him crying out for you. Not in your mind, this time. The word singing in the frozen air: '*Maty!*'

And directly beneath you is a face. Denis. His desperate features so clear it's like a reflection in a mirror. He's made it to the surface too. And his body is contorting – just like yours. Only he hasn't found the opening. His fingers scratching frantically at the underside of the ice. The last convulsions. A final sigh of bubbles. Then a faint look of surprise. His tiny, easy, meaningless death.

As if he realised, at the last, that's it?

You roll to your knees, still crunched in a cannonball. Your hair already stiffening, freezing in the sub-zero air. Crystallising around your head in a crown of spikes and barbs. You work to control your spasming muscles, stretch your arms forwards to counter the contractions. Palm the ice. Transfer weight to your arms. Push. Get a leg under you. The other. Each body part functioning in isolation, stiff and disconnected. Your joints rusted hinges. But obeying. Heeding your need. You straighten your knees. Somehow. You stand.

At the back of your mind, this thought: don't stay in the waterlogged clothing. It will kill you. The water, the freezing temperature. Get the outer layer off, at least. You tug your sweatshirt over your head. And your long-sleeved shirt. The skin of your arms bone-white and bare to the elements. Impossible to get free of your frozen jeans, or tank top. Leave them.

A gust of cold air ghosts across your shoulders. All sense of feeling gone. You are totally numb, on the outside and within. All emotions and feeling pared back to one single driving feral impulse: where is he? Find him. Save him.

Look around. A few hundred metres away you see two lumps on the ice. Two bodies. Pavel, and Marta. You sent Gogol the other way. You turn. See the red flare of Valerie's hair. Her figure stooped, crouched beside her truck. Struggling with something. Trying to drag somebody out from beneath it. Gogol. He didn't get into the cab. Maybe he wasn't able to, or decided hiding under the truck was better, safer – saved by his innate ability to evade.

You know then. What has transpired, and what you must do.

the snow queen

Crossing the ice with a sense of purpose that is close to divine. Having reached this frozen state, partially hypothermic, your nerve endings numb, barely able to feel. As if you're now beyond physical sensation and pain and emotion, and all things human. As if you're now solely a creature of the cold, having taken it into you, absorbed it, accepted it as your own.

The lake smooth and glassy underfoot. The winter winds swirling around you, catching in your frozen hair. You are walking on water. Floating like a wraith. Focused entirely on that truck, the child beneath it, the red-haired woman intending him harm. Everything else is hazy, blurred. Nothing else matters.

In the sky, no movement. No definition at all. Just that same grey glaze. As if there's a mirror up there, or another frozen lake, reflecting the world back down on itself.

You reach the shore, the path of trampled snow. You step on to it. Feeling the granular bits of ice beneath your feet. A heightened sense of awareness. Attuned to the snowy landscape. Only twenty steps from Valerie, who is sprawled flat by the wheel – her head partially under the chassis, her arms reaching underneath. Gogol has positioned himself between the rear wheels. He's clinging to part of the undercarriage, holding on while she tugs and yanks at his ankles. Something comical about her posture. Like a vexed mother trying to drag her misbehaving child out from under a table.

Valerie is so engrossed with Gogol that she doesn't hear you, doesn't notice you coming up. It occurs to you then, maybe you *did* die, down there. Maybe you didn't survive. Maybe this is your death-vision: a miraculous escape, and rescuing Gogol. Delusions of salvation.

You hold up your hands, study them. Gauging their corporeality. They are frozen, clutched in claw-like shapes. But you can move them. They are real. You are here. You take the last few steps and say her name softly: 'Valerie.'

She hesitates, still holding on to Gogol. As if unsure she has heard. As if maybe your voice is the wind hissing over the lake surface, stirring the snow. As if her brain is perhaps playing tricks on her. Her guilty conscience. Scorpions in her mind.

Until you say it again. Rasping the name through your throat.

'Valerie.'

She looks up then, lets go of Gogol, turns and sits with her back to the truck, her mouth half-parted in horror.

You will never understand what you look like to her, in this moment. Your clothing frost-stiff and stuck to your skin. Your hair a crown of ice. Your lips blue. Your feet bare

300

and frostbitten. You must look like the undead, a nightmare vision. An impossibility. The spirit of all those she has had killed and submerged beneath the ice. Risen up for vengeance. The snow queen that Mario called you, christened you, predicted you would become.

This is not a time for words. There is no language left. Nothing now but to act, the final action. Valerie attempts to get up and you fall upon her, pinning her, getting your frozen fingers around her throat. Feeling the heat of life there as you squeeze, tightening your grip like a torque, only dimly aware of her struggles, clawing and clutching, scratching at your face. To such resistance you're oblivious, impervious, too numb to feel pain, to feel anything but the flutter-pulse beneath your thumbs that is slowing, diminishing, ending.

Gogol is peering out at you, from beneath the truck. His wide brown eyes like those of an animal in its den. Wondering if the threat has passed. You must look as fearsome to him as you did to Valerie. But he would never, will never, be frightened of you. Even now. Having seen what you've done.

'It's okay,' you try to say, and find you cannot speak.

So you think it instead: *It's okay – you're safe now.*

And as if understanding he crawls out. The look on his face puzzles you. Relieved, but also concerned. Of course. He is saved, but are you? Not if you stay there, exposed, in the cold.

The truck. The keys.

You try to clutch the door handle, find you can't, your fingers fail you. You signal to Gogol you need him to open it. He pulls on the lever – using the full weight of his body – and the door swings wide. The heater is still on low and the released air exhales outwards like a breath. That single sensation – the possibility of warmth – sets you shivering again.

You crawl inside, on to the front bench seat. The keys are waiting there, in the ignition. You paw at them, can't turn them. Give up, clutch at yourself. Your body beginning to curl and contort again.

Look at Gogol helplessly. Please. The keys.

He gets in next to you, reaches across you. Twists the keys in the ignition. The engine starts easily, smoothly – a soft purr. The force of the heater increases, boosted by the engine, and you fumble at the controls, crank the fan even higher – as high as it will go. Hot, painful blasts of air gust over you.

Without you asking him, Gogol shuts the door.

You slump sideways on the bench seat, shuddering as you begin to thaw. There's an ominous tingling in your hands, your feet. You test your fingers, move them experimentally, and see that your fingertips are completely black – as if burned. Frostbitten, dead skin. The same sensation in the soles of your feet. Your toes. As these damaged parts of your body warm up, the pain is excruciating. You curl up and cry out, weeping. Gogol holds your head in his lap, cradling you and stroking you, as you once did him. In this moment, you have become the child, and he the parent.

Lying there in his arms you know that you will live, that you have prevailed, the two of you. You have faced and escaped death. And, with the clarity brought back from the depths of that frozen void, you understand what comes next. As soon as you have warmed up you will take Valerie's clothing. Dress in her coat, her scarf, her shirt, her trousers. Her boots. You will roll her, and Pavel, into the hole in the ice. And Marta, too. They deserve the ignominy but it will be a dismal burial for her, for such a true friend. But necessary.

One day you will find her family, if she has any. Explain how she died saving Gogol, saving you.

You will take whatever money they had on them and you will get in Valerie's truck with Gogol and you will drive it back to the highway and from there you will have an open and uncertain road ahead of you. There will still be so many variables, so many challenges, to get home, to get *him* home with you. First to London, then on to Wales. But those obstacles will be overcome. You will make it, eventually.

You will pick a secluded place in the countryside, in Mid Wales. Settle there with him. Legally change your name. Apply for guardian status. Make up lies to tell your friends, your own mother. Nobody will ever know. He will be a normal boy. Or almost. This secret of your shared past never hidden from him, never forgotten by either of you. But the trauma won't be a weakness, it will be a strength. A bond that will always hold you together, keep you united. You'll send him to the village primary. Buy him his school uniforms. Make him packed lunches. Sign him up for sports. For music lessons. Take him on trips and holidays. Take him, finally, to Disneyland. And so many other places. Get treatment for his leg. Heal him. Nourish him. Watch him grow. Watch him thrive. Nobody will come looking for him, and if they do nobody will ever hurt him. You have made sure of that. You *will* make sure of that. You are his parent and protector, both mothering and murderous, caring and vicious, tender and wrathful. Willing to fight and kill out of love, to ensure the survival of your child.

You know all these things with the power of prophecy as you lie in the truck with your head tucked against your son's chest, feeling the surge of blood returning to your veins, the strength of your own heart, beating in time with his, bringing you back to life.

absolution

I want to leave you there, end the story on that note – a moment of hope. Imagining your future with Gogol. The possibility of happily ever after is all we really ask for, in stories as well as in life. Do we really want or need a denouement?

But, of course, that is not the end. There are certain facts, certain truths, that need to be told, for the purposes of resolution. I have been assiduous and diligent, in that respect; I have researched every angle, found out – as near as I can – what actually happened.

I know, for example, that a year after you came to my apartment, and these events took place, the lake and their cabin was found. By two hunters who had trespassed on to the private property, property no longer guarded or secured, property owned by the woman who had called herself Valerie, though it emerged that was an adopted name.

An investigation followed. Soon, they uncovered the horrors that took place in the cabin. Despite Mario's claim that the job was a rarity, a 'one-off', it was, in fact, as common as their other smuggling activities. Adults and children. Evidence of harvesting. Body parts and organs sold on the black market. The lake filled with the bones of their victims. And also those of their other enemies, or people who gave them problems. A convenient way of making them disappear.

Not all the bodies were identified. But some were.

Marta was.

Marta Novotný. Her name is in the police records. A landlady, from Prague. And along with her a man named Mario – who apparently used his real name. Not so Pavel, or Denis. But among the bodies were 'known associates' of an established criminal organisation, including the woman who owned the lake itself, the cabin, the surrounding land.

Since not all the victims were identified, it might have been possible that you were among them: you and Gogol both. But, of the children, none had a bad leg. Gogol got away, and you did too.

But then, I know that, for a variety of reasons.

I have gone through the news articles, the case files, the police reports. I told the Czech government that I'm a writer, investigating these incidents. And, of course, my story checked out, because I am. The boy you met in the language class grew up, eventually, and did become a writer. The authorities accepted that this was all research for my new project. I went back to the school, too. To check their enrolment records. To find out the full name and contact details of the British woman who took the beginner's course, studied in the same class as me. I didn't necessarily expect them to have all that information, but they did – probably for tax purposes, in case of an audit. And I didn't expect them to readily hand it over to me either, but they did. My writing project providing justification enough.

The address you'd given was your old one in London, where you'd lived with Tod. Useless to me, but now I had your full name. I contacted the Home Office and Border Control, to see how much I could uncover about your movements. I didn't get far, but with the support of a missing persons charity, and a little help from a sympathetic contact in the immigration department, I managed to check border crossing records at the time to at least establish that you did make it back to the UK. Crossing from Calais to Dover. No mention of Gogol, of course, but he would have been hidden – in the back, or the trunk. Not the first time you'd used that trick for him. It must have felt like déjà vu. And from Dover, presumably on to London, and then to Wales.

I searched for you in Wales, scoured electoral rolls and directories and even enlisted various people-tracing organisations, but continually came up against dead ends. It took me a while to deduce you changed your name. A precaution to hinder Valerie's associates from potentially doing exactly what I was trying to do – track you down, find you and Gogol. It's simple enough to change your name in the UK, and there are ways to ensure a name change is kept private. You could have, for example, told them you or Gogol had previously been the victim of abuse, that you'd escaped a violent relationship. But just because the process was straightforward doesn't mean it was easy. To choose your new name, decide who you would become. I dwelled on this. Pondered if you would have gone with something practical, commonplace – as a way of blending in – or picked something more distinct, maybe even symbolic. I created lists of names, weighed up what might appeal, though of course had no way of knowing. Eventually, I had to accept

I wouldn't be able to find you, and that was when I began to write this. As a way of working it out, making sense of it all.

I wonder if you've spent time doing that as well.

You must. You must think back on what happened. When Gogol is at school, perhaps, or playing with his friends. And one thing might bother you. How did they know you were going to Dresden? How did they find out? There was the inn, where you docked overnight. The owners, other boaters – the person standing on the porch. Any of them may have been working for Valerie, or inadvertently provided information about you.

But that wasn't the case.

I had hoped to tell this whole tale and leave my role out of it, or mostly out of it. But I see now that is impossible. Part of the impulse to write this stems from my need to confess.

I told them, of course. When they came to my flat. Pavel and the other man, the crooked cop. They didn't even have to do very much. Nothing physical. Just Pavel's soft-spoken promises. The threat of violence, of pain, a display of his surgical tools. Enough to make me break. Like so many others before me. Predictable and pathetic. In my case, all I had to say was one simple phrase: 'They're going to Dresden, by boat.' Six words. Pavel smiled when I said it. It had been so easy. He thanked me. He actually thanked me.

I am a weak man.

I know that. I live with that.

There have always been people like me. Easy to scare, easy to coerce. All too willing to turn in somebody else to save their own skin. Like the informers who reported their neighbours, sent whole families to Terezín. We are the ones who make evil possible. I am culpable. I sent you to your death, and that little boy too.

Only, somehow, you escaped your fate. I know this not just because I tracked you to Dover, but because I received a follow-up visit, from the crooked cop. Alone this time – and clearly desperate. He demanded to know if I had heard anything else, if you had contacted me again. He said his employers were furious. Telling me more than he should have, in his anxiety. That somehow you and the boy had gotten away. That Pavel was dead, and others too. He threatened me again, but I couldn't betray you a second time, simply because I didn't have any information to give. If I had, I like to believe I would have resisted – been able to stand up to him, to them, and make amends when given a second chance.

It's reassuring to think so.

We have countless names for a coward: craven, weakling, faintheart, skulker, chicken, poltroon, recreant, dastard. Titles I must accept, and tarnish myself with. I've pondered over it and wondered about it endlessly: how can some of us be so feeble, and others so fearless? Why will some do anything to save their own skin, and others risk everything to save another?

I don't know. I simply don't know.

Maybe that's partly what this has been about – trying to find out what motivated you and drove you on. I live with my cowardice like a wound, like a hidden deformity that marks my body under my clothes. I hide it well. Nobody can tell. Not when they read my words; not when I stand in front of them reading extracts and signing books. Not until now. Until this. Here I am, exposed as a coward, with a heart full of fear and frailty. Or perhaps readers will interpret this confession as a clever twist – an authorial device.

Regardless, I needed to put it all down. I needed to get it off my chest. I have carried it for too long. But the point hasn't only been to confess. It's also been to compose a tribute, to you. You did not bend or break. You did not flag or fail. I envy you and admire you and idolise you. Even if I never find you, I hope you find this, or that this finds you. But the truth of the matter is, I may never know, and that you don't need to know. My weakness couldn't stop you. This is all in your past. Your future – the future you fought for, and earned – is wherever you are now with Gogol, living in your new home, sharing your new name, carrying on with your new life, leaving behind your old self, and this story.

acknowledgements

The support I've received throughout the development of this project has been tremendous, and I'm grateful and indebted to a number of people. Thank you very much to early readers Carly, Francesca, Jeremy, Katherine, Marilyn, Rebecca, and Richard; to Becky for your constant belief and guidance, and Hélène for being such a staunch advocate of this story; to Candida for your compassion and understanding, as well as Corinne, Emma, Lauren, Anna B., Dawn and all the good people of team Myriad; to Anna M., for designing another standout cover; to Blanka for the help with translation; to Vicki, a truly exceptional and gifted editor; and to Naomi, who has shown me the meaning of courage.

Sign up to our mailing list at

www.myriadeditions.com

Follow us on Facebook, Twitter and Instagram

about the author

TYLER KEEVIL grew up in Vancouver and moved to Wales in his twenties. He is the author of three previous novels, including *The Drive*, as well as the story collection *Burrard Inlet*. His short fiction has appeared in a wide range of magazines and anthologies, and he has won a number of awards for his writing, most notably *The Missouri Review*'s Jeffrey E. Smith Editors' Prize, the Wales Book of the Year People's Choice Award, and the Writers' Trust McClelland & Stewart Journey Prize. He is the director of the MA in Creative Writing at Cardiff University.